For Susan,

who believed.

# PRAISE FOR STACEY COCHRAN'S NOVELS

"The strength of this book is the story and level of suspense. I didn't want to put this one down simply because of the suspense and wondering who would make it out alive."

—SciFiChick.com

"An entertaining, fast-paced read . . . Highly recommended."
—Jeremy Robinson, bestselling author of *The Didymus Contingency*

"Nonstop action . . . powerful!"
—*Brew City Magazine*

"A unique blend of fantasy and suspense, *The Colorado Sequence* builds a strong female character in Amy Levine."
—Julio Vazquez, author of *Death at Disney*

"I have sacks under my eyes because I have been up late the last few nights reading *The Colorado Sequence*. I finished it last night at 2:31 A.M. because I simply could not put it down. I so enjoyed this book!"
—Ericka Jackson, author of *A Mansion Mindset*

"With all the action scenes, running gun battles and explosions this story has all the makings for an action packed, big-screen movie."
—Gene Curtis, author of *The Seventh Mountain*

"[I]ntrigue, adventure and thought-provoking speculation on the nature of the universe."
—Mark Jeffrey, bestselling author of *The Pocket and the Pendant*

"Thrilling, action-packed!"
—Hannah Stone, author of *Remembering Our Angels*

*Stacey Cochran*

# CLAWS

## STACEY COCHRAN

*Bouchercon 2009*

*Thanks.*

*Sara.*

KITCHEN TABLE BOOKS

ISBN: 1440495343

Cover design by Mimosa Mallernee

Manufactured in the United States of America

First Edition: May 2009

For more information, visit StaceyCochran.com

And e-mail the author via stacey@staceycochran.com

Once in a while a puma appears to have an insatiable desire to kill well beyond the limits of its food requirements. The remains of 275 sheep that had been killed in two nights by a puma in the vicinity of Strawberry Reservoir, in Wasatch County, Utah, were viewed by W.O. Nelson, supervisor for the Predator and Rodent Division of the U.S. Fish and Wildlife Service in Utah. On another occasion, Nelson counted forty-eight sheep killed in a single foray by another puma.

—*The Puma: Legendary Lion of the Americas*


They brought Daniel and threw him into the lions' den, and the king said, "May your God, whom you serve continually, rescue you!"

—Daniel 6:16

# ONE

Dr. Angie Rippard became an expert on mountain lions, when at nine years old, she and her twin brother were attacked by a young male four miles north of their Tucson, Arizona home. Her brother lived, but he lost his left arm and he carried the facial scars from the attack the rest of his life. For Angie, the scars were more psychological in nature because she never understood why the animal maimed her brother and not her.

"What do we got, Robert?" Angie said into the headset.

The helicopter swung around the northeast side of Rice Peak and started cruising up toward the nine-thousand-foot slopes near Mount Lemmon.

"*Felis concolor*," Robert's voice squawked excitedly over the headsets. "Looks like a mother with cubs."

Robert Gonzalez was her top grad student at the University of Arizona, and he and his team were tracking a mountain lion on foot, three miles west of the ski resort at Mount Lemmon.

"*Hot damn*," Angie said to herself.

"I didn't quite catch that, Angie. Over."

Angie said, "That's excellent, Robert. Hold your position and keep your satellite link-up clear."

The helicopter raced out to the north, high over the green sea of ponderosa pines, which was finally beginning to show green color again. The previous summer, the Santa Catalina mountain range suffered its worst wildfire in over a century, burning more than two hundred and fifty thousand acres of land.

To the west, Tucson sprawled northward through a fifteen-mile-wide valley, the Saguaro Wilderness and Tucson Mountains to the southwest, Pusch Ridge Wilderness and the great Coronado National Forest to the northeast. Multi-million dollar homes lay perched on the southern slopes of the Coronado National Forest, some situated nearly three thousand feet above sea level. They were built within a hundred yards of the National Forest Land boundary.

It was a hotly debated topic for Pima County officials. Three acres of land with sixty-mile views bordering National Forest Land would sell for more than nine hundred thousand dollars, and that was just the land. Several movie stars actually kept homes near the Ventana Canyon Resort north of Skyline Drive, such was the draw of the desert sunshine during the day and the spectacular view of city lights at night.

"Give me a reading on the cubs," Angie said.

The helicopter hovered along the steep cliffs east of the Catalina State Park. Pilot Dave Baker spotted the ground team on infrared and pointed to the screen for Angie to see. She smiled, and her blue eyes filled with excitement.

Angie had shoulder-length brown hair that was pulled back in a ponytail. The large gray headphones looked funny on her head, and a thin line of sweat formed on her upper lip. She had a smallish round nose, a prominent round chin, and the bridge of her nose was spotted with a half dozen freckles. Several strands of brown hair hung down past her ears behind the headphones, and a thin line of sweat showed through the back of her white cotton button-up blouse.

Angie looked at him and pointed toward the cliffs.

Robert Gonzalez's voice came through the headset, "Looks like a litter of three." There was a long pause. "Check that, Angie. We got a litter of five cubs. Three male, two female."

"*Five cubs.*" Angie was astonished.

The helicopter hovered a quarter mile out from the cliffs. Angie could see the bright orange climbing ropes Gonzalez's team had used to rappel down the cliffs.

"All five have opened their eyes, Angie. Repeat, all five kittens have opened their eyes."

"Can you see their teeth?" Angie said into her headset. "Have they cut their first teeth?"

"Negative, Angie."

"About fourteen days old."

Gonzalez's voice squawked back, "Looks like it's been a good year for momma."

# TWO

Johnny Watkins was a homeless drunk who had seen more of the United States than most RV owners. He was forty-three, weighed one-thirty, and carried all of his earthly possessions in a dirty green hiking backpack. His face was covered with soot and dirt, and he wore a beard that stretched down to his dirt-stained T-shirt. He had electric sky-blue eyes, and he talked out loud to himself when in public. It was like whistling in the dark for a man whom no one in this world cared.

He spent a month last fall up near Monterey in California, sleeping on seaweed-strewn beaches near the Pebble Beach Golf Resort. He hitch-hiked his way southeast through Bakersfield in October, went northeast up to the Sierra Nevadas near Olancha in November and nearly froze to death, and then headed southeast and walked across the Mojave Desert in late December and early January.

He spent his nights in rest areas, truck stop parking lots, or out under the wide open heavens. Had he looked a little cleaner (and saner), carried a guitar, or been able to explain what the hell he was doing, he might have impressed a few people with his travel stories.

He came south along State Highway 95 from Needles, California to Blythe, where he spent a few nights begging for change at the 7th Street Chevron and the Dairy Queen on Lovekin Boulevard. Then, he headed east for Arizona.

From Blythe, it took seven days to reach Phoenix, and had he held up there, everything would have been fine. Phoenix, Arizona had one of the highest populations of winter indigents in the United States. Nights were cool but reasonable, and the daytime highs and the rain-free weather made for fine living from November to May.

Numerous city parks, safe street corners, and a city of three million too caught up in its being the eighth-fastest growing city in the U.S. to bother with policing homeless folks made it something of a winter paradise for Johnny Watkins.

He spent late January and February strolling from street corner to street corner, convenience store parking lot to convenience store parking lot, from Sun City to Paradise Valley, from the Tempe Town Lake to Mill Avenue. He headed east toward Mesa and then south through Gilbert and Chandler, and from there, he walked southward along State Highway 79.

He reached the northern edge of Tucson four days later on March 9. The highest peaks east of the city were blanketed with snow, and clouds formed from the moisture atop the peaks like sky islands.

He stumbled and staggered up into the mountains and made his way south along a ridgeline that gave him views clear down to Nogales, Mexico. He passed giant Finger Rock and bulky Table Mountain.

Johnny Watkins felt like a General high atop a battlefield, looking out across the great sea of homes, cars, and civilization. He talked out loud to God. He communed with pine trees. And on the morning of March 11th, he started down from the mountains along a well-worn hiking trail south of Mount Kimball just a mile from official Tucson city limits.

• •

The big cat lay sleeping. He'd taken down a mule deer around midnight and had eaten until he was sated. The sun was now up, and he'd found himself a rocky outcropping, curled up, and drifted off to sleep. Curled up like that, the big cat was as large as a hood on an economy car, but when he rolled onto his back and stretched out, he was as long as a car from his head to the tip of his tail. He licked his paws and then began working the fur on his abdomen. His tail thumped up and down like a firehose, and he yawned.

Suddenly, he detected movement up the hill from the rocky outcropping, and he sprang silently to his feet, sniffed the air, and crept up into the woods.

• •

Johnny Watkins was lost in his own world, singing *Amazing Grace* aloud. He staggered down the trail.

Giant ponderosa pines rose on either side of the soft, bark-chip trail. Farther up the hillside, he caught glimpses of snow on the ground through the trees. But the forest was thick, and he couldn't see very far in any direction. He started whistling.

The big cat was forty feet to Johnny's back and right, the distance of three car-lengths parked at a stoplight. The man smelled strongly of sweat, his odor filling the forest all around him. The cat walked slowly, tracking the man with his eyes through the trees, his huge paws deftly moving over the ground, instinct keeping him downwind from his prey.

Johnny saw something shiny on the ground. It was about thirty feet down the trail, and it glinted in a ray of sunlight that reached through the trees. Johnny squinted and scrunched up his nose.

"What in the world," he said.

He walked up to it and realized it was a pocket knife. Someone had dropped a pocket knife on the hiking trail. It was a black enamel lockblade about six inches long, and the silver blade was locked in its casing. Johnny squatted down and picked it up from the soft earthy ground. He popped the blade out, and it locked firmly into position.

He touched his finger to the blade and felt that it was plenty sharp. All the while, Johnny remained knelt down. He turned the blade over in the sunlight, smiled, and then locked it back in its casing.

"Must be my lucky day," he said. He started to stand up.

The attack came without a sound.

Johnny was knocked forward onto his hands and knees, the knife hit the ground and skidded under a green bush, and then something had hold of the back of his neck. He screamed out and flailed his arms all around, but the big cat had hold of the back of his neck, and it wasn't letting go in this lifetime.

The cat dragged him up the hill away from the trail and the recent smell of other humans. Through the trees, the cat dragged Johnny Watkins up the hill. Johnny screamed. Something near the base of his skull cracked, and his vision went black, but he could still feel with his hands as he was dragged up the hillside. Johnny kicked at the ground, and the cat clawed at his side to turn him over.

They were now two hundreds meters up from the hiking trail, and the cat twisted him around. His backpack made it impossible to roll completely over, but the big cat's head popped up a split second and then lunged forward at Johnny Watkins's throat, its powerful jaws locking firmly onto the man's neck.

His voice was now gone. He was blind. His legs thrashed and kicked, but the cat held his neck in its mouth while its powerful forelimbs balanced the struggling man, holding him in position.

The cat held Johnny Watkins that way for another ten minutes, until it was certain that he was dead.

# THREE

"The attack," Dr. Rippard said, "comes from the front left."

The auditorium classroom was filled with senior level undergraduates and first year graduate students. Ninety-eight students total; only two were absent tonight. It was the single most popular upper level biology course at the University of Arizona. Dr. Rippard stood at the front of the room, a huge sixty-inch plasma TV screen to her left. She held a remote, and she paused the digital video.

The screen showed a grassy field and a single dirt road winding ahead no more than twenty meters, where it curved out of sight to the right. A tree line stood in the distance about four hundred meters away, and the grass in the field was seventy-five centimeters tall, about hip height on an adult.

Rippard looked around the auditorium and said, "Who can tell me the native region *for* and name *of* this grass species?"

Only three hands rose up in the auditorium. Rippard waited for more.

"Come on, people," she said. "Midterms are in one week; you've got to know your grass species."

Up came a few more tentative hands. Rippard frowned. She pointed seven rows up to Jenny Granger, one of the smartest girls in class. Jenny had shoulder-length red hair and a soft round face with light freckles and dimples.

"That's a field of mostly *Danthonia spicata*," Jenny said, "commonly known as 'poverty grass'."

Rippard looked impressed. She said, "And where might you find poverty grass, if you were so inclined?"

"Well, it's a native of North America," Jenny responded.

"What kind of soil?"

"Mostly acidic," Jenny said, "you find it in old, worn out fields."

"Hence the name," a girl on the second row whispered to a neighbor.

Rippard went back to the video. She waved the remote around like a wand.

"Anybody know where this was shot?" she said, looking at the screen.

"I believe that's South Carolina," Nick Jacobs said.

Nick was Jenny's boyfriend, and they sat next to one another in class each day. Nick had the piercing blue eyes of a likeable troublemaker and the lanky, lithe body of a cross country runner. His wavy brown hair was long enough that he fidgeted with it so that it wasn't over his eyes.

"Close, Nick," Rippard said. "It's actually North Carolina. A little farm in the eastern part of the state about an hour southeast of Raleigh. Nearest town is called Warsaw."

She turned and looked at the class and smiled. The image on the TV screen was still paused, but with the high-definition plasma TV and digital video, it might as well have been a crystal clear photograph.

"I'm surprised nobody's seen him yet," she said.

A stir went through the room. Heads turned.

"Seen what?" one student said.

"He's right there on the screen," she chided.

Everyone looked at the TV screen. They all saw a field of grass, the thin dirt road through the field, the trees in the distance; nothing special.

"If you were walking on this road," Rippard said, "and you were carrying this video camera, as this boy was doing, every one of you would be attacked within a minute."

A whispering buzz went through the auditorium. Rippard turned back to the giant TV screen. She said, "He's right there on the screen, just as plain as day."

These were the moments she lived for. Rippard had to pull some strings to create BIO 436, "Predators, Prey, and Their Habitats," but it had turned into one of the most popular classes at the university. And it was moments like these when Dr. Angie Rippard knew she *loved* teaching.

"Come on, people," she said. "He's on the left side of the road, about twenty feet up." She looked around at them, but no one could spot the big cat. "There's a predator that weighs one hundred and thirty pounds, waiting for you twenty feet up on your left."

She pulled two tables together and placed them end to end. Each table was about ten feet long. She stood at one end and pointed across to the other.

"You're out hiking with your girlfriend," she said, pointing to a twenty-two-year-old who tried to shrug off the sudden spotlight. "And you got a male cat—how much do you weigh?"

The guy sounded tough. He said, "One ninety-five."

"You got a male cat that weighs two-thirds your body weight," she said, "from this end of the table to that end of the table. It's got a bite powerful enough to snap your neck like a twig, and you can't even *see* him."

She looked around the room at everyone.

With the remote, she put the video on one/sixteenth-speed slow motion, and everyone in the classroom gasped as frame by frame an Eastern cougar, *Felis concolor cougar*, rose up from the grass at the side of the road and came right at the boy holding the camera.

Rippard paused it as the cougar prepared to pounce. The cat was huge, easily nine feet from head to tip of tail. Its shoulders were powerful, and in the paused onscreen image, its mouth was opened in a snarl, whiskers wide, eyes focused dead ahead on its prey.

"Eastern cougar," she said, somehow emotionally detached, like a state trooper at the sight of a terrible car collision. "This guy only weighed about one-thirty."

She stood there for ten seconds, staring at the cat, and students began looking at one another. She stared at the cat another few seconds— an image of her brother's face in her mind the last time she'd seen him— and then she clicked the TV off. Surprisingly, a groan of disappointment rippled through the auditorium. They *wanted* to see the attack.

"Learn your grasses," she said, calm and scholarly now. "Particularly the North American variety; they might show up as a bonus question on your midterm. There will be a section on birds, a section on bears, and you better know every snake in the Willard text. Be able to tell me poisonous from non-poisonous. And for those who want to read ahead, we'll be starting up after midterms with sharks, the Hollis textbook."

# FOUR

Maggie Eiser steered the Ford Taurus station wagon carefully up the dirt road. In the passenger seat beside her, Chip sat up and tried to see over the dashboard. The pop-up camper creaked and moaned on the trailer hitch, and Maggie gave the station wagon just enough gas to keep the tires from spinning underneath them.

"It's steep, Mom," Chip said.

"I know it is, honey."

Chip was six, but Maggie was amazed almost daily at how intuitive her son was. He sensed danger well before adults thirty years older than him, and he understood people in a way that was eerie for a boy his age.

"You shouldn't hang out with her," he'd told Maggie a year earlier, when she became close friends with a realtor in their Muncie, Indiana neighborhood. "She's bad."

Of course, Maggie thought it was absurd. Three months later, though, Vivian Hornet (pronounced Hor-*nay*) was pulled over for driving recklessly, and the cops found eight ounces of cocaine in her glove compartment. Vivian was sentenced to three years in the state women's correctional facility, and Maggie started listening to her son's ideas more seriously.

"We're almost there, baby," Maggie said. With both hands on the wheel, she glanced at Chip and gave him a smile. Chip looked at her, and then his gaze went back to the steep, rocky road in front of them.

The speedometer had stayed between five and ten miles per hour since the road turned to gravelly sand, ten miles southeast of the little mountain town of Oracle, Arizona. They'd stopped at a Circle K in Oracle for charcoal and sodas, and the store clerk had told them the turn for Old Mount Lemmon Highway was two miles down the road. But this was anything *but* a highway; they'd passed a large yellow sign that read "4x4 Only Next 25 Miles." Chip asked Maggie what "4x4" was, and she said that it was a car with a back area like their station wagon.

11

The car came out on a ridge,
the right. To the left, there was a
three hundred meters. Beyond that,
six miles to the San Pedro River. They
the Galiuro Mountains on the opposite si...

Old Mount Lemmon Highway was
and Maggie figured they were about a mile abo...
were down, a cool breeze wafted in through the
green trees in a canyon about a quarter mile in front o...

"I think that's it, Chip."

"That's Peppersauce?"

"See how it curves inward? There are lots of trees. The...
that comes down out of the mountains."

Maggie *hoped* it was Peppersauce Canyon because she coul...
what looked like a footpath rising straight up out of the canyon on t...
other side, and she knew her station wagon would never be able to make
it up that incline.

The road wound slightly downhill into the canyon, and soon they
were under the forest canopy. The campground was on the left, and
Maggie hit the brakes and said, "Look, Chip!"

Chip sat up in his seat and looked out the driver-side window. A
small herd of mule deer grazed in the campground.

"Cool!" Chip said.

There were four doe and one young buck, and they looked at the
station wagon with their ears perked up. Maggie frowned because there
didn't seem to be anyone else in the campground, and the deer stared at
Maggie's car. Slowly, the deer started walking downhill toward the creek.

"Looks like we've got the campground all to ourselves," Maggie
said. She proceeded over a cattle guard into the Peppersauce
Campground, deep in the heart of the Coronado National Forest.

• •

The female mountain lion had trailed the deer for more than two
hours. It was careful to stay uphill and downwind of the small group while

em, but the noise of the car made her wary, and she
st their scent.

young cat was on a forested hillside about two hundred
from the station wagon and camper. She stood still and
e car crawling slowly along, down near the creek.

•   •

Maggie did a slow circle around the campground. It was cool in
forest's shade, and late afternoon sunlight dappled the grassy floor. A
tle breeze stirred the tree leaves, and Maggie began to worry that the
mpground was out of business.

"I don't know, Chip," she said. "It looks kind'a empty to me.
What do you think?"

Chip unfastened his seatbelt and leaned up against the dashboard.
He looked out the window.

"Do they have a bathroom?" he said.

Maggie looked at him and smiled. Across the creek, she saw a dark
wooden building with a restroom sign hanging on the front door.

"There's one right over there," she said.

She crossed a wooden bridge over the creek. The pop-up camper
creaked and jostled, and it shook the Taurus. She pulled on across and
started up toward the restroom. The dirt road leveled out.

She parked in front of the bathhouse, and Chip got out and
walked around the front end of the car. Maggie watched him, and he
glanced up, smiled, and waved.

He said, "I gotta *go!*"

Maggie smiled. She noticed a blue payphone outside the
bathhouse.

While he was inside, Maggie pulled out her map. The road up to
Peppersauce Canyon was marked by two close parallel lines, which
indicated that it was a dirt road. It ended at the Peppersauce Campground.
She glanced up and looked at her reflection in the rearview mirror.

*Jesus*, she thought. *You look tired, Maggie. You look absolutely worn out.*

Deep lines surrounded her otherwise pretty eyes, attesting to the
countless sleepless nights she'd had of late. She looked like she was at the

end of her rope, that it would only take a gentle push to put her over the edge. She'd lost her husband, and the only thing that kept her from ending her own life was her son, a little boy whose hope and optimism knew no bounds.

Around her, Maggie saw there were about seventy campsites, and each site had a fire pit, a picnic table, a grill, and a little water spigot. There were no electricity or cable outlets.

This was a "primitive" campground in R.V. jargon, and Maggie was just happy to see that there was a bathhouse in which they could shower.

She saw a brown wooden bulletin board up near the entrance into the campground, and she started to get out of the car. Chip hit the door of the bathhouse and said "All done!" The screen door creaked shut and closed with a slap, and Chip walked around the front of the car and climbed into the passenger seat. Maggie saw that the screen door remained open wide enough to get a foot in the door.

"Did they have showers inside?"

"Two," he said.

"Did you check to see if they had hot water?"

"Yes, ma'am," he said. "They do. And they're clean."

Maggie looked at her son and smiled. She reached across and ruffled his sandy blonde hair.

"Come here, kiddo, and give your momma a kiss."

Chip leaned toward her and kissed her on the cheek. Maggie noticed Chip's resemblance to his father in his cheekbones. He had his father's personality, too: that endless optimism in his eyes no matter how dark or bleak the future.

She said, "Now, let's see what we gotta do to stay here."

• •

The mountain lion walked cautiously toward the campground. She kept her eyes on the car and watched the little boy run around the front end of the car up to the bathhouse.

The female cat lowered her shoulders and stalked in absolute silence. The brown fur on the back of her ears twitched with every little shift of sound and wind, and the cat changed her position accordingly.

She drew into some brush at the edge of the forest about thirty meters from the car, and she lay down in utter camouflage and watched the humans below her.

• •

There was a sign on the bulletin board that said "Campground Open All Year," and Maggie saw a metal box attached to one of the posts holding the large bulletin board. Chip stood on his toes and peered through the slot into the metal box, while Maggie filled out the camper registration form. The state of Arizona requested a ten-dollar-per-night fee per campsite, but they were obviously working on the honor system at this particular campground.

Maggie put the ten dollar bill in the envelope with her registration form, and she handed it to Chip.

"Just put it in the box, honey."

Chip beamed at getting to do this, and he slipped the envelope into the metal box. Maggie leaned over his shoulder and frowned when she saw there were no other envelopes inside the locked box.

*Maybe somebody comes by to pick them up daily*, she thought.

"Come on, honey," she said. "Let's pick us out a site."

• •

They decided on site seventy-three because it was adjacent to the creek and not too far away from the bathhouse. A dark brown post had a white number "73" etched into it.

Maggie checked the site's water spigot and saw that it functioned, and so she backed the camper up into the site. Then she got out Chip's bike from the back of the station wagon.

"You can ride it around the campground."

"Thanks, Mom." He pedaled down the narrow driveway at their site and onto the main dirt path that looped around the campground. He thought it would be cool to ride across the wooden bridge, and so he pedaled feverishly in that direction.

Meanwhile, Maggie laid the wood blocks around the camper's wheels, and then lifted it up from the back of the station wagon with the camper jack. She'd gotten proficient at setting up camp by herself since Frank had died three years ago.

When he was alive, Frank loved to take Maggie and Chip camping around the Midwest and as far west as Colorado. But when the cancer got into his lungs, his death came mercifully swift. There was a six-month period after the funeral when folks from the church and around the neighborhood really rallied to support her, but eventually, there were other issues to attend to, and people slowly started backing away from Maggie Eiser.

Kids around the neighborhood looked at her strangely, as though at a dog they were trying to figure out. Most of the families in her Muncie neighborhood were married and a good number had kids, yet Maggie found herself living alone with a toddler in a huge lakefront house that she and Frank had planned to grow into. Neighborhood kids thought it was a little weird. Truth was, she couldn't imagine moving onto another man, and she doubted that there were any guys interested in a widow with a young son in tow.

Eighteen months after the funeral, she went on her first date as a single woman in more than ten years. She was still using her married name, and she felt so out of the loop she didn't know whether to talk about music, work, or sports. The guy was okay, but he was coming off of an emotionally difficult divorce, and there were just too many issues.

"Honey!" Maggie called. "Don't go off too far. Okay?"

Chip parked his bike on the bridge, and he started wandering down the creek. He turned, looked at her with a smile, and waved.

"I won't," he called up to her.

Maggie stood there, her hands akimbo, and she watched him. She thought she saw something moving on the hill across the campground, but it might have just been the wind stirring tree branches and the bushes on the forest floor. She stared a moment more, but she didn't see anything move.

The pop-up camper opened with a hand crank below its license plate, and Maggie got it up and open, and then stepped up inside its door. She only stayed inside five minutes.

She made the beds at either end of the camper, and she stepped out and got the water from the spigot attached.

"Chip?" she called.

She walked around to the front of the Taurus.

She saw his bright red children's bike standing up on the bridge against the railing, but she didn't see Chip.

"Honey?" she said.

It was beginning to get dark, and Maggie wanted to get a campfire going before night set in, but she didn't see her son anywhere at all.

"Chip, honey," she called. "We need to gather wood for a fire."

There was no answer, and she walked down toward the bridge and his bike. A breeze started from high up in the mountains and swept down over the treetops, rustling the branches. Now that the sun was setting, it was beginning to turn cool in the high country. Maggie bent down and steered his bike around.

"Chip?" she called.

She stood up in the middle of the bridge and looked around the clearing. She didn't see a sign of her son anywhere.

His scream ripped the wind right out of her.

Maggie leapt down off of the bridge and started running along the creek's bank toward the sound of her shrieking son. She rounded a corner on the creek and saw her son staggering toward her. Tears streamed down his face, and in the fading twilight, Maggie saw the swarm of bees ten feet beyond him, pouring out of an old log.

"*Chip*," she said, and she ran to him.

Chip wailed, and his eyes were blind with tears and fright.

"Mommy!" he cried, and Maggie picked him up in her arms and carried him as swiftly as she could away from the swarm of bees.

"Oh, baby," she said. "Oh, my God. I'm so sorry. Oh, my God."

Chip continued to scream, but he was already calming down in the comfort of his mother's arms. Maggie led him up to their campsite, and she sat him down on the picnic table. Quickly, she retrieved her first-aid kit from inside the camper and returned to him.

"Where did it sting you?"

Chip pointed to his left bicep. "*Here*," he wailed.

She rolled up his shirt sleeve and saw the lump already forming. She turned on a flashlight and held it up to his arm. His skin was red and swelling where the bee had stung him.

"Okay, I'm gonna need to take the stinger out," she said. "Did they sting you anywhere else?"

"*Here*," he wailed, and he pointed to the back of his neck.

Maggie held the flashlight up and looked at the spot, and sure enough, another red lump of skin was swelling up where he'd been stung. Maggie removed a pair of tweezers from the first-aid kit.

"I need you to hold still," she said.

Chip sobbed, but he tried to calm down. He cried, "*It hurts.*"

Maggie leaned in toward his neck. She held the flashlight in one hand and the tweezers in the other.

"I know it does, baby," she said.

With perfectly calm hands, she reached the tweezers forward and removed the tiny stinger from the back of his neck. It came out cleanly, and she applied a dab of Sting-Aid to the wound.

"That's cold."

"That'll keep it from swelling up too much," she said, "and it should help with the pain."

Chip could already feel a difference in the back of his neck, and he wasn't crying as intensely.

"Now, let me see your arm," she said.

It had gotten so dark in the past ten minutes that Chip couldn't see all the way across the campground, as they both had been able to do just thirty minutes earlier. The flashlight beam was very bright, and Maggie knelt down and inspected the sting on his arm. She faced his torso with her back towards the center of the campground, and Chip sensed the mountain lion before he actually saw it. It came to him in a quick flash that sounded like his daddy's voice in his mind, as clear as a ringing bell. *Look out, Chip,* that voice said.

The mountain lion stepped out from the shadows down by the bridge. Chip saw it in the darkness.

"Hold still," she said.

The cat Chip saw was not the warm and friendly animal he had seen in calendars and on posters, pictures where an adorable mother lion licked her spotted kittens with affection and sunshiny love.

What he saw was a large animal with tight skin over its ribs. This cougar was not plump like the ones he had seen in the Indianapolis Zoo. It was skinny and undernourished.

The cougar stopped at the edge of a dirt path that came up from the creek. It stared at Chip and his mother, not with hatred nor with compassion, but with quick analytical eyes that looked at these two creatures twenty-five meters uphill from it.

"It's a cat," Chip said.

Maggie's focus went to Chip's eyes, and she immediately swung around.

"Where?" she said. "What?"

The mountain lion had stepped back down into the shadows along the creek.

"It was right there by the bridge," Chip said.

Maggie looked hard into his eyes and realized he believed he'd seen something. Her head swung back around, and she scanned the darkness, but she didn't see anything that looked like a cat. She heard the roar of the creek, the rustle of tree branches in the breeze, but she saw no cat. It was an hour past sunset and growing cold, and Maggie still had a stinger to remove from her son's arm.

They hadn't eaten since the Burger King up in Show Low, Arizona over seven hours earlier, and they were both hungry. She needed to cook dinner, start a fire, and she wanted to take a hot shower. She needed to make certain that her son was alright and that the bee stings would not grow any worse.

"What'd you see, Chip?"

Chip looked into her eyes and said, "It was a big cat."

Partly from the cold and partly from the conviction in his voice, Maggie shivered reflexively. Again, she scanned up and down the creek. It was dark and her eyes had been staring at his arm in the bright flashlight's shine, so everything along the creek looked pitch black to her. She didn't see anything.

"Come here, honey," she said. "Let's finish up with this arm."

And, rather fluidly, she reached the tweezers forward and removed the stinger from his swollen bicep. She quickly applied the Sting-Aid to the red bump, and she said, "Did they sting you anywhere else?"

"I don't think so," Chip said. He kept looking at the shadows down by the creek over his mom's left shoulder, but he didn't see the big cat anymore.

# FIVE

Jenny Granger and Nick Jacobs were two of the brightest stars Angie Rippard had seen come up through the biology department in a long, long time. They were both nineteen, both majoring in biology, and both making perfect grades in the honors program at the U of A.

Jenny had first heard about making out on the fourteenth green at Ventana Canyon from a hall mate who lived three doors down in the Arizona-Sonora honors dormitory. Nick thought the idea sounded cool, so the young couple rolled three joints, packed a thick blanket and a six-pack of Coors Light, and drove up into the hills north of Skyline Drive.

Jenny parked her convertible Jetta in a public lot just off of North Kolb Road, and the couple carried the blanket, beer, and marijuana a quarter mile through the shadows adjacent to North Resort Drive and then walked out onto the Ventana Canyon Golf Course. Once out on the sixteenth fairway, they could see the city lights spread out below them for thirty miles to the south. The lights glimmered in the night.

The air was cool, and the starlight was peaceful. Nick grabbed Jenny's butt, and she turned, smiled, and they started kissing. Nick's hand rose up to her breasts, and she put the beer on the ground and threw her head back. Nick began kissing her neck. His hand caressed her red hair.

Suddenly, her head snapped up, and she looked around them.

"What was that?" she said.

Nick didn't even look up. He was unbuttoning her blouse, and his mouth was on the warm flesh of her neck.

Jenny whispered, "Nick, I think I heard something."

"Yes," Nick said. His hands continued southward.

Jenny grabbed his hands in both of hers, and she stepped back away from him. He finally looked up and into her eyes.

The warm lights of large homes glowed just a couple hundred meters away.

"What if somebody is out walking," Jenny whispered.

"At eleven o'clock at night?" Nick said.

Jenny stood there looking at Nick a few seconds more. She thought, *he sure looks good*. Nick had a charming, devious look about him that excited Jenny. Her head pivoted from right to left, but she didn't see any further sign of movement.

"Come on," she said, and she picked up the beer and started forward across the fairway.

Nick grabbed the blanket and followed after her.

Ten minutes later, they found the fourteenth tee box, and they started uphill along the fairway in the direction of the green. There were no houses along the fourteenth, and it was far enough away from the clubhouse that they felt safe.

Up behind the green, there was a eucalyptus tree that gave anyone on the green total privacy from the rocky hills up above. A giant rock formation stood twenty meters left of the green. It climbed up more than forty feet above ground level. There was a pond back behind the tree, and a ten-foot-wide waterfall poured down from the mountains into the pond.

They were well up above the city lights and not far from the National Forest Land boundary. Jenny ran up the giant rock formation and got out on top of it.

She could see over the trees and mansions built farther down the course. Nick spread the blanket out at the back of the fourteenth green in the shadows near the tree. A gentle breeze rustled the leaves. He gazed out at the pond and saw moonlight rippling on the water's surface. He knelt down and touched the water with his hand; the water was warm enough for a swim.

He turned and started to say as much to Jenny, but she waved him up onto the rock, and he came to her.

They both stood there atop the giant rock, looking down the fairway and out over the city lights. Jenny cracked open a can of beer and felt certain that no one would find them (or hear them) this far up on the golf course.

They could see the nearest home was a hundred meters or so beyond the fourteenth tee, which itself was five hundred yards downhill from the green. The house was almost a half mile away. Jenny sipped the beer and felt completely at peace. She handed one to Nick, and he too cracked open a beer.

They both sat down on the rock, and neither said a word. The view was spectacular. Nick put his arm around Jenny, and she draped her left arm over his lanky right thigh and wrapped her hand up around his knee. They just sat there and sipped the ice-cold beer and enjoyed one another's company.

"You feel like getting high?" Nick whispered.

Jenny looked into his blue eyes and smiled. "Come here," she said. She leaned forward, and they kissed.

A minute later, she said, "God, I love you." She looked at his longish brown hair, then into his eyes. "You know that?"

"Yeah," he said. "I think I do. I really think I do."

She sipped the beer, and Nick fired up the joint. He handed it to her, and she took a good draw from it. She held the smoke in her lungs a moment, and then exhaled through her nose. She passed the joint back to Nick, and she sipped her beer.

She glanced back around and down the rock at the blanket laid in the shadows toward the back of the green. Nick inhaled deeply and then exhaled.

"Look at you," Jenny said, feeling giggly. "Settin' up a picnic down there."

Nick handed her the joint and finished off his beer. He cracked open another, while Jenny worked the rest of the joint.

"Yeah, I'm getting kind'a hungry," Nick said.

"Not much left," Jenny said, holding the end of the joint in her fingertips.

"Just put it out on the rock," he said. "We don't want to start a fire up here."

Jenny put the joint out on the surface of the rock and just sat there staring out at the city lights, feeling the buzz coming on. The lights seemed to kind of swell and move, and it seemed funny to her. She smiled.

Jenny pushed Nick backward on the rock, so that he lay back, and then she caressed the denim fabric over his thighs. She felt his cell phone in his right front pants pocket, and she eased her hand up under his shirt and felt the warmth of his skin. He had the lean muscular stomach of a distance runner.

She started to unbutton his jeans with one hand but could not, and so she had to reposition and use both hands. Nick leaned up and started to unbutton her blouse. The rock was beginning to hurt his back.

"Let's go down on the blanket."

"Okay," she said, feeling somewhat awkward with her blouse half open and with Nick's pants unzipped.

They both stood up. Nick held his unbuttoned pants, and they walked down the rock toward the blanket. Jenny lifted her blouse up over her head, unsnapped her bra, and ran up behind him and hugged him. She let the blouse and bra fall on the grass near the back of the green. Nick turned around and started kissing her.

She lifted up his shirt, and they had to stop kissing a moment while the shirt came up around his face and over his head. He threw the shirt on the soft, green grass, and the young couple embraced one another skin to skin in the moonlight.

# Six

Chip fell asleep next to his mother in the warm glow of a campfire. He'd eaten an amazing two cheeseburgers and two hotdogs, a small bag of Ruffles, and he'd finished off a can of Sprite, and now he lay asleep in a lounge chair ten feet from the soft warm glow of a crackling campfire. Maggie sipped white wine from a plastic cup and stared into the fire as if in a trance.

It was completely dark around the campground, but their fire was bright and warm, and Maggie sat there in a fold-out chair with her feet propped up on the picnic table bench. She sipped the wine and stared into the fire.

Chip had quieted down, and Maggie was planning to put him to bed inside the camper. Chip was the kind of boy who would roll up inside a sleeping bag and not make a sound until eight A.M. the next morning. She thought of taking a hot shower, and she glanced over her shoulder at the bathhouse across the creek.

A single bug-repellent, yellow light bulb hung to the left of the bathhouse door. She saw the payphone, and she saw the crooked sign hanging from the door, and she finished off her cup of wine. Sparks shot up into the air above the campfire, and Maggie toed open the cooler with her hiking boot. She saw that she'd finished half the bottle of wine, and she told herself that she deserved it.

It was not easy being a single mother, and this vacation was as much for her as it was for Chip. She'd been living with the moniker "widow" attached to her name for so long it was making her a little crazy in the head.

She'd kept her nursing job at the hospital in Muncie, but she hadn't been able to afford the mortgage payments on the big house (nor did she and Chip need a five-thousand-square-foot lakefront home anymore) and so six months earlier, she'd moved into a townhouse a mile from the hospital. After the sale of the big house, she had enough money to trade up and buy a nicer camper, and she'd done it, pledging to Chip to work less and to spend more quality time with him. And so, they'd planned this twelve-day spring break vacation out of the lingering gray winter of Indiana on across Illinois, Missouri, Kansas, Colorado, and southwest into Arizona.

The camper had heat and air conditioning, a TV, a stove, a fridge, an internet outlet, two full-size beds, a utilitarian shower, toilet, and "sleeping room for eight" (or so the owner's manual described). Insurance on the camper was thirty bucks per year, and the gas stove could cook up a scrambled egg in just under five minutes.

Maggie stood up and swayed a little, braced herself with her left hand on the picnic table, and then placed the empty cup of wine atop the table. She looked at her sleeping son. He wore a Harry Potter sweatshirt, jeans, and his longish blonde hair hung disorderly down over his forehead. Maggie crossed to him and brushed his hair back. The fire crackled and popped.

She knelt down and hefted him up in her arms. Chip was getting bigger and heavier each and every day. She cleared her mind and walked to the camper. She opened the door and stepped up inside. She kept her balance inside the camper and carried him to one end and placed him on the mattress.

She unzipped his jeans and pulled his pants off.

Chip mumbled something in his sleep, and Maggie unzipped his sleeping bag and struggled to get him inside.

"What's going on?"

"Hush, now," Maggie said. "Put your feet down here."

She got him inside the sleeping bag and zipped him up. Chip looked up at her and smiled sleepily. The shadows of the campfire danced on the wall inside the camper. Maggie leaned over and brushed his hair back. She kissed him on the forehead.

"I love you, baby," she slurred. "Now you gesh some sweet dreams."

"I love you too, Momma," Chip said. He curled up inside the sleeping bag and rolled over.

Maggie stood there looking at her son with so much love that it made her heart ache, and for some strange reason she wanted to cry. He was so clear headed and brave, had so accepted his dad's death and had moved on, and he was only six years old. Maggie was filled with pride, pity, a touch of envy, and love, and each of these emotions came together in a moment of confluence inside her mind, and she couldn't hold them down. Maggie stood there looking at her son, and she cried deeply peaceful and cleansing tears.

She cleared her throat lightly, and she swung around toward the other end of the camper.

She whispered wearily to herself, "I need a shower."

She undressed at the far end of the camper and put on her white terrycloth bathrobe. She eased her feet into her flip-flops, and she picked up her bathroom kit, a clean towel, and a clean pair of underwear. She rolled the underwear up inside the towel and stepped down out of the camper.

She couldn't see the cat that stood in the shadows twenty yards away from her.

Maggie looked once more at her son and closed the camper door. She saw the cooler still open and crossed to the picnic table, picked up her empty cup, and filled it anew all the way to the brim. She stood there in her white bathrobe and sipped the wine down enough that she could walk without spillage.

The mountain lion watched her.

Maggie stirred the campfire around with a stick, centering the glowing embers. She grabbed her flashlight from atop the picnic table, turned it on, and then started down the little driveway of site seventy-three. At the bottom of the drive, she turned and looked at the fire. It looked like it would be okay, and she thought it might be nice to take a hot shower and then lounge in a chair by the fire afterwards. She took another long sip of the wine, and she started off in the direction of the bathhouse.

The mountain lion leapt silently to its feet and watched her from the darkness.

Maggie crossed the wooden bridge, lingered for a moment, and saw the moonlight reflecting off of the creek. She took another sip of wine and started up the hill toward the bathhouse.

She saw the yellow light bulb to the left of the door. She saw the payphone. She saw the sign hanging crookedly from the door. And then she heard something back behind her. Maggie turned and looked down toward the creek.

She saw their campfire and camper up on the little hill across the creek.

She started to say "hello?" but then thought that whatever she'd heard was just her imagination. She turned and walked up to the bathhouse door. At the doorway, she saw that the screen door was open about four inches wide. The lights were off inside the bathroom. Standing outside, she reached her hand inside and felt for a light switch on the wall. The wall inside consisted of cold, square bathroom tiles.

Again, she thought she heard something, and she peered over her left shoulder down at the creek. And again, she saw nothing. She saw the glow of the campfire up at their site, the rushing water in the creek, the rustle of leaves in the treetops, but that was it.

Her hand hit the light switch inside. She flipped it up, and fluorescent lights came on.

She turned once more, and this time, spoke in the direction of the creek, "Is anybody there?"

As if in reply, the wind in the branches died down, and everything in the forest became still. There was only the sound of rushing water in the creek. She shrugged her shoulders and stepped inside the bathhouse.

She was pleasantly surprised to see that the bathhouse was clean. There were two toilets over to the right, and she stepped up to the double sink in the center. The mirror was spotless and shiny clean, and the sink looked as though someone had given it a good scrub with Comet in the not-too-distant past.

Maggie looked at herself in the mirror.

She had blue eyes and was beautiful in that curious way that only occurs when a young woman does not know that she is beautiful. She had the beauty of a young woman who had been through some crazy shit in her lifetime and was working to keep her failed family together. There was something deeply piteous about her, but of course Maggie didn't see this at all when she looked at herself in the mirror. She saw a woman who was cracking up, tired, goofy looking, unkempt, slightly drunk. She had a smudge of black soot on her cheek. She opened her bathrobe, and she gazed at herself calmly.

Maggie Eiser was proud of her breasts and slightly ashamed of her little paunch. She sipped the wine and then tried to smile at herself, but it felt awkward and she sort of smirked at her own inability to look genuinely happy.

She turned and saw that the screen door into the bathhouse was open a few inches, and she wanted it closed. Mosquitoes were not a problem in Arizona, but she was sure there were other bugs, and they'd be attracted to the fluorescent lights. She put her towel and shower kit in one of the two shower stalls over to the left and then tried to pull the bathhouse screen door closed.

She pulled it shut and let go of the handle, and the door creaked slowly open about four inches. It was built on a tilt, she realized, and the door was going to stay open just a few inches. Maggie sighed.

She crossed to the shower stall, pulled back the clean plastic shower curtain, and turned on the hot water.

She removed her bathrobe and hung it on a shower hook. She placed her soap, shampoo, and white washcloth inside the shower. A few seconds later, the water turned hot, and she adjusted it to just the right temperature. She stepped inside the shower and pulled the clear plastic shower curtain closed behind her.

The mountain lion came up from the creek, and it walked up the dirt path toward the bathhouse.

The light inside shined through the screen door. The mountain lion took three cautious steps, then froze and listened to the sounds coming from inside the bathhouse. It heard the hiss of the showerhead and the water pattering off of the woman. The young female hadn't made a kill in ten days, and she was tense with hunger.

Maggie rinsed the shampoo from her hair, leaning backward toward the showerhead. The water was warm and clean, and it felt good on her skin on her back. She took the bar of Ivory and lathered up her shoulders. She turned and faced the shower and let the hot water spray down over her forehead and face. She leaned back and let the hot water shower her chest, and she lathered the bar of soap up underneath and around her breasts and let the water rinse her off.

The mountain lion stepped up to the screen door. It sensed that the woman was completely unaware, but the young cat was still very cautious. It nosed its head toward the opening in the screen door, and it realized that the door would part for its head and body. It eased its head inside the door and peered from right to left.

Maggie dropped the bar of soap and squatted down inside the square shower stall to pick it up.

The mountain lion lowered its head and looked underneath the wooden stall outside of the shower. It saw the woman's legs, and its head rose up, poised, realizing that the woman was utterly unaware of its presence. It took three silent, cautious steps into the bathhouse. The floor was cold and slippery, and the cat's claws emerged from its paws and felt the hard surface of the tiled floor.

Maggie glanced over the top of the shower curtain and saw the screen door swaying.

"Honey?" she called.

There was no response. Maggie stood still, and her brow furrowed over with worried curiosity, her lips dropped open ever so slightly, and she wiped the water back from her eyes.

The screen door's swaying settled, and Maggie moved her head to see better, realizing that the door would not have moved like that unless someone had opened it.

"Baby, is that you?"

Maggie stood there in the shower, waiting for a response.

Then, through the somewhat clear shower curtain, she saw the mountain lion step around the corner of the wooden locker right in front of the stall. Its head peered up at her. Maggie's chest felt like it was injected with a massive needle of icy helium, and her lips tingled.

All the blood rushed out of her face, and she felt raw panic like nothing she'd ever experienced in her life.

Something primal clicked inside her, and she realized that she was cornered, pinned in a little ceramic-tile cell, and that a large predator stood there three feet away. She realized that the next ten seconds would determine whether she lived or died.

The cat took two steps forward into the wooden locker area and then lunged at the clear plastic shower curtain. Its claws did not grab well on the tiled floor, so the lunge was partly a slip. It hit the shower curtain, and Maggie fell backward in the square shower.

She screamed, and she beat at the plastic curtain.

The cat fell to the floor inside the wooden locker area but outside of the actual shower. There was a bench on either side of the locker area, and Maggie's towel hung on a hook on the right side, and her bathrobe hung on a hook on the left side.

The cat tried to spring to its feet, but the floor just outside of the shower was wet, and the cat had difficulty standing balanced. It slashed at the shower curtain with its right front paw, and the claws tore through the plastic.

Maggie screamed and batted dumbly at the plastic curtain and at the cat's clawing paw.

"Get out!" she screamed. "*Goddamn it, get out!!*"

Her voice was an animalistic shriek.

The cat crouched down and leapt into the shower curtain again. This time its claws caught the plastic, and its weight tore out four of the eight shower curtain rings. The cat's two front paws came down inside the shower.

Water sprayed all over the place, and the cat was somewhat tangled up in the half-fallen shower curtain, and its right forelimb came up and slashed through the air inside the shower.

Its claws swept powerfully across Maggie's front left thigh. She was backed up as far inside the stall as she could stand, and she screamed and batted at the mountain lion's head.

The cat bared its teeth and tried to take a bite at her hand. Maggie screamed at it, and the cat lost its balance and fell on its side. It immediately tried to leap up onto its feet, but it slipped and fell down again. Its left front paw clawed around wildly, and it tore down the rest of the shower curtain.

Suddenly, the cat was blanketed by the curtain, and it just went crazy, screaming a wildcat scream like nothing else Maggie had ever heard. It thrashed wildly and powerfully to get free of the curtain, and in this action, it swept Maggie's legs out from under her.

She fell hard inside the shower, her head struck the wall, and everything faded into white dizziness for a moment.

The cat retreated into the locker area, thrashing around wildly. It tore through the wooden locker wall on the right side, and it tried to swing completely around, which it could not do, and so it swung back the other way.

Finally, the shower curtain fell away from the cat's head. The mountain lion stood there, staring at Maggie Eiser who was now seated inside the shower. Blood flowed from her left thigh.

Maggie sat there, staring at the lion.

"Come on!" she screamed. "*Finish it off!*"

But the cat stepped back away from the stall. And as swiftly as it had entered, it turned and exited through the screen door, vanishing into the night.

## SEVEN

"You want to do it again?" Jenny asked.

She lay cradled beside Nick, her head and her right arm up over his chest. Nick lay on his back staring up at the millions and millions of stars in the night sky. She took his silence to mean "no," though he hadn't really heard her. Nick was imagining them making love on the moon where they'd both weigh like twenty-five pounds and could float around.

He started to laugh.

"Oh, you think that was funny?" Jenny said.

She grabbed hold of his penis and flipped it around.

"Now, *that* is something to laugh about," she said.

Nick rolled over to reach for one of the last two beers, and it kind of pushed Jenny backwards.

"Well, aren't you Mister Sensitive," she said.

"Excuse me," he said, and he cracked open the beer.

"Let me have a sip," she said, and he handed her the beer.

She sat cross-legged on the edge of the blanket, sipped the beer, and gazed down the fairway and across the glimmering city lights of Tucson.

"Do you want to live a long time, Nick?" she asked.

"I guess so."

"It's just we don't get many years, you know?"

"That's life."

"Sometimes," she said, "I'll get to thinking about what happens when I die, and it's like a black grip of fear comes over my mind. I'll start twitching and shit, and my heart will feel like it's about to explode, and I think 'What if this is it, man, you know?' What if this is all there is? The thought is so frightening and lonely, it scares the hell out of me."

"*Damn*," Nick said.

"I'll be alright. I'm just telling you that it happens sometimes. You ever feel like that?"

"I don't know," he said. "Maybe. What do you do?"

"When I get scared like that?"

"Yeah."

"You're gonna laugh," she said.

"No, I won't."

"Yes, you will."

"I swear I won't," he said. "What do you do?"

"I pray," she said. "I get down on my knees, and I pray."

"Does it work?"

"Sometimes," she said.

They were silent a moment.

"What do you do if it doesn't work?" Nick said.

Jenny thought about it. She said, "I go hang out at Wal-Mart."

Nick laughed.

"I'm serious," she said. "I'll go walk around Wal-Mart, talk to employees, ask them questions about toothpaste and shit. Make some good eye contact and just talk to other people, or just *be around* other people. I don't think about dying when I'm around other people."

"You're crazy."

"Maybe," she said.

She looked at him. And then she noticed that he was getting aroused again.

She said, "Well, look who decided to stand at attention."

"Come here, baby," he said.

She put the beer down and got on top of him. She wasn't quite ready yet, but she rubbed up and down on him until she was. She eased her way down and felt him filling her up inside. The sensation was raw pleasure, and she felt comfortable enough to want more, faster.

"Oh, God," she said.

They held one another's arms while she rode up and down on top of him.

*"Oh, my God!"*

# EIGHT

Maggie Eiser lay on the cold tile floor inside the bathhouse. She glanced at the front door and saw that it was still open four inches. She expected the mountain lion to nose its head inside that door at any moment, to look at her bleeding on the floor, and to realize that it had almost passed up an easy kill.

She reached across the demolished wooden locker and grabbed the white towel. The towel was now damp with water that continued to spray out of the shower. Her leg was bleeding badly, and she had zero movement south of her left kneecap. The wound was so messy that it was difficult to tell just how deep the gash went, but she knew that if she'd lost musculature movement below her knee that it was pretty deep.

She grabbed the towel, and with both hands positioned her legs out in front of her. The general plan was to wrap up the leg in order to stop the bleeding. Her face and hands felt pale and cold, and her whole body felt weak. Again, she glanced at the screen door into the bathhouse. It swayed just a little in a breeze that stirred up from outside. She could see nothing outside the bathhouse, in part because it was dark and in part because of her angle on the bathroom floor.

She padded the wound area lightly with the towel. The towel soaked up the blood, and Maggie grimaced seeing just how deeply the mountain lion's claws had torn through her thigh. The muscles were cut in two like a rubber band that had been snapped.

She groaned, "*Son of a bitch.*"

And she held the towel firmly on her thigh, applying pressure to the wound.

• •

Chip Eiser awoke inside the camper. He lay in his sleeping bag, but his eyes opened and looked across the camper.

"Momma?" he said.

Through the dim light, he could see that there was no one on the far side of the camper. He rolled over and looked out the mosquito-netting window down past the creek and on up to the bathhouse. He saw the light on inside the bathhouse through the bathhouse's screen door. He saw the single bug-repellant yellow light bulb hanging just left of the screen door.

He quieted himself and listened for any sound.

He heard the steady rushing water of the creek, and faintly (maybe just his imagination) he thought he heard the sound of a shower. Again, he glanced at the far end of the camper toward his mother's bed, but he could see in the dim light that there was no lump where her body should be.

He said a little more urgently, "*Momma?*"

And again there was no answer.

Chip sat up in bed and shivered. He unzipped his sleeping bag and stepped down onto the floor of the camper. He was wearing a white pair of underpants and white socks with little blue stripes. The camper smelled of wine and the lingering odor of campfire smoke. And it was cold.

Chip could see his breath in the air, and he turned and pulled his sleeping bag over him like a blanket. He opened the door to the camper and looked around outside at the dying embers of the campfire. He saw the picnic table with a two-liter bottle of soda on it, a roll of paper towels, the red forty-gallon Igloo cooler, and an empty bottle of wine.

He called out into the darkness, "Momma?"

He thought he saw something moving down by the creek, and he suddenly remembered the big cat he'd seen earlier when his mom took the stinger out of his arm. His mom hadn't seen the cat, but *he* had.

*Or had he dreamed it?*

Chip rubbed sleep from his eyes, pulled the sleeping bag a little more snugly around his shoulders, and stepped down out of the camper. He closed the door behind him. The sleeping bag dragged behind him like a lumpy cape, but it kept his shoulders warm. He stepped out into the middle of the campsite and looked around him in the darkness.

Chip was the kind of child that ordinarily felt fine when he was alone. He was a quiet, intense boy at school, and while he had friends, he was almost as happy playing in the sandbox alone. It was just a part of his fiber to not be afraid of being alone, but standing there in the middle of the campsite, his mother nowhere to be seen, Chip began to worry.

"Maybe she's taking a shower," he said to himself.

And he considered a walk across the campground, up to the bathhouse to see. It was dark and he didn't have a flashlight, but he thought there was one inside the camper.

He walked back over to the camper door, opened it, and stepped up inside. He grabbed a red flashlight, hit the switch and saw the beam come on. His breath steamed in the cool mountain air. He pivoted around and found a pair of sandals, slipped his feet into them, and then stepped back outside of the camper. He closed the door behind him.

The air was cool, but Chip was worried and he was alone, and he was a resourceful young boy, so he started across the campground. He held the flashlight beam on the ground in front of him, and he walked down toward the bridge. The water glistened in the moonlight that reached through the treetops.

Chip saw something large and sleek move across the path on the other side of the bridge, and he froze in his tracks. Whatever it was, it moved across the path very quickly and back down under the bridge. Chip stood there five feet from the bridge.

He shined his flashlight across the bridge and its wooden railing. He saw dirt on the wooden planks of the bridge. He saw car tracks through the dirt. The bridge was about twenty feet across, and the wood was painted an aged, rust-red color. There were dead leaves scattered on the bridge.

Chip shined his flashlight on either side of the bridge, but he couldn't shine it down under the bridge where there were shadows. His breath steamed out into the cold night air.

"Hello?" he said.

There was no answer, but he was certain something had gone down under the bridge, and he was afraid to cross over it. It might reach up and grab him around his legs and pull him down into the shadows. He would go screaming and kicking. His flashlight would fall and hit the floor of the bridge, and that would be all anyone would ever find of little Chip Eiser.

"Momma!" Chip called out.

He stood there at the foot of the bridge and looked up at the bathhouse. He saw the light inside shining through the screen door, and he was certain he heard the shower on inside now, but the rushing water of the creek was loud, too, and there didn't appear to be any movement inside the bathhouse.

The fear that gripped him was unlike anything he'd ever felt in his life. He was just frozen, frozen between moving and running and staying perfectly still. His mind flooded with panic and the horrible realization that no one was here to protect him. His dad had "gone to heaven." His mom was not answering him, and he was all alone in the middle of a campground five days away from home, and there was no one here to help him.

"Momma," he whimpered, and tears began to form in his eyes.

He took one step, then another. His left foot came down onto the wooden planks of the bridge. He tried to straighten himself up to see over the sides of the bridge. Something was down there; he just knew it. Some kind of monster. It looked like a cat, a big giant cat, and it was going to reach up and grab him by his ankles and pull him down into the shadows under the bridge and do horrible things to him.

He took another step across the bridge. The light from the flashlight shook, as much from the cold as from the icy fear that trickled down his spine. He held the flashlight up and shined it into the trees. The trees seemed to stand over him with branches like spindly arms.

He was midway across the bridge.

"Chip?" The voice sounded weak and tentative.

Chip looked up toward the bathhouse. "Momma?" he said.

And then he saw shadows moving inside the bathhouse. He shined the flashlight up the path on the far side of the bridge, and his mother stepped into the doorway of the bathhouse.

Chip was not prepared for how she looked—she wore a bloody white towel wrapped around her thigh, and her bathrobe was soaked with water and spotted with blood. She staggered forward like something from a nightmare. He ran to her, ran up from the bridge, up the hill.

"Chip!" she cried.

# NINE

The big cat came often to the pool in the early morning hours between three A.M. and four A.M., but tonight there was something down there. He was high up on the rocks, and he stepped onto a rocky outcropping and looked out at all the twinkling lights.

To the cat, the city smelled alien and foul. It was like some legion of locusts surrounding his home, and he was at once fearful and ready to fight.

He heard water splashing at his regular watering hole.

Without a sound, the big cat leapt down from the rock and walked silently down the hill.

．．

Jenny stood ten feet from shore, the water up to her abdomen. The bottom of the pond was smooth, sandy, and clean, and she ducked her head back, wetting her hair, then shook her head and swept her hair back with her fingertips.

"Come on, Nick," she called up to him.

Nick was asleep on the blanket. He'd pulled one side of the blanket up over him and was rolled up inside its warmth dreaming of pistons and roller coasters and a clown that became himself then Jenny looking at herself in a bathroom mirror.

"Stop licking me," he mumbled.

Out in the middle of the pond, Jenny turned and dove underwater. She started swimming for the waterfall on the far side of the pool.

The big male cat stood over Nick, purring. Its head came up at the sound from the middle of the pond. It watched the figure swimming across the moonlit water, and then it returned its gaze to the sleeping human. It tilted its head toward him, sniffed, and then winced backward, shook its head and licked its nose.

"Leave me alone," Nick mumbled from the depths of sleep.

The cat leaned in toward Nick's face again. It was not accustomed to prey that showed no sign of awareness and lay there so completely vulnerable. The big cat was used to chasing its prey, but this creature just swatted at its head dumbly.

The big cat started pawing at the blanket around Nick, trying to cover him up. It scraped up the leaves of the eucalyptus tree and piled them on and around Nick. It grabbed twigs in its mouth and placed them on him.

"I said go away," Nick mumbled.

The cat raised a paw up and licked it, then placed the paw on the left side of Nick's head. The paw covered his head from the back of his skull all the way around to the bridge of his nose. The paw was almost twice the size of an average human hand.

Nick felt the paw on him and slowly opened his eyes.

All at once, he tried to scream, scramble away, and bat at the mountain lion's right forelimb. Claws emerged from the paw sinking deep into his skin.

The big cat's mouth came down and clamped powerfully around Nick's neck, silencing him.

Jenny was under the waterfall, feeling the water pouring all around her, its sound roaring. At the waterfall, the surface of the pond was thigh high, and Jenny stood there taking a natural shower.

She thought she heard something over the noise of the waterfall, and so she stepped out away from it.

"Nick?" she called across the pond.

There was no answer.

*Sleeping*, she thought. *The lightweight.*

She craned her head to see up to the blanket. It was in the shadows and too far away to see very well, but she didn't see a lump where his body should have been. She started toward the shore.

"Fell asleep on me, huh?" she said.

And she came up out of the water.

Nick was not there. The blanket was bare where she'd left him just a couple minutes earlier. Her chest immediately seized up with adrenaline. She stood in the moonlight, looking around wildly in every direction.

*"Nick,"* her voice cracked. *"This isn't funny."*

She glanced beyond the blanket and saw his jeans, socks, tennis shoes, and pullover shirt.

She was getting cold, goose bumps rising up on her bare wet skin. "Nick?"

Her first fear was that some nut had taken him, some stalker, but then she said to herself that Nick was just screwing with her.

*"Nick,"* she said with urgency.

Her pulse was doing one-forty, and her hands shook. Suddenly, she was surrounded by shadows. There were shadows on either side of the putting green. She hadn't really noticed them before, but they were all around her. She'd heard stories her whole life about serial killers who did just this kind of thing, and suddenly she was racked with red hot shame, vulnerability, and fear.

*But he was just playing a prank on her, right?*

"Are you taking a leak or something?" she said.

Silence.

Her bare feet took a few steps out toward the putting green. The shadows from the eucalyptus tree stretched midway out onto the green, and she walked to just beyond their edge. She was cold and so held her arms close to her chest. Water still trickled down her face and back, and she could smell the fresh algae scent on her skin and in her hair. She started shivering.

She wanted the police. At this moment, she didn't care if she got caught for trespassing, for underage drinking, for the marijuana, for *any* of it, she just wanted safety. She wanted someone who would carry her safely out of this situation.

But there was no one.

She thought of running down the course to one of the million-dollar homes and banging on a door. But there were too many unknowns, and all of her courage seemed to vaporize into a wicked butterfly feeling of nervousness gnawing her stomach.

*"Come on, Nick,"* she said, more to herself than to Nick.

And then she remembered the cell phone.

Nick had a cell phone in his front jeans pocket.

She felt safer standing out in the middle of the putting green under the moonlight as far away from the shadows as possible, so she ran quickly over to the pile of clothes and just grabbed Nick's jeans and ran quickly back out into the moonlight in the middle of the green. She held his jeans in her hands.

She felt around the loose denim for the cell phone, and she immediately felt it inside the front right pocket. She reached inside and pulled the cell out and let his jeans drop to the ground.

"Nick?" she said one last time.

There was no response, only the sound of the waterfall and the wind rustling through the tree branches behind the green.

She knew Nick's cell pretty well and punched 9-1-1 and hit send. She raised the cell to her right ear and glanced around her quickly watching the shadows. And she waited for a ring.

Five seconds passed.

"*Come on*," she said.

She held the phone in front of her and tried to see what kind of signal she was getting. The L.C.D. indicated the signal strength was at its lowest, and she realized she was too far up inside the canyon. She stepped out toward the front of the green, holding the phone out in front of her trying to get a better signal.

Suddenly, she heard something very much like a domestic cat's caterwauling, only about five times louder and deeper and held out longer, for nearly seven full seconds.

"*What in the world*," she said.

The sound came from the shadows to the right of the putting green. It was no more than twenty-five meters away from her, and it was the unmistakable sound of a very large, wild animal.

Her first impulse was to stand her ground, to stand tall and erect, and to make herself look as large and calm as she could. To not seem threatening and to not seem threatened: her mind found that balance, and she stood there in the middle of the fourteenth green.

The big cat emerged from the shadows, looked at her, and then turned its head and started walking toward the pond. It stopped ten feet farther on, turned, and looked at her again.

Jenny remained perfectly calm: do or die calm.

The cat just stood there, twenty feet away, its body pointed toward the pond, its head turned over its left shoulder staring at her. Jenny slowly raised her arms up over her head.

The big cat licked its lips and sniffed at the air. It seemed utterly unafraid of her, even nonchalant and disinterested.

With her hands raised up above her head like that, Jenny slowly walked backward.

She spoke firmly, slowly, and clearly, "Hey, big fellow. We're both just gonna take it *real* easy."

The cat looked large enough that it would not have been able to stand in her dorm room without curling its tail, but she wasn't thinking about anything like that. She was standing there looking at a very large wild animal that could kill her, and her instinct kicked in: she was remaining calm, alert, and non-threatening.

"This is your watering hole," she said calmly and clearly, taking two slow steps back away from the pond. She kept her hands up above her head. "Ain't nobody gonna mess with your watering hole."

She took another two steps backward.

The cat looked at the pond, as though considering it, took two steps toward the water, and then turned around and started coming toward Jenny.

Jenny immediately wanted to turn and run, but some part of her mind knew that *that* would trigger an attack. So, she shot her hands up as high as she could, and she shouted firmly at the cat: "No! Back away!"

The big cat veered over to her left, standing on the fringe of the green. Suddenly, it let go a stream of urine, and then it continued around the left side of the fourteenth green.

The cat seemed somewhat confused that this creature didn't turn and start running, and it veered again—this time to the right—and it crossed over the putting green to the right. It seemed to be measuring her up.

Jenny continued backing slowly away, while facing the cat. She spoke firmly and clearly, and she reached the fringe at the front of the green.

She glanced over her right shoulder to see what was behind her. At the exact moment that her head turned, the mountain lion quit zigzagging and came straight toward her. Jenny's head came back around, and she saw the giant cat coming at her.

It was ten feet away, and Jenny turned and ran. She sprinted hard down the fairway, but the chase didn't last two seconds.

The cat lunged onto her back, its weight staggering, its claws searing into her flesh, and Jenny immediately hit the ground. The cat flipped over in front of her, skidded around, and then regained its balance.

Jenny popped up in a push-up position, the cat five feet in front of her. She thrust herself backward, and the cat leapt.

She screamed and swung her arms at it, and the cat didn't have a good balance on her. Jenny managed to swing both hands at the cat's head like a double-gripped forehand, and she knocked it off of her momentarily, its claws tearing over her chest.

She screamed and got to her feet and just started yelling at the giant cat. The cat backed away a moment.

And then in one fluid movement, it coiled down and leapt up at her from ten feet away. The weight and force of the forward attack knocked Jenny backward, and she hit the ground very hard. It was like being tackled at full speed by a professional defensive end with claws and incredibly dexterous agility.

The cat was on top of her, and it suddenly lunged forward at her face. Jenny had no time to think, no deep realizations at the moment of death, no life flashing before her eyes or long white tunnels. She had perhaps a quarter of a second to exhale a partial scream, and then was quickly silenced.

## Ten

Angie Rippard's black Porsche raced up the mountain. Her boyfriend John Crandall sat in the passenger seat, the lights from the dash illuminated his face. He looked worried. Angie glanced down at the speedometer in front of her, saw that she was doing one-forty, and pressed the accelerator a little harder.

"How far is it past Oracle?"

"It's only about ten miles," John said. "But you're not going to be able to do one-forty."

Angie's eyes were ice blue, like the eyes of a Siberian husky. They were mesmerizing in their utter clarity, and her straight brown hair fell back over her shoulders. Her hands gripped the steering wheel, and she felt irritated that her boyfriend lacked the necessary courage and conviction to arouse her. John was thin and had a large nose, and theirs was a relationship which caused people to ask themselves: What does she see in *that* guy?

They raced past the Biosphere out on Highway 77 and saw the green signs for Oracle. Homes glittered up the mountain to the right of the highway, and Angie downshifted and quickly brought her speed down under one hundred.

"This is it up here," John said, pointing to a single flashing yellow light.

There was a sign that read:

Oracle →

Angie hit her turn signal and slowed for the turn. They saw singlewide trailers on the right and a Circle K convenience store on the left, a video store, and a Mexican restaurant. The mountainside town looked sleepy, but a sheriff's deputy pulled onto the two-lane street a block uphill from them, turned on its blue lights, and took off, racing further up the mountain.

"Keep up with him," John said. "He's probably heading up to Peppersauce."

••

There were more than twenty spinning blue lights of sheriff's deputies, spinning red lights of ambulances and fire trucks; Angie steered her car down the last stretch of dirt road into Peppersauce Canyon. She parked over to the right, giving plenty of room so that other cars could get past her, and she and John got out.

The campground was shining with car lights, police, ambulance, and fire truck lights, with shining search beam lights. There was a steady crackle of CB radios, and there were upwards of one hundred people on the scene.

Angie saw the woman sitting near the back of an ambulance. She wore a bathrobe, and a doctor inspected her son. Angie recognized one of the sheriff's deputies, and then she saw Robert Gonzalez coming up from a creek in the middle of the campground.

Gonzalez wore an orange ball cap and spectacles. Angie thought he was a nice looking guy. His legs were muscular, and his arms were strong . . . a very fit specimen. She liked his self-assured attitude and the way he walked. And working with him, she knew he was a good listener, too. Attentive and humble. He saw Angie and John and waved.

"How're you doing?" he said.

Angie said, "Who's in charge here?"

"We've got a problem with jurisdiction," Gonzalez said. "This is National Forest Land, but the sheriff's deputies were the first on the scene. It'll take rangers three hours to get down here from Lemmon. Ever gone up the north route?"

"A couple times," Angie said. "That's the closest ranger we got?"

"We've got two state park rangers from Oracle." Gonzalez pointed them out for Angie. "But they've got no jurisdiction here, and they just want to help the sheriff's deputies."

"This is National Forest Land," Angie said. "It comes under Game and Fish jurisdiction. We need a ranger."

A large man spoke up from near one of the ambulances. "You must be the Cat Woman," he said.

Angie's blue eyes met his. The man's first impression of Angie was that there was something almost wolf-like in her gaze. He wore a grizzly beard and had clear brown eyes. His expression was sober, and he had a kind of weary affability about him. He had been talking to a younger sheriff's deputy who held a clipboard and was taking notes.

"Sheriff Graham Tucker?" Angie said.

She approached him and held out her hand.

He said, "How was the drive up the mountain, Doctor Rippard?"

Angie said, "You realize this is National Forest Land."

They shook hands. Angie looked into Sheriff Tucker's eyes, and she saw one tough son of a bitch, but she saw, too, someone for whom loyalty was prerequisite. This was a man who had been elected sheriff of a county by people who didn't give a damn about money, fads, and trendy liberal thinking, which at first glance made him look like an enemy of Angie Rippard. But Rippard and Tucker were of the same blood; they were people who could see many sides to an issue and would reserve judgment until a well-formed opinion could be made.

"You'll probably want to speak with the victim," Tucker said.

"Yes," Rippard said. "You realize we need a National Forest ranger. Has anybody contacted Barbara Tonapaw up on Lemmon?"

Tucker glanced at Gonzalez and John Crandall. "You're that nature writer," he said, "the one who writes all those exposés about encroaching on animal habitats."

John said, "I wouldn't call them exposés exactly."

Tucker didn't seem impressed. He said to Angie, "We've got two state park rangers here, Doctor Rippard. It'll be several hours before National Forest rangers can get down the north side of the mountain. They'll probably have to go all the way around to the south. Until they get here, this is my investigation."

"They may not be up here until morning," Rippard said.

"Calm down, Doctor Rippard," Tucker said. "We ain't gonna be putting a hunting party together just yet."

He led Angie Rippard toward the back of the ambulance.

"Miss Eiser," he said. "This here is our resident mountain lion expert, Doctor Angie Rippard. If you feel up for it, she's probably got a few questions for you."

"Okay," Maggie Eiser said.

"Thank you, Sheriff," Angie said.

Sheriff Tucker looked into Angie's eyes long enough to let her know that he was in charge, but that he appreciated her presence. He managed a smile.

"How you feeling?" Angie said.

"I think I'm gonna be alright."

Maggie Eiser sat at the back of the ambulance. An EMT was dressing the wound on her leg, but he was intensely focused on his work.

"How's your son?" Angie said.

Maggie glanced at Chip. A doctor listened to his breathing with a stethoscope.

"He's a little shook up," she said. "But we should be alright."

"Did the mountain lion seem strange to you?" Angie asked. "Did you notice any erratic behavior, foaming at the mouth, a staggering gait."

"No," Maggie said. "It wasn't rabid from what I could see. It looked undernourished."

"How big was it?"

"Probably about six feet from its head to the tip of its tail."

"Six feet?" Angie asked. She pulled out a pocket notebook.

"Five or six feet," Maggie said.

"If you had to estimate a weight," Angie said.

"Oh, I don't know about that; that'd be kind'a hard to do."

"Would you say less than a hundred pounds, less than two hundred?"

Maggie said, "Definitely less than two hundred. Maybe a hundred pounds, not much more."

Angie made a note and underlined it twice. "How did it approach you?"

"I was in the shower," Maggie said. "The screen door up there"— she nodded in the direction of the bathhouse—"it doesn't close all the way. I figure it nosed its way in."

Angie wrote this down. She'd only once heard of a mountain lion attacking someone like this, but she didn't say anything to indicate that to Maggie Eiser. Mountain lions were solitary, and they generally hunted their prey by stalking and ambush, in open spaces but where camouflage was readily available, not by boldly walking into a confined bathhouse. It was the fourth largest cat in the world, but it was probably the most wary of all the big cats. Angie had once watched a one hundred and sixty-pound male stalk a herd of elk in Summit County, Utah for four hours before it made a decisive move. It would creep a few feet at a time and was extremely patient.

"You're sure it wasn't rabid?" Angie said.

"It didn't look rabid," Maggie said. "Now, tests may prove otherwise"—she glanced at her leg—"but I'm a registered nurse, and I've seen two rabid animals before. This cat didn't look like any of those. If anything, it just looked undernourished and very hungry."

"And it approached you while you were in the shower?"

Maggie nodded her head.

"How did you scare it away?" Angie asked.

"To tell you the truth, I don't know how I scared it away. It attacked through the shower curtain, and it knocked out my leg. I fell to the shower floor. The shower curtain came out from its rings. I think the curtain kind'a netted the cat, and it scared it. And then the cat went crazy and demolished the locker in there. I was just lucky, I guess."

Angie asked Sheriff Tucker to show them the bathhouse, and so Tucker led her, Crandall, and Robert Gonzalez up to the bathhouse where the attack had occurred.

"Mind your footing," Tucker said. "The floor's slippery."

Angie stepped into the bathroom. She saw the demolished locker to the left and the water and blood on the floor.

Gonzalez said, "She says the cougar just nosed its way inside?"

Angie pointed to the screen door. "It wouldn't be difficult."

John asked, "Have you ever heard of a cougar doing something like this?"

"Once," Angie said.

"What were the circumstances there?" Sheriff Tucker asked.

"Not unlike this one," Angie said. She knelt down and looked closely at the screen door. "It was a campground inside Banff National Park. In that case, a cougar actually went into a person's camper, killed two children, badly wounded the kids' father, and dragged one of the kids out of the camper."

Gonzalez stepped over toward the demolished locker. "This cat must have gone wild," he said.

Angie stood up and brushed her hands off. She looked Tucker in the eyes.

"Last summer," she said, "we had the worst forest fire to hit the Coronado in a century years. More than two hundred and fifty thousand acres of land burnt to the ground."

"Would that account for this attack?" Tucker said.

"There's no way to prove it," she said. "But it's likely a contributing factor. A hungry cat, driven out of its home, its normal food sources depleted—it may attack someone in a remote location like this."

"You thought it was rabies?" John said.

Angie said, "A rabid cougar's liable to do anything, but that doesn't seem to be the case here."

"What would you recommend, Doctor Rippard?" Sheriff Tucker asked.

Angie looked around the bathhouse at each of them.

She said, "At first light, we need to get a helicopter up in the air. With tranquilizer darts, we can relocate our cougar across the San Pedro Valley. That's sheer wilderness area over there. Our cougar will avoid human contact from this point forward."

Sheriff Tucker looked interested but skeptical.

"You think a cougar will be able to survive," he said, "if we just up and move him seventy miles away?"

"What would you recommend?" Angie said.

"Well, I can tell you one thing," he said. "The cattle farmers in this county ain't gonna lose any sleep over one less cougar."

"That's unacceptable, Sheriff," Angie said. "This is National Forest Land. It's a protected wilderness area."

"And we got a cougar that almost killed a woman and her six-year-old son, Doctor Rippard."

"If you put it to the voters in this county," Angie said, "what would they say? Relocate or exterminate?"

"I don't know what the voters in this county would say," he said. "But this ain't an election. We got a cougar up there that tried to kill a woman."

"And so you just want to *exterminate* it?"

"All options are on the table at this point, Doctor Rippard," Tucker said. "I'm a sheriff, and I'm trying to deal with the situation that's in front of me."

"We need to wait until the National Forest rangers get down here," she said. "This is National Forest Land."

"Fair enough," Tucker said. "But tell me one thing, though. How far can a cougar move, if given five hours?"

Angie knew the answer to this because one study she'd done tracked dozens of mountain lions with radio collars. Sometimes they stayed put for days. But sometimes an animal could move as much as fifty miles in a single night.

"Chances are," she said, "our cougar will stay in the area. I can have a man with a helicopter up here by sunrise. I've got the equipment to relocate any animal we find in the morning."

"How many animals survive relocation, Doctor Rippard?" Sheriff Tucker said. "From what I've read, the percentage ain't that high, and a death by relocation is a tortuous death. Starvation, thirsting to death. Which would be more brutal?"

"You're misinformed, Sheriff," Rippard said. "It's the only way this cougar will have a chance to survive."

## ELEVEN

Ernesto Torres wore headphones while riding the single-seat John Deere Tri-Plex Greens Mower. He'd gotten the new Sean Paul CD from his twelve-year-old daughter for Christmas, one of those curious gifts that a kid buys her parent when it's obviously what the kid wants. And sure enough, he'd heard Christina listening to it in her bedroom in their two-bedroom Meridian East apartment three days after Christmas. The CD remained there for six weeks, until one day in mid February, when Ernesto came home and found it lying upside down on the coffee table in the living room.

Someone had used it as a drink coaster, and Ernesto picked the CD up, carried it over to the kitchen sink, and washed it with warm soap and water. He dried it off with a paper towel and then carried it across the dirty living room and put it in the Wal-Mart Sanyo they had underneath their TV. He pressed play, turned the volume up to seven, and immediately fell in love with Sean Paul and Beyoncé.

Since then, Ernesto had been listening to the CD almost every morning while he mowed the fairways and greens at the Ventana Canyon Country Club.

"What the hell," he said.

He'd been hauling up the fourteenth fairway about nine miles per hour, and he came up over one final hill and saw a blanket and clothes at the back of the putting green. An hour before sunrise, the sky was the color of gunmetal, and Ernesto steered the John Deere around to the back of the green. The grass was still wet with dew. Ernesto killed the John Deere's engine, removed his headphones, and leapt down to have a better look.

There was a large thick blanket, a pair of jeans, a pair of men's briefs, women's panties, bra, tennis shoes. Ernesto stepped up onto the right side of the putting green. He saw a second pair of jeans right in the middle of the green. He turned back toward the fairway and saw something shiny just beyond the fringe.

He picked up the jeans.

"Hello?" he called out.

There was no reply.

He carried the jeans toward the front of the green and realized that the shiny object he'd seen was a cell phone. He picked it up, pressed a button to turn it on, and saw that the battery was still half charged.

He wheeled around and called out, "Anybody here?"

*Strange*, he thought.

And he started back toward the blanket and the rest of the clothes near the pond. He was going to pile it altogether at the base of the tree and go on with his job, but he suddenly had an idea. He held the cell out in front of him. Christina carried one like this, and so he tried to navigate the commands.

Sure enough, he found it; "Recently Called Numbers" flashed on the L.C.D. He pressed "send," and another list came up. It read "Last Ten Numbers," and there at the very top was the last number punched into this cell phone: 9-1-1.

Suddenly, Ernesto realized something bad had happened here, and he was hit with the impulse to just drop everything and move away from the green. He'd seen enough crime scenes down at Meridian East to know that he'd already traipsed over far too much of the green to remove the signs of his presence.

He tossed the jeans back toward the pin flag, close to where he'd picked them up, and he carefully placed the cell phone on the grass at his feet. He made a straight line for his Tri-Plex Greens Mower.

Ernesto grabbed the two-way radio clipped to the side of the bright yellow John Deere seat, switched to channel fourteen, and said, "Roger, this is Ernesto—come back."

Roger Saunders was the sixty-three-year-old course ranger who worked the morning shift Monday through Friday. The course ranger job paid no money, but Ventana Canyon gave their four rangers free greens fees. And, as the golf course's green fee was two hundred and twenty-five dollars during peak season, the job had its advantages. All four rangers were retirees who did the job as much to stay in contact with other people their age (kind of like volunteer librarians in a small public library) as to be able to play golf for free on their days off.

Ernesto waited ten seconds and tried again. "Roger, this is Ernesto, do you read me?"

A voice squawked over Ernesto's radio: "Ernesto, this is Roger, go ahead."

Ernesto's brow furrowed with worry. He glanced at the jeans in the middle of the green. He looked at the blanket and clothes near the eucalyptus tree.

"This is gonna sound odd," Ernesto said into the radio. "But we got something up here at the fourteenth green."

There was a pause. Then, "Go ahead, Ernesto."

Ernesto held the back of his right hand against his forehead, gripped the walkie-talkie in his left, and said, "There's a bunch of clothes up here on the green."

Roger's voice squawked through the radio, "Clothes?"

"Yeah," Ernesto said. "It looks like some kids might have been partying up here last night."

"Oh, shit," Roger said wearily.

"No, it's not what you think," Ernesto said. "Their clothes are still here."

There was a pause. Ernesto could picture Roger standing there beside his white golf cart near the club house and first tee.

"I don't understand," Roger finally said.

Ernesto said, "There was a cell phone on the front of the green. I checked it. The last number dialed on the phone was nine-one-one."

Ernesto waited for this to register in Roger Saunders's mind. He stayed close to his John Deere, but he pivoted his head around to see if he noticed anything else out of the ordinary.

"Should I call the police?" Roger finally said.

"I think we may need to," Ernesto said.

"Give me a minute," Roger said. "I'll let Paul know."

Paul G. Knowles was the course pro; he was a former NCAA second team All-American who'd taken over as Ventana Canyon's Golf Pro back in 1998. Knowles was in the club house, greeting the morning's first golfers and answering phones to take tee times for guests of the posh Ventana Canyon Resort.

A minute later, Paul Knowles's voice squawked over Ernesto's two-way radio.

"Ernesto, this is Paul. What do you got?"

"I don't know," Ernesto said. "There's a bunch of clothes. There was a cell phone. I checked the last number; it was nine-one-one."

"Is there anyone up there?"

Ernesto looked around, his head pivoting. "I don't think so," he said. "I've been up here about ten minutes, now, and I haven't seen anyone."

"And their clothes are there?" Paul asked.

"Yes," Ernesto said. "*All* of their clothes. There's a bra and underwear. Looks like it might have been a guy and a girl."

There was a pause. Ernesto imagined Paul Knowles rifling through his options.

Ernesto said, "Whoever left here, left without any of their clothes."

"I'll be right up," Paul said. "Give me five minutes."

# Twelve

Sheriff Graham Tucker stood by an ATV on a ridge that jutted out from the mountains. He sipped coffee from a dark blue Thermos. The sky was just beginning to lighten with the first signs of dawn. The air was cold. The coffee steamed, and Tucker watched a hawk soaring on an updraft from the San Pedro Valley. His radio crackled.

"You want me to get that, Sheriff?" Deputy Andy Jones asked.

Tucker was with four of his best boys, and Andy Jones was the best of the four. They had six hounds and six pointers, and Sheriff Tucker had a single rifle strapped to the side of his ATV because that was all it would take to kill a mountain lion.

Tucker's radio crackled again: "Sheriff Tucker, this is Angie Rippard. We've got a lock on your position."

Tucker grabbed the radio and said, "Go ahead, Doctor Rippard."

And at just that moment, they heard the helicopter come over the top of a ridgeline just north of them.

"We have the tranquilizer darts ready, but it's hard up inside the canyon," she said. "There's not a lot of room. How many of your men have tranquilizer guns?"

"Doctor Rippard, we may need to use more than darts with this cougar."

"If you kill that animal, I'll make certain you never get re-elected, Sheriff. Is that clear?"

Tucker clicked off his radio just as Robert Gonzalez said, "They've got an animal about two hundred meters south, southwest of their position."

Each of the deputies heard it.

Tucker glanced from the LANSAT monitor on his ATV, to the narrow ATV trail. The mountain rose up steeply above the ATV trail, and the hillside above the trail was forested.

Tucker looked at his four sheriff's deputies. Everyone suddenly looked alert, realizing that a cougar was close. Tucker scanned the hillside above the ATV trail, but the light was still too dim and the hillside too forested to see anything other than trees.

A cloud rolled over a high peak to the south.

Tucker glanced at his rifle strapped to the side of the ATV. Andy Jones held his rifle up and scanned the hillside through the rifle's scope.

Tucker said, "See anything, Andy?"

Andy just shook his head. "Nothing, Sheriff," he said.

Tucker turned back on the radio and said, "What would you say it's doing?"

Angie Rippard's mouth dropped open when she saw the mountain lion's signal blinking on the screen. Inside the helicopter, there was a little video display monitor, and the mountain lion was represented by a small white dot on the green screen. Pilot David Baker saw it, too, and he looked into Angie's blue eyes.

"It's hunting them," Baker gasped.

"Can we get in close enough to fire the Telazol?" Angie asked.

"I can't push it up any higher into the canyon, Angie," Baker said. "The canyon's too narrow. It's just too tight."

Gonzalez leaned forward from the backseat and looked at the monitor.

"Those boys are going to kill that cougar," Angie said.

Baker thrust a finger at the monitor. "The cougar's hunting *them*, Angie."

"That's impossible," Gonzalez said. "They've got dogs. Cougars are terrified of dogs."

But everyone in the helicopter stared at the screen, and they saw the little white dot moving closer and closer to the bunch of green and blue dots that were Sheriff Tucker and his four best deputies.

Angie spoke into her headset, "Sheriff Tucker, you're not going to believe this, but it appears that the mountain lion is hunting you. Look alive."

On the ground, Sheriff Tucker clipped his radio to his belt and strode over to his ATV. He removed his rifle from its case on the side of his ATV. He put the rifle to his shoulder and scanned the hillside. He saw nothing but trees.

One if his deputies, Dale Bachman, started walking up toward the ATV trail.

"Careful, Dale," Tucker said.

Deputy Jones said, "Sheriff, I think we ought to release the dogs. We could tree this cat in a matter of minutes."

Tucker stared hard at the hillside.

"*Sheriff,*" Andy said again.

"Yeah," Tucker said, his eyes not leaving the hillside.

"The dogs," Andy said. "I think we should release—"

Tucker raised a commanding index finger to silence him.

Angie's voice cut through the static of the radio: "Sheriff, the mountain lion is about fifty meters southwest of your position."

Tucker looked at Andy. "Release the hounds," he said.

Andy nodded and then let go of the dogs. The pack started barking wildly chasing down an old scent, and they took off running up the ATV trail.

When they got two hundred meters away, Tucker said, "Where the hell are they going?"

The four deputies watched the hounds vanish down into the canyon about four hundred meters away from them.

"The mountain lion is about thirty meters southwest of you, Sheriff," Angie's voice said over the radio. "Can you see him?"

All of the deputies scanned the forest hillside with their rifles. Dale Bachman was about thirty meters up from the group on the trail. He stood on the trail looking straight uphill into the forest.

Angie's voice was urgent over the radio: "Oh, my God, look out!"

The attack came so fast it was a blur.

Dale Bachman was standing on the narrow ATV trail. Behind him the mountain sloped down into a deep ravine, and right in front of him was a rock wall about fifteen feet high.

The mountain lion came from the forest. Like a flash, it hit Dale Bachman, and both Bachman and the lion went over the trail and tumbled down into the steep ravine.

"What the—?!" Tucker said.

All four remaining men ran up the trail. They ran to the spot where the cougar hit Bachman, and they raised their rifles and scanned down into the ravine. They saw Bachman lying motionless a hundred meters down the hillside, and they saw no sign of the mountain lion.

"Dale!" Tucker shouted, and he shimmied down the steep rocky hillside.

Angie's voice squawked, "The lion has moved up into the canyon!"

But Tucker wasn't listening. The hillside was extremely steep, but he and the deputies made it down to Dale in a matter of seconds, sliding and tumbling along. Tucker knelt down and touched Bachman's neck, feeling for a pulse. There was none.

"Damn," he said, and he stood up and fired three shots into the canyon.

Tucker started up a narrow trail into the canyon, along a worn cattle path that climbed as it went into the canyon. Deputy Jones followed him.

Tucker heard the dogs barking farther up in the canyon, up on a hillside. Desert bramble branches slapped at him. Foliage grew bushy and thick on either side of him. He pushed his way higher into the canyon, now a distance from Dale.

The walls on either side of the canyon were steep, but Tucker stayed in the wash in the middle. He was out of breath and sweating, and he saw something move across the path up in front of him.

"Look out!" Andy shouted from behind.

Tucker wasn't sure what he'd seen, but he raised his rifle and fired two shots into the thicket. The sound of the gunshot echoed off of the canyon walls, a sharp *crack!* echoing over and over. Smoke cleared from his rifle, and Tucker pushed harder into the bushes.

Suddenly, there was a terrible scream, and Tucker swung around. He looked back toward Deputy Jones.

Andy Jones was screaming.

Tucker raised his rifle up on his shoulder and made his way through the bush toward the sounds of Andy Jones's screams. He saw something flailing around in the bushes ten meters in front of him, and he pushed through the last bit of foliage.

"Oh, my God," Sheriff Tucker said.

Lying on the ground, Deputy Andy Jones had been ripped open. Andy had a horrified look on his face, and he was trying to put his intestines back inside his body.

"Oh, my God, boy," Tucker said.

He knelt down over Andy, whose face had gone pale. Tucker grabbed his radio.

"We need an emergency helicopter in here, now," he shouted into the radio. "We got another man down!"

He clipped the radio back on his belt and lifted Andy's head up off of the ground. Andy looked up at him.

"I don't want to die, Sheriff," he cried. He tried to hold his stomach together. "I'm afraid," he said.

"Hold on, boy," Tucker said. "Hold on, Andy."

"I don't want to die," Andy said. "*I don't want to die.*"

"Shut up," Tucker shouted. "Shut up, damn it!"

Andy coughed and a deep red burst of blood shot up from his mouth. Tucker helped him turn his head to clear his throat. Andy coughed again, and his cough was thick with blood.

"Hold on, now," Tucker said, but he knew it was too late.

He turned Andy's face back toward his, and he saw the lifeless blank stare in his eyes.

Tucker roared, "Goddamn it, no!"

He stood up, grabbed his rifle, and fired up into the canyon. He fired again and again, until the gun was empty, and then he picked up Andy's rifle and took off running up into the canyon.

Tucker pushed through sharp and thorny bushes and stepped out into a clearing that allowed him to see up the canyon hillside. The grade was steep, but Tucker used his left hand to balance himself, and he climbed up the rocky slope. He got up above the tree line and saw his two remaining deputies heading up into the canyon toward Andy Jones.

He grabbed his radio and said, "We have two men down up here. Repeat, two are dead. We're about a quarter mile southwest of trail junction F.R. 4472 and F.R. 29. The mountain lion is on the loose. And it's hunting us."

Immediately, voices crackled back from his three other teams and from the helicopter, and they were all speaking at once.

"Emergency helicopter on the way," one shouted.

"Stuck on F.R. 4472," another said.

"How far south?" yet another said.

Sheriff Tucker's breath was truncated and thin. He scanned the opposing hillside, and he wiped sweat back from his bearded face. His hands shook, and his eyes darted around nervously.

Then he saw the cat.

It was on the opposite side of the canyon, about fifty meters up from the thick bush along the base of the canyon. It was fully exposed, and it moved along the steep canyon hillside. Tucker raised his shotgun up, but his arms suddenly felt like lead.

He squinted his eye and stared through the rifle's scope. At first he saw nothing but naked rocky hillside. He wiped sweat back from his eyes. He looked over the scope and saw the mountain lion still on the hillside. It climbed up the hill, moving farther up into the canyon.

Tucker looked through the scope again and tried to find the cat. He passed over it once and then inched the rifle back to the left just enough, and he found the magnified image of the mountain lion within the scope of his rifle. The lion moved quickly up the hill, but it stopped every ten feet and glanced back down into the canyon.

"Kill it," Tucker said to himself, his hands shaking. "Bear down and kill it."

Tucker followed the cougar a moment more, inhaled, and let out a long breath that tasted coppery. At the end of the exhale, he pulled the trigger. His rifle kicked back hard against his shoulder, the sound of its firing loud. Pungent gunpowder smoke filled the air a moment, and Sheriff Tucker immediately looked up to see if he'd gotten the cougar.

A cloud of rocky dust exploded where he'd hit the ground, and the cougar still moved quickly up the hillside.

"*Damn it*," Tucker said. He ducked back down behind the scope of the rifle again and found his mark. Inside his scope, there was a series of three little blue rings, and Tucker forced himself to bear down and be calm. He found the mountain lion and got the innermost ring located up toward the front right shoulder of the animal. He steadied himself, channeled his adrenaline, inhaled, exhaled, and fired the rifle.

He knew the cougar was hit before he looked up.

He looked across the canyon and saw the mountain lion slumped on the ground. Sheriff Tucker fell back in a kind of *whooshing* motion, his legs giving out from under him.

He took his radio from his belt and said, "I got him."

## THIRTEEN

The reporters were local, but the story was going national. Angie Rippard stood on the sidewalk in front of Hildreth's Market in the mountain town of Oracle, ten miles north of Peppersauce Campground. Two sheriff's deputies were dead, and a woman had been attacked.

One reporter said, "Can you be certain that the mountain lion you killed was the same one that attacked the woman and her child last night?"

"Let me get something straight," Angie said. "I did not advocate the killing of this animal. It was my recommendation that we *relocate* the animal."

"But an animal was shot and killed?" another reporter said.

"That is correct," Angie said.

"What can you tell us about this animal?"

"It was a cougar," Angie said. "A mountain lion. *Felis concolor*."

"What does that mean, '*Felis concolor*'?"

"Cat of one color," Angie said.

"How big was it?"

"The animal Sheriff Tucker was forced to shoot and kill was a female," Angie said. "She weighed about a hundred and five pounds."

"Is that normal?"

"Yes," Angie said. "That's a normal weight; maybe even a little on the low side. Mountain lions can weigh up to two hundred and seventy-five pounds, though, that's rare."

"And a mountain lion and a cougar are the same thing?"

"Yes," Angie said. "Mountain lion, cougar, puma; they're different names for the same species of animal."

Angie looked out at the ten reporters. There were three television cameras. An occasional flashbulb flashed. She saw Graham Tucker on the far side of the parking lot, standing near a cruiser. John Crandall and Robert Gonzalez were talking to him.

The reporters were friendly enough, and so Angie stayed on to answer their questions. Cars slowed down, and drivers tried to figure out what was going on at Hildreth's Market. Oracle was a sleepy little town of peaceful people, working class folks and a high number of artists and writers.

Angie pointed to one reporter whose hand was raised.

"Is it normal for these animals to confront people?"

"No," Angie said. "It's not normal. It does happen, but cougars tend to shy away from people."

"Any idea why this animal didn't shy away?"

"It could be any number of things," Angie said.

"Such as?"

"Well, last year's forest fire burnt more than two hundred and fifty thousand acres of land, as you're all well aware," Angie said. "A shift in the local ecology could account for erratic behavior."

"Did you see the animal?"

"I did," Angie said. Then she added, "After it was killed."

"Why weren't you able to relocate the animal?"

"The animal attacked the sheriff's deputies," Angie said. "They reacted, I presume, in the manner that they saw fit. We were unable to get the helicopter up into Peppersauce Canyon."

"Wait a minute," one reporter said. "You're telling me that you had a helicopter up in the air *and* you had a tranquilizer gun?"

"We had Telazol tranquilizer darts in the helicopter," Angie said.

"And you failed to dart the animal?"

"We couldn't get the helicopter up into the canyon," Angie said.

"Two men are dead, Doctor Rippard," the reporter said. "And you're telling me you could have prevented it?"

The cameras recorded every gesture, movement, and every emotion. Angie looked worried but tried to compose herself.

"The animal attacked the men," she said.

"And now the animal is dead, correct?"

"Yes," Angie said. "I've said that already."

The reporter held a thoughtful finger to his lower lip. He had short red hair, a flattop cut, and piercing blue eyes. "So," he said. "Two people are dead. A cougar is dead. A woman and her six-year-old son are in the hospital. And all this was because you couldn't get a helicopter up into the canyon?"

"Well, the attack on Maggie Eiser occurred last night," Angie said. "I wasn't notified until after the attack."

"Is it fair to say that you were the most knowledgeable person on the scene with regard to mountain lion behavior?" the reporter said.

Angie seemed shocked by the question's implication and was speechless.

"Would that be a correct assumption, Doctor Rippard?"

"Yes, I suppose so," she said.

"And two people are now dead?"

"We've been over that already," Angie said.

"Please answer the question, Doctor Rippard."

"Yes, two sheriff's deputies are regrettably deceased," Angie said. "There was nothing we could do. The attack happened too fast. The men were on the ground. I was in the helicopter. No one expected a mountain lion to attack them the way that it did. It was just unfortunate."

"*Unfortunate?*" the reporter said. "Two people are dead. You were the expert on the scene, Doctor Rippard. You could have prevented it. You could have told those men not to go up there."

"If you're implying this was my fault—"

"Are you, or *aren't* you a mountain lion expert, Doctor Rippard?"

An embarrassing chill went through the crowd. Angie's face turned bright red with humiliation and shame. She was stunned.

And in the heat of the moment, she said, "I can tell you, this; this just doesn't happen. Mountain lions just aren't supposed to attack people this way. What happened here this morning was an unfortunate tragedy— a rare, freakish unfortunate tragedy. And we are all deeply saddened by it."

# Fourteen

Officer Jim Kleifelt had been with the Tucson Police Department for seven years, and there was not much that would rattle him. He and Officer Holly Newton rode in a golf cart beside the fourteenth fairway. In front of them on the cart path, golf pro Paul G. Knowles led the way. In the cart with Paul was groundskeeper Ernesto Torres.

"What is this all about?" Holly asked.

The golf cart bounced along the asphalt cart path, climbing higher up into the hills. Behind them, the city of Tucson spread out wide in the valley below. A city of nearly a half million situated two thousand feet above sea level, Tucson had largely retained its flavor as a desert town in the American Southwest.

"Groundskeeper called in a situation," Kleifelt said. "Apparently some kids were up here partying last night on the fourteenth green."

"So, that warranted a call to Tucson Metro?" Holly asked.

Jim shrugged.

"We'll check it out," he said. "He found a cell phone, and the last call was nine-one-one."

The golf carts swung around a curve in the cart path, and everyone saw the bright yellow pin flag up on the hill. There was a navy-blue "14" on the flag. The putting green had a two-tier surface area, and there was a huge bunker that wrapped around the left side. It looked like there was a pond up behind the green, a eucalyptus tree over on the right, and a waterfall at the back of the pond where the sheer rocky cliffs north of Tucson began the rugged climb up into the mountains.

They saw clothes in the middle of the green.

The carts pulled over to the right side. Officer Kleifelt locked the brake and frowned at the scene.

"I just came up over the hill here," Ernesto said excitedly. "And I saw the clothes. There was a blanket at the back. And I said, hey, you know, someone was partying."

"Where did you find the cell phone?" Officer Newton asked.

"On the front of the green," he said. "I picked it up, so it's probably got my fingerprints on it. It's over here."

Kleifelt said, "Don't come any closer. We're going to have to call in an I.S.B. unit. This is a crime scene."

Holly looked at him. He hadn't consulted her at all and had made a quick decision. She wasn't pleased.

Paul Knowles said, "I've already got golfers out on the course. Do you think we can have this cleaned up by ten?"

Kleifelt removed his radio from his belt, and he made the call. Holly walked over toward the blanket under the eucalyptus tree. She saw the girl's panties and the men's briefs, and she felt an immediate chill. No one would leave here without their clothes, she realized.

She started back around the right side of the pond. Golf pro Paul G. Knowles was pleading his case to Kleifelt. He had golfers out on the course, he said. It would take them a couple of hours, but eventually they would make it up here to the fourteenth, and the last thing he wanted was to explain to them that they'd have skip the fourteenth, the signature hole.

"*Oh, my God,*" Holly said.

All three men looked up and saw her. She was about thirty meters away, over on the right side of the pond. There were bushes and a footpath up into the hills, but Holly was frozen standing there in front of the bushes. She swung back to her left. Her hands came down to her knees, and she vomited.

## FIFTEEN

Angie received the phone call as she was listening to Sheriff Graham Tucker navigate his way through the reporters' questions. She thought the phone call was a hoax because the woman was telling her there had been another attack.

"Who is this?" she said.

Both Gonzalez and Crandall looked up, hearing the alarm in Angie's voice.

Assistant Chief Jane Kennedy told Angie who she was.

"Commander of I.S.B.?" Angie said into her cell phone.

"Investigative Services Bureau," Chief Kennedy said. "It's one of four bureaus within the Tucson Police Department."

"How did you get my number?" Angie said.

"Somebody from the Office of the Medical Examiner recommended you as a specialist," Chief Kennedy said.

Kennedy explained briefly that Tucson I.S.B. had three divisions: central investigations division, forensics, and special investigations division. C.I.D. handled all violent offenses, and was itself organized into five details, one of which was homicide. The folks in homicide often worked closely with the Office of the Medical Examiner, and Angie had twice served in courtroom litigations as an expert wildlife biologist for the Office of the Medical Examiner.

"I see," Angie said.

"We've got a full-scale crime scene down here in Tucson," Kennedy told her. "Two kids are dead."

"Jesus," Angie said.

"It looks like an animal attack," Kennedy said. "And we sure could use your experience."

"Chief Kennedy," Angie said, "are you aware that there was a mountain lion attack up here in Oracle last night?"

Kennedy said she was not. The news hadn't made it down to Tucson yet. Angie explained that she was standing at an impromptu press conference right that moment about the attack that had occurred at Peppersauce Canyon.

"Two sheriff's deputies are dead," she said. "Local press is up here right now."

"Jesus," Kennedy said.

"Yeah," Angie said. "This is gonna turn into a hurricane of a media frenzy. You're sure it was an animal attack?"

Kennedy said she could not be certain, but that she had never seen a homicide scene like this one, and that that was why she was calling Angie. She needed her help.

"Give me an hour," Angie said. She glanced at Gonzalez, John, and Dave Baker. "I've got a couple of good people with me."

Kennedy explained where the Ventana Canyon Golf Course was located. Angie knew the place well. They had a five-star West Corp. hotel that had ignited fierce controversy ten years back when it was built because of its proximity to protected lands. Angie even remembered the billionaire developer because of his notorious nickname "The Chopper," which was not earned for his *planting* trees around the globe.

Angie glanced at her wristwatch and saw that it was nine-thirty in the morning. *It's been a hell of a twelve hours*, she thought.

But nothing could have prepared her for the next twelve.

## SIXTEEN

Angie sat up front in the helicopter in the seat beside pilot Dave Baker. Robert and John were in the back, and all four enjoyed the view from ten thousand feet as they came over Mount Lemmon and saw Tucson spread out far below. Baker communicated with local air-traffic control out of Davis-Monthan and learned they could put down on the golf course.

"A guy had a stroke in the middle of a tourney back in December," Baker said to Angie, Robert, and John. "They had to airlift him out. We can land on the twelfth fairway."

The helicopter came down the mountain like a fly down an elephant's back. They could see traffic moving up and down the residential streets north of Skyline Drive, where the homes started at a million and went as high as fifteen. A three-acre lot with sixty-mile views could sell for a million bucks, and as such, developers like Charlie "The Chopper" Rutledge had little reservation about parking homes and lavish resorts as high up the mountain as county, state, and federal ordinances allowed.

Some houses bordered National Forest Land, and the encroachment into preserved lands was a non-stop war between billionaire developers and conservationists living from paycheck to paycheck. For the past thirty years, it seemed that the developers had been winning.

"There's the course," Baker said.

From the air above the land, Angie saw just how much the Ventana Canyon Resort encroached on the Coronado National Forest. There was a line of homes—literally a swath—cut into the side of the mountain along a ridge from southeast to northwest.

"It's no wonder people are being attacked," John Crandall said. He leaned forward and looked at the hillside. "They're building homes right into the National Forest Land."

Baker said, "Ten years ago, the boundary was two miles further down the mountain."

Gonzalez said, "You mean to say they've built everything up here in the past ten years."

Baker nodded, and each of them was stunned. There were easily two thousand homes in the area he pointed out.

"This section here was National Forest Land a decade ago," Baker said. "Each of these homes goes for about two million, on average. You do the math."

Angie did. "Four billion dollars of development," she said.

"*In ten years?*" John said, taken aback.

"I'd say that's a reasonable estimate," Baker said. "You see, that's just the homes. You add in local businesses, road construction, the new hospital. All total it's probably twice that amount of money that has gone into this area in five years."

"All of which was National Forest Land," Angie said, "a decade ago?"

Baker said, "It's tough to compete against that kind of money if your only cause is preservation."

# SEVENTEEN

Police Chief Jane Kennedy approached the helicopter in a stretch golf cart that had front and back seats. She had short brown hair, brown eyes, and a slight nervous tic that made her look like she was smiling with the right side of her mouth when she actually was not. She locked the brakes and stepped out of the cart to greet Angie Rippard.

"Doctor Rippard," she said loudly over the helicopter.

The two women shook hands. Angie introduced John Crandall and Robert Gonzalez, and all four walked toward the golf cart. Angie rode up front with the chief, and John and Robert sat in the back. It only took about a minute to get up to the green, and Jane explained that they'd found the two bodies about thirty meters from the green.

"Just beyond a row of bushes," she said.

Angie asked, "What makes you think they were attacked?"

"They were partially buried."

Angie nodded and glanced back at Robert.

Jane said, "But it doesn't look like any kind of *human* burying."

And she looked into Angie's eyes to make certain that she understood what she meant.

"I see," Angie said, and she glanced back at John. "You may want to sit this one out," she said.

"You bet," he said. "I'll just hang out here by the golf cart and keep an eye on things. You go ahead."

Jane led Angie and Robert up through the crime scene. There were two dozen officers, detectives, medical technicians, forensics investigators.

"We've been able to hold the press up at the clubhouse," Jane said. "But I think you were right, Doctor Rippard, once the national media gets wind of two separate attacks—if that's what we have here— we'll have to hold some kind of press conference."

"How's the golf course management doing?"

"So, far, they've been very cooperative," Chief Kennedy said. "We'll hold the conference at the club house. You'll want to speak?"

"Let's take a look at the bodies," Angie said.

Jane led her toward the row of bushes back behind the pond.

•  •

Angie noticed paw prints along the bank of the pond, and she glanced up ahead beyond the bushes where the hill rose up steeply into the rocky cliffs.

"Have your people seen these?" she said, kneeling down to inspect the prints.

Jane Kennedy said they hadn't and then waved for one of her people to come over. To an untrained eye, the tracks looked like large dog prints. Everyone knelt down and looked at the tracks in the drying mud.

"See how the heel pad is lobed here?" Angie said. She removed a pen from her shirt pocket and pointed to an impression in the mud. "A dog's heel pad curves upward here. A cougar's"—she looked into Kennedy's eyes—"are flat along the back with this lobe, here and here."

"So, these are cougar tracks?" Kennedy said.

Robert Gonzalez said, "Large cougar tracks."

Everyone stood up. Angie traced it out in her mind, searching the mud for front and back paws. She pointed to a spot on the ground.

"Here's the front right paw," she said.

Robert said, "Here's the back left."

He looked up at Angie, and they both realized what they were seeing.

"Jesus," Angie said.

Gonzalez asked, "Have you ever seen this broad a gait?"

Angie shook her head.

"What does that mean?" Kennedy said. "Broad a gait?"

Angie said, "Let's see the bodies."

She glanced at the sand near the bushes and noticed drag marks. All the police standing near the bushes looked up at Chief Kennedy, Angie, and Robert.

"We found the bodies—" Jane started to say.

But Angie saw Nick Jacobs and what was left of Jenny Granger—two of her brightest, most delightful young students—and nothing in all her years of biology training and wildlife experience could have prepared her for that.

"*Oh, my God,*" she said.

The bodies were partially buried in a shallow grave. Angie had seen enough attack scenes that the gruesomeness of the bodies didn't bother her. But she had been completely unprepared for the fact that she was going to *recognize* the victims, and it was all she could do to steel her will.

Her hand came up to her mouth. "Has anybody notified the families?" she said.

"We're working on it," Chief Kennedy said.

Angie's eyes were somewhat wide and wouldn't meet Jane's. It was as if she didn't want the police to see that she—a professional biologist—was appalled. Methodically, Angie began to explain what had happened to the best of her ability. Method kept her from being floored by emotions.

"The cougar began feeding mid thorax on the female victim," she said. "It ate the liver, the spleen, and then began on the victim's lungs. Death was likely instantaneous, delivered by a crushing bite to her face and head."

Robert stepped back away from the bushes and tried to keep from being sick. Angie coughed twice to keep her stomach down and circled the shallow grave. Chief Kennedy and the forensics detectives watched her.

"The male victim," she said, "was likely killed by strangulation. Notice the puncture wounds here, and here. The cougar simply locked onto his throat and choked him to death."

# EIGHTEEN

Angie recognized several of the reporters from earlier in the day. She stood over to the left of an improvised stage where they'd set up a podium and more than two dozen microphones. It was the front landing of the clubhouse, and the reporters stood at the base of the steps, excited to hear the official report from the authorities. Chief Kennedy had held back the press conference as long as was feasible, and late afternoon shadows were creeping across the parking lot behind the reporters.

"I guess I'll start things off," she said.

Camera shutters clicked. Flashbulbs flashed. There were about two dozen reporters, and another dozen or so people stood at the base of the steps looking up at her.

"Two people were attacked last night," Kennedy said. "Our initial indications are that it was an animal attack. Apparently the two victims were on the golf course after hours when they were attacked. Tucson Metro was first notified by officials here at the golf course this morning. Two officers were sent out. One discovered the bodies."

"Can you tell us the victims' names?" one reporter asked.

"At this time, we cannot," Kennedy said. "We are still in the process of contacting the victims' families."

"Is this attack related to the attack near Oracle?" another reporter asked.

Chief Kennedy glanced over at Angie. She said, "That's under investigation. We have experts in the field who have seen both attack sites, as well as all of the victims. Certainly, it's unusual for this many separate attacks to occur in this time frame."

"Was it a mountain lion attack?" one reporter said.

Kennedy nodded. "Initial indications point to that," she said.

"What kind of 'indications'?" the reporter said.

"Evidence found at the scene," Kennedy said, "indicates that it might have been a mountain lion."

Kennedy pointed to one raised hand.

"Could you speculate as to the victims' ages?" the reporter asked.

"Not at this time," she said. "I can't answer any specific questions about the victims at this time. We're still in the process of contacting their families."

"What state were the bodies in?"

Kennedy took a deep breath, exhaled. She said, "They were partially denuded."

One reporter launched, "In recent months, there have been a number of cougar sightings in the Ventana Canyon area. Some biologists have pointed to human encroachment into preserved lands as the reason for these more and more frequent sightings. Could you speculate as to why these mountain lions are behaving this way? Is it because of human encroachment? Is it because of last year's wildfire?"

"That's not a question I can answer," Chief Kennedy said.

She pointed to another reporter whose hand was raised.

"What do you intend to do at this point?" the reporter asked.

Kennedy said, "We are working with wildlife authorities, National Forest Rangers and with the sheriff's department involved in the Oracle attacks. One cougar was already killed today. We'll draw up some kind of plan this evening. I don't know whether it involves relocating the animal or exterminating the animal. We need to talk with Arizona Game and Fish, and we need to talk to the governor."

"But you say that one animal was already killed?"

"That is correct."

"Well, how many animals are up there?"

"In the Coronado National Forest?" Chief Kennedy said. She glanced at Angie. "I really couldn't speculate how many cougars are up there."

"Do you have the authority to hunt these animals?"

"It's really up to the National Forest Rangers," Jane said, "because we believe that the animal has moved up into National Forest Land."

"And how far is that?" one national reporter asked. "How far is the National Forest Land from the site of this attack?"

Chief Kennedy said, "About fifty meters."

A ruffle of murmurs went through the crowd. A good number of non-local reporters thought they had misheard her.

"I thought the attack occurred on the golf course?" the national reporter said.

"It did," Kennedy said.

"But you just said it was fifty meters from the National Forest Land," the reporter said.

"That's correct," Jane said. "Parts of golf course are very close to the National Forest Land. The two share an invisible fence, you might say."

## Nineteen

Angie got the helicopter up an hour before sunset. Chief Kennedy rode with her, and they searched the mountains due north of Ventana Canyon. But they were unable to locate an animal. Kennedy pushed her to keep the helicopter up until darkness had fallen on the mountains, but eventually pilot David Baker insisted that they put in for the night and resume the search first thing the next morning.

Angie treated everyone to dinner that night at a Chinese restaurant on the corner of Sunrise and Swan. She explained to Chief Kennedy that relocation was not always the best alternative for these animals. She presented the case to her and explained that she understood that sometimes it was necessary to put an animal down. Angie explained that in all but the most extreme cases, though, she advocated relocation over extermination. She explained that the real issue was much more complex.

"If it gets to the point of relocate or exterminate," she said, "then there was a breakdown somewhere further back."

Jane said, "It may well be encroachment."

"Too many people are living in locations that were once wilderness areas," Angie agreed. "You should realize, too, that mountain lion populations are at their highest in a hundred and fifty years; some researchers estimate their numbers total thirty thousand in the U.S. and Canada."

"Really?" Jane said.

"But even with numbers like that it's a delicate balance, one that requires vigilance and awareness. That the five fastest growing states in the U.S.—Nevada, Arizona, Colorado, Utah, and Idaho—are all home to thriving cougar populations is cause for concern. Every year more and more people move to the American West, and every year cougar populations increase in areas where humans weren't living twenty years ago."

The next morning they put the helicopter up in the skies north of Ventana Canyon again, but they were unable to locate a single cougar. The official decision to relocate the animal came from the governor of Arizona, but the decision was made via the Arizona Game and Fish Department's five-member commission. No one considered the possibility that the cougar might elude them, until night set in on the second day.

They'd brought in professional trackers late that afternoon, but even the trackers with their hunting dogs were unable to follow the mountain lion's tracks more than a couple miles up into the Coronado National Forest. Angie spoke several times to members of the news media, and her image was broadcast a number of times on national news outlets. She advocated relocation of the animal before extermination, but she voiced her concerns that they might be unable to locate the mountain lion that killed Jenny Granger and Nick Jacobs.

That night, she received phone calls from people who had seen her name and face on TV and looked up her phone number. The furthest call came from Miami, Florida, and it was clear that she was going to have to change her number. A few people were hostile with her, and she finally unplugged her phone line at three in the morning.

The next day, she went to campus and found her email inbox flooded with email from concerned citizens all over the country who had seen her on the news and wanted to voice their opinions. Most of these were supportive, but a few were downright scary.

By the fourth day, the story lost its front-page status at cnn.com as well as at other national news outlets. Angie suspected that the cougar that killed two of her best students had begun to move north. Each night she had nightmares that involved Jenny and Nick, and each day she woke less refreshed and more afraid. There were rumblings that she wasn't doing her job, that she was sabotaging the investigation, that her love for these animals biased her against making the right decisions to find them.

"She wants these animals to go on killing," one pundit said, "because it affords her a spotlight in which to speak her liberal politics."

Another said, "She's quite possibly the only person who gains something when these animals kill innocent people."

The guilt began to gnaw at Angie, and she woke from a terrible dream the fourth night wherein a mountain lion was eating her alive. Finally, her boyfriend John Crandall asked her to put aside her work for the weekend and spend forty-eight hours as far away from anything resembling mountain lions as she could. She promised to do that, but she silently considered every tracking map she'd ever made of a cougar.

She reasoned through the possibility that the mountain lion may have moved north. And she began to worry that the next attack would come from a more populated town closer to Phoenix. She kept all of this inside her because she knew that John was a sensitive man, and she didn't want to burden him with her guilt and fear. She held it in. She breathed. And she made it through the weekend without once mentioning a word of her inner turmoil to John or to anyone else.

## TWENTY

Dr. Angie Rippard exited her office in the Easton-Howell Science Complex and strode confidently down the hallway. It was hot outside, but the AC was on inside the building and it felt cool and good. Angie could see through the glass double doorway at the end of the hall, and students were busy walking up and down the sidewalk just beyond the door.

"Doctor Rippard?" the voice came from behind her.

Angie had a tall stack of papers in her arm, and she turned around and saw police Chief Jane Kennedy coming up the hallway. Angie hadn't seen Kennedy since April 8th.

"Chief Kennedy," Angie said. She produced a hand from under the stack of papers, and she and Jane Kennedy shook hands.

"How've you been?" Kennedy asked.

"Busy," Angie said. "This is finals week."

They started walking up the hallway toward the double doors.

"Would you let me buy you lunch?" Jane said.

Angie glanced at her wristwatch. "Sure," she said. "What's up?"

· ·

They ate at a little deli across from campus. There were tables inside and tables outside, and they took a table outside under the shade of a patio umbrella. There was a steady breeze, and Angie had to place her plate on top of her paper napkin to keep it from flying away.

"There were two different mountain lions," Kennedy said.

"Nick and Jenny were killed by a different mountain than the one that attacked Maggie Eiser."

"Right."

Angie nodded from behind her sandwich. "Yes," she said. "We weren't misleading anybody. Every spot I had on TV, I said that it was two different animals. It's just an unfortunate coincidence, but the cougar that attacked Maggie Eiser—that killed those two deputies—it was not the same cougar that killed Nick and Jenny."

Jane Kennedy stared into Angie Rippard's blue eyes. She noticed the lines around Angie's eyes. She noticed the lack of sleep that those lines suggested. She felt an intense emotional tug, and she wanted to make it better for this woman. There was something about Angie that made Kennedy want to help her, though it was only in the color of her blue eyes, the exhaustion on her face.

Angie said, "But the general public, well, they seemed satisfied that *a* cougar was killed. Any cougar."

"But it means that we still have a cougar up there," Jane Kennedy said, "that killed two people."

"Two people that we know of," Angie said.

"Well, yeah."

"There are a lot of cougars up there," Angie said. "Animals pass across the San Pedro Valley a lot, so that means we have a few cats up in the Galiuro Mountains. From there, the animals have a much better range. There's a lot of untouched land east of the San Pedro, and the big male cats—the adults—have large seasonal ranges."

"So, what're you saying?" Kennedy asked.

"Well, the cat that killed Jenny Granger and Nick Jacobs was not the cat that attacked Maggie Eiser in that bathhouse. I'd bet my life on it. The bite wounds, the paw prints, the cougar mounds; all indications are that there were two different animals. Sheriff Tucker killed one of those animals. The other one—quite possibly the largest mountain lion I've ever heard of—is still up there. But a cat like that has a huge seasonal range. We may find that cat a year from now as far north as Payson. And, too, we may never hear from it again."

"Payson is over two hundred miles from here," Kennedy said.

"There's a lot of unspoiled land north of the San Pedro," Angie said. "There's a perennial water source in the Gila River. There's a plentiful deer population. A cougar could live in sheer isolation north of Winkelman and Hayden and never be seen by a human."

"And that's what you think has happened?"

Rippard started to reach for her drink. The outside of the glass was wet with condensation in the warm sunlight. "It's what I hope has happened," she said. She picked up her drink, and the little square napkin stuck to its bottom. "Most of the time, cougars don't get much larger than a hundred and forty pounds. For those animals, it's rare that they'll attack humans, particularly adult humans. But a cat that gets larger than one-sixty is capable of taking down a six-hundred-pound elk. To that kind of cat, a human is very real prey. And the cat that killed Nick Jacobs and Jenny Granger was probably much larger than that, trophy size, as sport hunters like to say. So, yeah, it's my hope that the cougar moved north. There are literally millions of acres in the Tonto National Forest that are inaccessible to humans."

"The Tonto?" Jane said, a little alarmed. "That's north of Phoenix."

Angie nodded her head. "It's the largest wilderness area in the state," she said.

"But that's north of Phoenix," Jane said again, still alarmed. "If a cat's capable of going that far north—"

"—they do it all the time—"

"—then that means that it could be near Phoenix."

Angie pulled one of her papers from her stack and turned it over so that the page was blank. She drew a map with her pen.

"Phoenix lies here," Angie said. "The Valley of the Sun. You have a couple of mountains in town here—Camelback, the Phoenix Mountains—and due northeast of Phoenix is this giant wilderness area, the Tonto National Forest: nearly three million acres of untouched mountainous land. There are lakes and mountain peaks and forests, and the total human population is less than a thousand. Now, if you're a mountain lion, where would you live: in this wilderness area where no human is ever going to see you, or close to a giant city of nearly three million people?"

"I'd tend to say that it would stay in the wilderness area," Jane said. "But this animal has clearly shown that it doesn't give a damn about the wilderness boundaries that we've set up. It killed two people on a golf course, Doctor Rippard."

"A golf course built within fifty meters of National Forest Land."

"And now you're telling me that the animal has moved north to one of the largest cities in the United States?"

"No, that's not what I'm telling you at all," Rippard said. "I'm telling you that it's *possible* for a male lion to move two hundred miles in a month."

"But Phoenix is only *ninety* miles north," Jane said.

"And chances are that mountain lion will stay as far away from the city as it can," Rippard said. "However, it *has* made two successful human kills that we know of; so it knows that people make a good food source."

"A good food source?!"

"On the record, Jane, my position should be crystal clear: I am for relocating these animals at any cost."

Jane gazed across the table at her. "But?"

"I don't know," Angie said. "The cougar that did that to two of my students, to two bright kids with their whole lives ahead them—maybe relocation isn't always the best solution."

## Twenty-One

Charlie "The Chopper" Rutledge was a giant bear of a man who once ran the two most expensive unsuccessful gubernatorial campaigns in Colorado state history. He was born in 1933 to a mining family that had been in the Denver region for more than sixty years. His father was president and CEO of West Corp., an innocuous name for the state's most notorious strip-mining company. In the 1920s, 30s, and 40s, though, Colorado was still a relatively uninhabited state and environmental consciousness was pretty much limited to knowing what the weather was going to be like for the next few days.

Charlie grew up going to the best schools and living in multiple homes around Colorado and the southwestern United States. By the early 1940s, West Corp. had diversified and branched out into Utah, Arizona, New Mexico, Wyoming, and Nevada, but a strange thing began to happen in the late 1940s and early 50s that impeded its progress. Average citizens became aware that companies like West Corp. were irreparably damaging natural resources in the region.

By the mid to late 1950s, state and federal legislation had gotten involved and laws were put into place to limit the amount of destruction a company like West Corp. could inflict on local ecosystems.

Young Charlie turned twenty-five in 1958, and he was bright enough to see that there was a hard future ahead for large mining companies in the state. He enjoyed hotels. He enjoyed skiing. He loved partying with the social elite, and in 1960, he talked his father into loaning him ten million dollars toward building a resort hotel in, what was then, the remote town of Aspen, Colorado.

The St. Chevis Hotel took three years to build and occupied twelve acres of prime real estate at the base of Aspen Highlands. It opened in October 1963 and was an immediate sensation. One of the chief consulting architects was a student of the legendary builder Frank Lloyd Wright, and the St. Chevis actually won several awards for its design. Fueled by that particular hype and poised at what was becoming one of the most popular ski resorts in the world, the St. Chevis proved a windfall for a young entrepreneur then only known as Charlie Rutledge.

What Charlie found in the early 60s and on into the 70s was that the state regulation for developing tourism destinations was much more lax than for mining companies; i.e., it was easier to cut down one thousand acres of trees, if the aim was to build a golf course and hotel, than the exact same thousand acres of trees if the aim was to strip-mine silver. It was a matter of less red tape.

By 1967, Charlie Rutledge had completed three similar hotel resorts following the success of the St. Chevis in and around Aspen, Aspen Highlands, and Snowmass. And no one complained; the hotels were a hit and it was a time when posh vacationing was popular. It seemed that the government even *encouraged* him because the Colorado governor, at the time, did television ads inviting tourists to Colorado, and in several of the ads, the governor was seen standing in front of a West Corp. Hotel.

Charlie did raise a few eyebrows in 1971 when his particular branch of West Corp. mowed down ten thousand acres of trees in north-central Colorado to begin building his own ski resort at Smuggler Mountain. Smuggler's Hole (as the resort was to be called) was ruthlessly designed and completed in under two years to coincide with the opening of the Eisenhower Tunnel on March 8, 1973. Charlie had the vision to build a ski resort less than three miles from Interstate-70, fully aware that the tunnel would significantly change traffic flow into the interior of Colorado. Denver's population was soaring, and Charlie believed that tourism should no longer be limited to those who could fly into Colorado.

Because of its timing with the Eisenhower Tunnel's completion, Smuggler's Hole became a phenomenon. Located an easy forty-five miles west of Denver, it hailed a new era for skiing tourism in the state. That people could easily *drive* to the resort seemed like a simple enough idea, but it was something that few real estate developers had cashed in on up to that point. There simply weren't enough accessible roads to Colorado's interior prior to the 1970s.

Charlie was the first. And by 1977, a half dozen more West Corp. resorts sprung up along Interstate-70, totaling fifty thousand acres of deforestation in the region, more land than West Corp. Mining had destroyed in fifty years of business. And all of it was presented in the form of trendy, popular ski resort vacations that the public loved. Charlie was a hero. And a billionaire.

By the early 1980s, West Corp. diversified by building resorts and hotels in Las Vegas, Tucson, Scottsdale and at Mammoth Mountain in California. He appeared on the cover of *Time* and *Newsweek* and became something of a public figure at major social events. He often wore a black cowboy hat and a rhinestone-studded necktie. He never married but did date one supermodel in the late '80s, and he even showed up in a couple of small Hollywood movie roles.

No one knows for certain who first coined the nickname "The Chopper," but its origins were likely the Denver *Herald*, where the first major criticism of Charlie's ruthless real estate development emerged. The public largely overlooked the criticism because Charlie was building some of the coolest jetsetter destinations in the country. They wanted more, and any criticism in the 1970s and 80s regarding the lavish lifestyles Charlie's resorts promoted were quickly dismissed.

It wasn't until the early 1990s that the cultural pendulum began to swing the other way, and people began to notice that Charlie's mountain resorts were scarring up the natural landscape. And so Charlie began branching out of the United States, first to Mexico, where West Corp. built a fabulous oceanfront resort in Cabo San Lucas called The Palace. In 1994, construction of resorts in Austria, Greece, Italy, Fiji, and New Zealand were mapped out. Maui and Oahu were added in '97, Sao Paulo, Brazil in '99, and by 2001, West Corp. was one of the largest global resort contractors on the planet.

Along the way, Charlie put his hat into the 1992 and 1996 Colorado gubernatorial races, spending a reported one hundred and thirty million dollars in two unsuccessful bids for the state's governorship. It was as much money as a national presidential candidate would spend on a run at the White House, and all of it was for naught. Colorado had gradually shifted to become a more liberal state, and Charlie "The Chopper" was seen as staunchly conservative.

He enjoyed sport hunting wildlife that, in states like California, voters were outlawing. He had stuffed grizzlies, elk, and mountain lions adorning his forty-five-million-dollar Aspen estate, and he was friendly with the National Rifle Association.

Perhaps the most damning photograph of the two elections was the result of poor campaign insight. The image showed Charlie wearing plaid flannel and hefting a woodcutter's ax up over a pile of logs. The intent had been to show Charlie as an "everyday" Coloradoan chopping logs (presumably) for his own little woodstove, but the final perception was quite different.

*Time* did an unusually vituperative article of his campaign for governor, and splashed "The Chopper Wants In" in massive forty-eight-point font above the full-page photograph. The article described West Corp.'s devastating deforestation as a "rape of the natural land," and with red, white, and blue schematics, it showed the regions where Charlie had cut down the most trees to build his lavish resorts. It was a period of strong environmental awareness, and Charlie was laughed out of both elections.

It was the first sign that he might be losing his Midas touch, but he countered his political defeats by diversifying his company, by going global. In the late 1990s, his name regularly showed up on America's wealthiest top-ten list, and he went ahead with plans to build a stunning quarter-billion-dollar resort community in Tucson, Arizona near Ventana Canyon.

Construction of West Corp.'s Ventana Canyon Resort began in 1994 and ignited outrage because of its proximity to National Forest Land. It was the first of his "planned communities," wherein an entire town sprung up around a golf course and fabulous hotel. Homes, pools, shopping malls all came together, and Charlie's original vision was exactly that; to develop small cities around his hotels and golf courses. If he couldn't get elected as a state leader, he'd build his own states within states and rule his empires that way.

## Twenty-Two

Jarvis Cole wheeled his red Nissan Sentra into Prospector Park and was somewhat surprised when he saw no one on the lighted basketball courts. It was a Wednesday night, about an hour past sunset, and a Little League baseball game was underway on the far side of the municipal park. Parents filled the bleachers behind home plate and along the first and third base lines. The lights on the field were bright, and Jarvis caught the scent of popcorn and hotdogs from the concession stand.

A P.A. announcer's voice said, "Number Nine, the short stop, Timmy Redfield!" Parents clapped for Timmy, who stepped up to the plate, tapped dirt from his cleats, and swung his bat a couple of times. He dug into the batter's box.

Jarvis grabbed his basketball, stepped out of the Nissan, and walked up to the courts. The courts were about two hundred meters from the baseball field, and the parking lot adjacent to the ball field was packed with pickups, minivans, and SUVs. The Apache Junction Little League games were made of a curious socioeconomic composition: working-class folks, yuppie transplants, and the super wealthy that lived at the base of the Superstition Mountains. Jarvis laced up his shoes, did a few stretches, and then began to shoot from around the key.

He heard the metallic *plink!* of an aluminum bat on the ball, and he looked up and saw the long fly ball to deep left-center. A roar went up from the crowd, and the ball hit the ground on the warning track, careened up off of a sign that said "Lloyd's Dry Cleaning," and Timmy Redfield rounded first and started running for second. Timmy slid into second base, popped up, and dusted himself off.

One of the parents shouted, "Way to go, Timmy!"

Jarvis smiled. He dribbled the basketball out to the three-point line, and practiced a hook-and-roll shot that he'd been working on the past few weeks. He hit three out of four and then got bold and took a couple of shots from the baseline.

The first baseline shot hit the rim and fired back to him. He let the ball hit his hands, spun it around, and went up for another jump shot. This time he was long, and the ball hit the back of the rim and took off bouncing toward the far side of the court. Jarvis trotted after it, and the ball rolled down a hill at the side of the courts and into the shadows.

"Damn," he said. He walked down the hill toward the ball. Regulars at Prospector Park's basketball court complained about the hill all the time, but no one seemed to be able to get the city of Apache Junction to do anything about it.

All they needed was a fence along the court's perimeter, but city officials thought an aluminum fence whose sole purpose was to catch errant basketball shots was an eyesore and a waste of money. And as Apache Junction had received a lot of heat about zoning codes and building regulations as one of Phoenix, Arizona's fastest growing suburbs, town officials were not just going to put up a five hundred dollar fence without due consideration.

Jarvis saw his basketball and bent down to pick it up.

Something moved in the shadows ten feet from him, and it sent a bolt of adrenaline through his body.

"Hello?" he said.

There was no answer. He craned his head to see better through the bushes in the wash, and he slowly started backing up the hill toward the lighted basketball courts. He heard something that sounded like a low growl, and he thought it was maybe some kind of dog, though it didn't sound like any dog he'd ever heard. The bushes shook, and the sleek figure moved farther up the wash, staying out of sight.

Whatever it was, it was moving in the direction of the baseball field.

Jarvis reached the edge of the basketball court, and he stood there, looking down the hill. He held the basketball on his right hip and stared into the darkness at the bottom of the hill. He stared for a good ten seconds, didn't see anything, and so turned and took a long baseline shot that hit nothing but net.

"That's right," he said.

• •

Miguel Priest stood at the fence just beyond the dugout on the first base line. He preferred setting up his lawn chair next to whatever dugout his son's team was playing out of, than to sitting in the bleachers with parents who looked like rejected models from a J-Crew catalogue. The white parents treated their kids' baseball games like it was a PTA meeting.

Jose Priest was playing third tonight and would likely come in to relieve the blonde-haired, blue-eyed Nelson Jacks who had gotten the start for Debruck's Cardinals. Debruck's Feed and Cattle sponsored the Little League team, and Jose was one of those rare twelve-year-olds of whom other parents quietly thought, *This boy's got potential.* Real *potential.*

Miguel leaned over the fence and took a long hard look inside the dugout. Head coach Mike Fox was in there eying his pitcher, chewing away at a wad of bubble gum and glancing at the boy who had just made it to second base.

"Okay, Nelson," Coach Fox said. "Dig in now and get this last out!"

The score was tied three-three, and it was the third of a scheduled six-inning game. Make it or break it time.

Miguel glanced across the infield at his son on third. Jose smacked his hand in his glove, shouted "Pitch it in there, Nellie," and crouched down into his third-baseman's stance. Nelson Jacks eyed the catcher's signals, nodded his head, and went into his windup.

"Oh, my God!" one of the parents shouted, standing and pointing toward the right-field fence.

Nelson delivered the pitch. The batter swung hard, and the ball smacked into the catcher's mitt, a puff of dust blasting up from the glove. Everyone started to clap.

But a ripple of fear was going through a pocket in the crowd because one of the parents was standing up shouting, his voice somewhere between a panic and a shriek. The parent was pointing out toward the right-field foul pole. And slowly, all eyes went to the spot at which the parent was pointing. There was a large opening in the fence where the groundskeepers could drive their riding mowers out onto the outfield, and because of the field lights, the opening looked like a large dark mouth.

A wave of shrieks went up, and suddenly all of the players and coaches turned and saw the mountain lion standing there at the opening of the fence just right of the right-field foul pole. It was the size of a Volvo.

The cat had golden eyes that glanced with utter calmness at the field of Little Leaguers as though they were a flock of sheep. Parents screamed and waved for their kids to run. The fenced-in ball field suddenly became a large prison cell, and the large cat singled out the weakest child on the field and began trotting toward him.

Miguel didn't even think. He placed his hands on top of the fence and leapt over onto the field. The mountain lion was only fifty meters away from him, but it was charging toward right fielder Zach Reynolds.

The place went nuts.

Everyone was screaming and running away from right field. Parents rushed the fence behind home plate and screamed at their kids. Everyone was running from right field except this lone man, Miguel Priest.

Little Zach Reynolds looked over his left shoulder as he ran away from the cat. The cat's stride was fluid and smooth, and it bore down on him.

"*Nooo!*" Miguel shouted. "Away!!"

Parents screamed. The P.A. announcer said, "Everyone, remain calm." And the mountain lion lunged onto Zach Reynolds's back.

Miguel was midway across right field. The mountain lion was on top of the boy. The little boy's limbs kicked and flailed, and then the lion lunged and grabbed the boy in its mouth, locking onto him under his left rib cage.

Zach Reynolds screamed.

His arms and legs shook, but the mountain lion had hold of his side, and it lifted him up completely off of the ground. The mountain lion was easily three times larger than the boy, and it carried Zach in its mouth. It turned and started heading toward the opening in the fence, the boy's kicking and screaming body bowed in the cougar's mouth.

Miguel roared and leapt onto the mountain lion's back.

The cat was huge. It tried to shake Miguel loose, but Miguel had hold of its tail in both of his hands. The lion didn't stop, though, and

Miguel was dragged behind the cat toward the darkness beyond the right-field fence.

One of the parents filmed the whole thing with an eight-millimeter Sanyo video camera.

• •

Jarvis Cole looked up from the basketball court and saw the mountain lion running across the outfield. He dropped the basketball and started sprinting toward the baseball field.

By the time he hit the fence along the first-base line, the giant cougar already had the boy in its mouth and another man was running toward the cat.

Jarvis leapt over the fence, grabbed an Easton thirty-four-inch aluminum bat from the on-deck circle, and started running toward the mountain lion, the boy, and the man who was now holding onto the mountain lion's tail.

"Look out, man!" Jarvis shouted at Miguel Priest, but Miguel was on full adrenaline and wasn't letting this animal get away with Zach Reynolds.

The mountain lion turned its head, the young boy in its mouth, and Jarvis swung down at it with the baseball bat.

The bat hit the mountain lion flush between the shoulder blades with a dull *pong!*

The lion dropped the boy from its mouth and staggered under the blow. Jarvis took another swing at the giant cat, flush against the animal's right ribcage. The cougar let out a fierce wildcat shriek, and it swung around.

Miguel tumbled away and hit the right-field fence, and Jarvis Cole stood there ten feet away from the mountain lion. He held the baseball bat up in front of his chest, slightly over his right shoulder.

"*Come on!*" Jarvis roared.

The cat stared at him and swayed from right to left, its golden eyes locking on him.

The little boy lay on the ground near the foul line. He was crying the terrible, shrieking cry of a child in serious pain.

The cat bared its teeth and shrieked again, a sound like nothing Jarvis Cole had ever heard; the wildcat's shriek was like a page-ripping-spitting sound, but deep and punctuated with a low guttural growl. Jarvis suddenly became very afraid.

"I'll kill you," he shouted. "I'll kill you!"

And he hefted the bat up, readying to swing.

The cat stared deep into his eyes, hissed and growled, and then it turned and trotted off through the opening in the fence, vanishing into the darkness beyond right field.

Only one parent had the presence of mind to immediately dial 9-1-1 on her cell phone.

..

By the time local authorities had a helicopter up in the air over the ball field, the mountain lion was four miles east of Prospector Park heading up into the Superstition Mountains. Of course, no one had any way of knowing this, and so the helicopter circled an area around the ball field shining search lights down on the ground from a couple hundred feet up.

An ambulance was on the scene much faster, and parents and coaches guided it over to the opening in the outfield fence where a large group encircled Zach Reynolds. Miguel Priest had received quite a knock on the head, and Jarvis Cole had cut his hand pretty severely somewhere in the melee, but both of these were nothing compared to Zach's injuries.

The mountain lion had locked onto the boy along his left side just below his ribcage and then had carried him for thirty meters like that. The bleeding was pretty bad, and the EMTs quickly assessed that there was serious damage to his renal artery and vein. The boy's floating rib and two of his lateral false ribs were crushed. There was possible damage to his ilium, and his screaming about the pain in his hip and his inability to move his left leg indicated a break in his femur.

This particular mountain lion apparently had a bite radius about the size of a football, and it had used all of that to hoist up Zach Reynolds in its mouth. The boy would probably lose a kidney, but the skilled surgeons at Banner Baywood would keep him alive.

A group of parents huddled around the fellow who caught the whole thing on his Sanyo video camera, and the guy seemed a little too excited with himself for having caught such a horrible thing on film. He actually said to his wife, "This thing is going to make us a *ton* of money." And he played it over and over again for the curious to watch on the camera's miniature video-display monitor.

The first news crew arrived ten minutes after Zach Reynolds was carried away from the ball field in the back of the ambulance, but within an hour, every news station in the greater Phoenix/Mesa area had a van and/or news helicopter on the scene. Reporters were getting eyewitness accounts from everyone they could, and the size of the mountain lion fluctuated with every parent and child's rendering of the story.

## Twenty-Three

Governor Horace G. Redmond III settled into bed with a paperback copy of Rosemary Kingston's *Beyond the Edge*. His wife smiled at him from her side of the bed, and she asked him about the book, rolled over, and snuggled up next to him.

"It's a pretty good book," he said.

Rosemary Kingston had been named to the Arizona State Literary Society, and the governor was scheduled to speak at her induction. His wife, Robin, however, aimed to kiss him on the lips, and the governor put the book down and embraced her.

Horace G., strange as it may sound, was thoroughly in love with his wife of twenty-three years, and he spent considerable time each day daydreaming about making love to her. In an era when politicians generally developed a strangely icy (or at least "aloof") public persona regarding private matters, Governor Horace G. (or "H.G." as his close compadres called him) was a bit of a flirt.

H.G. was a funny man, who could look at once boyish and deadly serious at the exact same moment. It was something about the way his mouth moved, a nervous smile, combined with extremely clear eyes that would lock onto you and not let you go.

People first meeting the governor didn't know whether to laugh or take him seriously, and that juxtaposition almost always set a person off balance, by which point the governor would say something so intensely earnest, warm and sincere that the person had nowhere to run *but to* accept him as a nice, pleasant, shrewd man. And people who went head on and attacked him with bitterness and vehemence were quickly made to sound negative or just plain angry. Some people felt that he could read their thoughts.

"What are you thinking?" his wife said.

She lay with her arm draped across his bare chest. His head was leaned up against the pillow in the bed, and he looked at her.

"I was just thinking about this book," he said, "thinking about the speech tomorrow."

Robin looked into his eyes a moment, smiled, and snuggled close on his chest.

He said, "What're *you* thinking about?"

After twenty-three years of marriage, they weren't always this compassionate and warm, but there were times when the stress of the job, the work, the worry over their children, when all of that subsided for a few hours and they were able to hold one another, and it all seemed somehow worthwhile.

"I was just thinking about how much I love you," Robin said. When she spoke, her breath made the hairs on his chest move slightly. "I feel like I'm the luckiest girl in the world."

She looked at him, and they both seemed like school kids again, not the fifty-somethings Arizona voters had elected to lead the state. There was so much energy and life in Robin's gray-green eyes, and that was something that age hadn't changed. They were both still kids at heart, and they loved each other tremendously.

"I think we're both lucky," H.G. said.

Suddenly, the phone rang, and Robin grabbed it. Horace could tell by her expression that it wasn't good news. It never was, at nine o'clock at night. Robin handed him the phone.

She lay back and watched him. She caught the words "mountain lion" and "attack," and she knew it was going to be a long night. She lay there seeing his expression grow more and more serious. He listened to the voice on the other end of the phone.

"What's the police chief say?" he asked.

Robin got up and walked over to the bathroom sink inside the governor's mansion master suite. She wore a white nightgown, and she started to brush her teeth.

"What about this expert down at U of A?" he asked.

Robin rinsed her mouth and put the toothbrush back in the toothbrush rack.

"And Charlie 'The Chopper'?" he said. "When will he fly in?"

"First thing tomorrow morning," the governor said, and he hung up the phone.

Robin climbed back into bed and turned out her nightstand light. Horace looked at her and realized they weren't going to be making love tonight.

"There's been another cougar attack," he said.

She nodded her head.

He said, "I'll need to address the media first thing in the morning."

They lay there silent for a while, neither one wanting to talk about the fact that they had just been getting warm and cuddly but were both now on edge.

Finally Robin said, "What about this hunter, this Charlie 'The Chopper'?"

Horace looked at her. She turned her head on her pillow and looked at him. Horace reached over and turned out the lamp on his side of the bed. He lay still in the darkness and silence of the mansion. Robin listened to his breathing.

"He's a hunter; he's a sport hunter. And he's ticked off at the bad publicity these attacks have caused at his resort," he finally said. "He'll be here. And he'll be ready to hunt a mountain lion."

## Twenty-Four

In Oracle, there was a rain storm overnight, and Angie woke in the bed next to John Crandall. She lay there listening to the rain hammer the rooftop of John's little home. It was a steady thrumming sound and to Angie it was peaceful and soothing. She got up from bed and opened the window in the bedroom so that she could smell the fragrance of rain in the high country.

"What are you doing?" John asked. He glanced at the clock and saw that it was just past three o'clock.

"It's a storm," she said.

She stood there naked by the window, the dim light casting her skin in a kind of soft, blue sheen. John looked at her, then he pulled up his pillow so that he could lean back against the headboard and listen to the rain. He watched the shadows of rain from the window move steadily over her skin.

Angie turned and looked at him in bed. She had a curious, eager look in her blue eyes.

"Make love to me," she said.

John laughed. "It's three o'clock in the morning," he said.

Angie crossed the bedroom to him. A strong gust of wind blew through the room, carrying the dampness of the pounding rain, and Angie climbed into bed and then onto John.

• •

By morning the storm had moved on, and the sky was bright blue. Angie woke and made a pot of coffee. She opened the windows in the house, and she turned the ceiling fans on to their lowest setting in the living room, the bedroom, and in John's writing studio. The air was cool and damp, the breeze stirred the curtains in the bedroom, and John woke to the smell of brewing coffee.

Angie put on a pair of sweatpants, a T-shirt, and a big ratty sweatshirt, and she took her coffee out onto the front porch. They had a glass mosaic café table on the porch, and the house was situated on a hillside with a view thirty miles down the mountain to Tucson. She set up her laptop on the table with the view, and she sipped her coffee from the steaming cup while she went through the morning's email.

She heard John rattling pots and pans inside in the kitchen, and a couple minutes later the fragrance of scrambled eggs and sizzling bacon came from the kitchen. Angie said loud enough for him to hear, "That smells really good, baby!"

The sunlight was warm and the air was cool, and Angie listened to the birds twitter in a tree over at the side of the yard, while she drank her morning coffee and responded to her students.

John brought her a plate of buttered toast, scrambled eggs, and three strips of bacon.

Angie's cell phone didn't work up in Oracle, which she actually kind of liked because she could escape "up the mountain" when the business of school and administration got too crazy. Angie was a good looking woman and there was a growing buzz, and it seemed a lot of people wanted to be a part of the wave that was her rising star. Some mornings there'd be twenty calls before ten o'clock at her home number thirty miles down the mountain in north Tucson. And that was just the people she gave her number out to; so John's cottage up in Oracle offered a much needed respite.

And so it was actually Robert Gonzalez who called up to John's house to let them know that there'd been another attack, this time at a Little League baseball game. John was cleaning the dishes in the kitchen when the phone rang, and he dried his hands off on a blue hand towel hanging from his fridge and answered the phone.

"What's up?" he said into the phone.

"There's been another attack," Robert told him.

"Oh, no," John said.

"Is Angie up there?"

"Yeah, she's just outside. When was the attack?"

"Last night."

"Where?"

"Up near Phoenix," Robert said, "at a Little League baseball game."

"A Little League baseball game?"

"The mountain lion walked onto the field and attacked a kid, the right fielder."

"Damn."

"The governor's going to address the media at seven A.M.," Gonzalez said. "That'll go live and national, at what, nine A.M. Eastern? We're going to pass through the eye of the hurricane between now and then, man."

Angie called from the front porch, "Who is it?"

"Let me hand the phone to Angie," John said.

"Hello?" Angie said.

Robert Gonzalez said, "There's been another attack, Angie. I think this is our cougar. He walked right out onto an outfield in the middle of a Little League game and attacked a kid."

"Oh, shit," Angie said.

"The governor's going to go live at seven," Gonzalez said. "I'm en route to Apache Junction as we speak. Karen Fowler's up there right now. There's a state park, The Lost Dutchman—"

"I know the Lost Dutchman State Park," Angie said.

"Karen says it's a media circus up there," Gonzalez said.

"I take it they haven't found the cat?"

"No, it's probably headed up into the Superstitions, the mountains east of Apache Junction," Gonzalez said. "It's like a city has sprung up at the state park. You don't have a TV up there in Oracle, do you?"

"No," Angie said.

"It's on every station," Gonzalez said. "This is huge."

"Third attack in just over a month," Angie said. "No one's going to go camping in Arizona for years."

"This happened in an urban area, Angie, a suburb of the fifth largest metro city in the United States. By ten A.M. tomorrow two hundred and fifty million Americans are going to know about Arizona's mountain lions."

"You've got a cabin up there don't you, Robert?" Angie said.

"No, that's up near Castle Peak in the Sierra Anchas."

"How far north?"

"The cabin's forty miles northeast of Lost Dutchman."

"That's where our cat will go," Angie said.

"Why do you say that?" Robert said. "The mountain lion was last seen in Apache Junction."

"The reservoirs that service water to Phoenix are to the northeast: Roosevelt, Canyon, and Bartlett. It's a huge wilderness area, the largest in the state. If we don't find our cat within twenty-four hours that's the place it'll go. He's cut off to the west by Phoenix. He'll go to the northeast."

"My cabin is in the woods north of Roosevelt. Castle Peak is northeast of that. That's mountain country, Angie. Ponderosa pine country."

"We need to get on the ground around Apache Junction and Prospector Park, but if we don't find the cat there, your cabin may be the perfect place for a base of operations."

"How long before you could make it up to Apache Junction?"

"One hour," Angie said.

"I'll see you there," Robert said.

Angie hung up the phone and looked at her wristwatch. It was a quarter past six.

Outside John's modest cottage, Angie's black Porsche glistened in the early morning light.

# Twenty-Five

The reporters were lined up outside of Prospector Park as though ready for a parade. Angie and her team were inside the park studying the tracks from the previous night's attack. Everyone else's eyes were on the governor, who stood over near the bleachers adjacent to the infield. It looked like Horace G. was getting an idea of what the parents had seen.

"He's coming this way," Robert said.

Angie looked up from the tracks they'd been meticulously studying just beyond the outfield fence.

"These tracks match the tracks from Ventana Canyon," she said.

"Let's hope there are no two mountain lions with paw marks that large."

Angie was knelt down comparing the tracks on the ground to the tracks in her palm pilot. She had a tape measurer and caliper ruler. She shook her head in disbelief.

"It's the same cat," she said.

"Doctor Rippard," the governor called. He stood at the opening in the outfield fence through which the cat had walked. Angie was in the dry wash twenty-five meters downhill. She rose up, smiled, and approached the governor and his entourage.

All of his men wore suits, ties, and sunglasses, and the governor extended a hand for Angie to shake.

She enthusiastically gripped his hand, smiled, and said, "It's an honor to meet you, Governor."

"It's a pleasure to meet you," the governor said. "That was some good work you did in Tucson. I wish we could have spoken sooner. I would have congratulated you."

"Four people died."

"And you handled yourself admirably in the press." Horace glanced over his shoulder at the police line that held the circus of news reporters, news vans, and television cameras outside of the main entrance to the park. There must have been thirty news vans and nearly four times that many reporters, cameramen, and pushy onlookers trying to get a better look into the park. "They can be vicious sometimes."

Angie looked into the governor's eyes and said, "You'll probably want to see what we've found."

"Yes."

Angie held up her palm pilot for the governor to see, and she led his entourage down the grassy hill toward the wash.

"The tracks we've found here in the wash lead to the northeast," Angie said. "As you're probably aware everything slopes from northeast to southwest into town, so this wash here flows through the park. During rainy seasons it'll fill with water. The tracks that we've found match the tracks that I found at the Ventana Canyon site."

"They match?" the governor said.

Angie showed him the palm pilot. Horace looked from the computer, to Angie's eyes, to the area her team had roped off like an archaeological site in and around the wash. There was an elaborate grid system with strings and wooden stakes, and a few of the paw marks were being filled with plaster cast. Angie had a team of a half dozen grad students working the site.

"This is my top grad student," Angie introduced, "Robert Gonzalez."

"It's a pleasure to meet you, Governor."

The governor shook Robert's hand and smiled solemnly.

"Robert's team was the first on the site this morning," Angie said. "We initially put six grad students on this grid here to map the tracks up the wash."

"And what do they tell you?" Horace asked.

"I'd say there's a ninety-nine percent certainty that the mountain lion that attacked Zach Reynolds is the same mountain lion that killed Nick Jacobs and Jenny Granger at the Ventana Canyon Resort. I'll need to enter the numbers into my computer, of course."

"What are the trackers telling you, Angie?" Horace asked.

"So far, there's no sign of our mountain lion."

"Well, can't we just follow the tracks?"

"They put dogs on it," Angie said. "Local authorities here in Apache Junction have been tracking since last night."

"And this mountain lion just disappeared?" Horace asked. "Does that happen?"

"It happened at Ventana Canyon."

"How do you explain it?"

Angie shrugged. "They're highly specialized predators," she said. "And typically the way they behave after an attack follows what this animal has done."

"How exactly?"

"Well, they don't hang around after an attack. It's a survival mechanism. A cat will make an attack—successful or no—and then move well away from the site. Sometimes they never come back; most times they'll return to a successful kill within forty-eight hours. But this wasn't a successful kill, and the cat probably moved on. It's one reason why *Felis concolor* is so elusive; they make an attack, and they move on. They stay alive by constantly moving, and a cat like this has a big range."

"Like ninety miles."

Angie said, "As much as two hundred miles sometimes."

"I'm sure I don't have to tell you how bad for business this will be. I want to be sensitive to this animal's habitat, but, well . . . What do you recommend, Doctor Rippard?"

"I'm for relocation above all else." Angie realized her own words rang hollow. It was like a political speech or broken record that had played over and over, but even she was beginning to have her doubts about relocating this particular animal.

"You don't sound too sure of yourself, Doctor Rippard," Horace said.

"No, I'm, uh," she stammered. "Yes, relocation. We can't just exterminate an animal. They have rights."

Her mind filled with an image from her childhood; it was when her brother was attacked, and it made her shiver. Something was happening inside of Angie. She was having a change of heart. Could it be possible that she was wrong about preserving this particular cat?

Horace glanced around at his men. No one said anything, but they all seemed to realize that Dr. Rippard's professional interest in this animal may be clouding her judgment. It was an awkward moment.

Horace was sensitive to her feelings but asked, "Would you ever support exterminating a cougar, Dr. Rippard?"

"I, I, I don't think so," Angie said. "I don't know. They're just harmless animals; they need our protection."

There was a commotion up by the gate into the park. People screamed and leapt out of the way, and a giant Hummer limousine crashed through the plastic barricades and yellow police tape.

"Now what?" Horace said.

They walked up to the top of the hill near the outfield fence. Angie stood down in the wash staring at the ground.

The white Hummer limousine raced through the parking lot. Police chased after it on foot, shouting and yelling. It was headed toward the baseball field. The governor's men started to grow tense and surrounded him for protection. Several of his men actually removed firearms from inside their suit jackets.

The Hummer limousine raced toward the right-field fence. It plowed over the curb and started down the hill. It was going to plow through the fence on the right-field line.

"Look out!" someone shouted.

The governor's men tightened around him.

The limousine plowed through the fence and raced out onto the ball field. It tore up grass and dirt and started heading towards the outfield opening where everyone stood. They leapt out of the way, and the limousine raced through the opening, down the hill toward Angie Rippard.

The biologist and her grad students jumped out of the way just as the Hummer limousine plowed through their grid system at the bottom of the wash. Dust filled the air, and the limousine came to a stop.

"What lunatic is driving that obscene automobile?" Horace said.

The back left door popped open, and a giant bear of a man stepped out from the darkness inside the limousine. He wore a black cowboy hat, black leather pants, black cowboy boots, a rhinestone-studded shirt that glinted in the sunlight, and on his right hip and left hip there dangled matching silver hatchets like a six shooters.

"*Yahoo!*" the man bellowed.

Angie muttered, "The Chopper."

"Just who do you think you are?" Horace shouted. His men were trying to hold him back, but he broke free and started angrily toward the man.

"Governor," the man said. "I'm the only person who can solve this problem."

The man thrust a hand forward for Horace to shake, but Horace declined.

"My name is Charlie Rutledge," he said.

"You mean 'The Chopper'," Angie said. "Do you realize you just ran over our site?"

"I'm terribly sorry about that," Charlie said. "It didn't look like the folks up there at the gate were going to let me through. And I don't have time for your bureaucracy. You must be the biologist that let two people die on my golf course."

"Excuse me," Angie said. She looked into his eyes and realized he wasn't wholly sane.

"Let me tell you something, Doctor Tree Hugger," Charlie declared. "You've let enough people die on your watch. It's what happens when women get into positions of power. You don't have the requisite— ah, *heart*—to follow through with the kill when it becomes necessary. And because of that, people die."

Angie said, "I don't know what Cro-Magnon universe you and your limousine just fell out of."

The man bowed up his chest. "I don't have time for you, Doctor Rippard, if you have the gall to actually call yourself 'Doctor.' I'm here because you've failed, not once, not twice, but three times, now, and because your failure is costing me a lot of money. People are canceling trips to my resort because of you, Doctor Tree Hugger."

Horace said, "Let's be reasonable."

"Reasonable has gotten four people killed, Governor," Charlie said. "I'm not letting you fail again. I'm going up in those hills"—he pointed toward the mountains to the east—"and I'm going to skin me a mountain lion. Now, if you get in my way, I'll skin you, too."

Angie's face turned red with anger. "Why you son of a—"

"*Angie*," Horace said. "I'm sure we can work this out. I'm sure Charlie here didn't mean it quite like that."

"I'll tell you how I meant it," Charlie said. Like lightning, he unlatched the hatchets from his hips. He pivoted around and hurled them like a pro twenty feet through the air. First one, then the other, stuck solidly into a dead log in the middle of the wash.

"Johnny Black," he called to the open door of the limousine. "Let's see the video."

A man with long black hair stepped out of the back of the limousine. He carried a video unit, and he stepped up to the group. Charlie retrieved his hatchets and used one like a pointer.

He proclaimed, "This here video was captured by a parent in the bleachers last night!"

"How did you get this?" the governor said.

Johnny Black pressed "play," and everyone watched the video screen as a mountain lion emerged from the open fence and charged across the outfield toward a little boy in right field.

"From what I understand, young Zack Reynolds may actually live. He was lucky."

"Jesus," Angie gasped.

"You're not supposed to have a copy of this tape," Horace said.

On the video, the largest mountain lion Angie Rippard had ever seen leapt onto Zach Reynolds's back. Parents screamed. Everyone fled the field, except one man, then another who charged right for the mountain lion.

"Look at the size of him."

"I see him," Angie said.

"Have you ever seen a mountain lion that big?"

Angie shook her head.

On the video, the mountain lion had the boy in its mouth and was trotting toward the opening in the fence.

With his hatchet, Charlie Rutledge closed down the video unit and motioned Johnny Black back towards the limousine.

"Now, maybe you think that monster is worth preserving," Charlie said. "I say it's a killer. It's killed four people, and it would have killed a boy last night were it not for two heroic men. I'm going up in those hills. And if you come up there and try to protect this animal, you better bring some mighty good ammunition because I'll become one with the woods, and I'll hunt every last one of you. My name's Charlie Rutledge. *Yahoo!*"

Charlie turned and strode toward the open back door of the limousine. He climbed inside, pulled the door shut, and the limousine roared on up the wash in the direction of the mountains. Everyone just stood there speechless.

## Twenty-Six

The helicopter swung out over the crystal blue water and started racing northeast twenty meters above the water's surface. On either side of the reservoir, desert mountains towered straight up from the clear blue water.

"It's seven miles up to Roosevelt Dam," Dave Baker said. "Are you familiar with it?"

Robert said, "I am. The cabin's just beyond the lake on the high side of the dam."

Angie said, "We'll be able to see Castle Peak once we get out above the—"

"*Damn*," John Crandall said. His mouth dropped open.

"Big ain't it?" Baker said. He glanced at each of them. "That's the world's largest cyclopedean-masonry dam."

"What is that?" Angie said.

"It's a style of building that uses huge irregular-shaped blocks," Baker said. "It's why it's curved."

The enormous convex dam was built between opposing canyon walls. It had a structural height of three hundred and fifty-six feet, as tall as a thirty-five-story building, and it was over twice that wide across the top, seven hundred and twenty-three feet.

"It's a hundred and eighty feet thick at the base," Baker said.

Everyone stared at it as the helicopter came closer and started to climb.

"Yeah," Baker said. "That's Arizona right there; that dam controls seventy percent of the water for Phoenix."

The helicopter came over the top, and everyone saw the huge arch back beyond the dam and then the stunningly vast Roosevelt Lake on the high side of the dam.

"What's the arch?" John asked.

"Highway 188."

And they all saw a single car hauling across the bridge, the arch high over it. The little white sedan looked like a toy car passing across the bridge.

"Depending on rainfall totals," Baker said. "Roosevelt Lake may be as wide as thirty miles from northwest to southeast."

It was huge from left to right, and on the far side of the lake, the enormous Sierra Ancha Mountains rose like a slumbering giant.

The helicopter raced onward across the lake and then began to climb up into the mountains. Giant peaks rose in the distance some eight thousand feet above sea level. The desert saguaro cacti gave way to shrub trees, and then to giant ponderosa pines. The forest was huge and on a scale for which John was not prepared. In either direction north and east, there was nothing but mountains and pine forests for hundreds of miles.

And then they all saw it. Castle Peak rose from the horizon, and it suddenly hit them how remote the location was. The nearest telephone would be more than a hundred miles away. Cars and roads would be non-existent. Angie swallowed down her fear and said, "Well, if I were a mountain lion, this is where I'd be."

Baker tucked the nose of the helicopter down, and raced onward over the sea of ponderosa pines, climbing higher and higher up into the mountains.

"I sure hope you're right, Angie," Robert said.

And they all fell into silence, listening to the rhythmic thump of the helicopter blades.

· ·

The helicopter dropped them off in a clearing a half mile from the cabin. Each of the three carried expedition-style backpacks loaded with enough clothing and food to last them seven days; pilot David Baker was instructed to return to the clearing at eight A.M. in exactly that many days, and the last thing unloaded from the helicopter was an unassembled steel kennel that Robert was already snapping into place.

John and Angie stood there in the clearing and watched the helicopter climb up into the sky overhead. John grimly waved goodbye to

Baker, and the helicopter swung around and took off over the tree line vanishing from sight to the south.

Robert assembled the kennel. It was about fifteen feet long by ten feet wide, and its grated steel roof was five feet tall. John looked doubtfully at it standing there at the side of the clearing. Robert opened and shut the door on one side.

John said, "How're you going to get the mountain lion inside is what I want to know."

Angie carried a Winchester .22 with two dozen Telazol tranquilizer darts strapped to the side of her pack. She also had twenty .22 shells in a pocket on her pack, but she didn't tell John or Robert about that.

"I've got two dozen Telazol darts," she said.

John frowned as Angie approached the assembled cage and shook it with her right hand. It seemed fairly sturdy.

"It'll hold together," Robert said.

Angie nodded her agreement.

"Are you kidding me?" John said. "That mountain lion will rip out'a that thing like it's Glad wrap!"

For his part, John carried a telephoto lens, a Nikon camera, and a Remington twelve-gauge, double-barrel shotgun. The shotgun was strapped to his pack. Robert looked at the cage and said heartily, "It'll hold."

He carried a hatchet, binoculars, and an old .357 in a leather holster on his right hip.

"Come on," he said. "That's the trail over there."

He pointed to a little rectangle sign that stood atop a three-foot-tall wooden post.

## CABIN ↑

The word was etched into the dark wood, and a worn path led uphill into the forest.

"It's about a ten-minute hike up the mountain," Robert said.

"I hope you know," Angie said, "if we make it through this, I'm making sure you get your Ph.D."

Robert smiled and said, "Good, because I might not ever finish up otherwise."

The group shouldered their packs and started up into the forest. It was a beautiful sunlit morning, and light danced through the shadows and on the red earthy ground inside the forest. There was a deep silence all around them, punctuated only by the sound of an occasional bird in the treetops, the wind rustling the tree branches, or a squirrel skittering over dead leaves and pine straw.

"It's peaceful," John Crandall said. "I just hope to get a good story out of this. Maybe I'll even turn it into a novel."

Angie smirked good naturedly at his eagerness.

John said, "If I could write a bestseller maybe Angie will stop flirting with you."

The comment caught Angie off guard because it had no grounding in reality, but she thought that maybe he was just trying to say something funny and that it came out the wrong way. She started to ask him what he meant.

Robert said coolly, "I think you'll really like the views from the cabin, John."

Angie ignored John's comment and said, "How so, Robert?"

"Well, it sits up on a clearing on the side of a hill," Robert said. "You can see down the mountain all the way to the lake; it's probably about thirty miles."

"How often do you come up here?" John asked.

"Three to four times a year," Robert said. "Ordinarily, I put in on the east side of the lake near Grapevine."

"Grapevine?" Angie said.

"It's a little campground area," Gonzalez said. "I keep two ATVs up here. One is in a shed down near Grapevine; one is up at the cabin."

"How long would it take us to get down to Grapevine?" John asked.

"By foot," Robert said, "it's a two-day hike. On an ATV you can do it in a few hours."

They reached a little stone stairwell up the side of the hill. The forest was thick with ponderosa pines, and they were each winded from the climb.

"I put in this stairwell a few years back," Robert said.

When they reached the top of the steps, they could see the cabin through an opening in the forest. The trail continued on ahead of them another forty meters, but there was a clearing up ahead, and they could see the cabin on the side of a grassy hill.

It was a two-story cabin with twin windows upstairs on the front. A wide running porch ran along the front and two sides of the cabin. The porch was screened in, and a wooden swinging chair creaked in a breeze on the front porch. Sunlight shone down on the cabin, and Angie could tell that from its perch, there was quite a view out over the trees.

"It's beautiful, Robert," Angie said.

Robert whispered, "Look!"

Everyone looked up and saw the herd of elk on the far side of the cabin. The elk were grazing on the grass at the edge of the clearing.

"They're huge," John said. He looked at Angie and smiled excitedly.

Robert said, "I'm afraid that's all we'll have in the way of neighbors for the next few days."

There were two adult females, one juvenile, and a month-old calf. The bull elk had an enormous rack of antlers.

"They're in the rut," Angie whispered.

"What do you mean?" John asked.

"Most of the year," Angie said, "elk stay in a loose female social order, and the males travel alone. You only see them like this when they're mating."

The humans stood there on the edge of the clearing, the cabin between them, and on the far side of the clearing the elk casually walked on up the mountain and into the forest.

"How much does the male weigh?" John asked.

"The bull's about seven hundred pounds," Angie said. "The two cows probably weigh about five hundred. The juvenile's about half that, and the calf weighs a hundred or so."

The group stepped out into the sunlight. A worn gray path led through the knee-high grass. A dozen wooden steps led up from the ground to the screen door on the front porch; their feet clomped heavily up the steps.

Robert unlatched the screen door, and they all stepped up onto the porch. John and Angie turned around and were stunned by the view.

"Oh, my God," John said.

The mountain sloped downhill thirty miles to the southeast. It looked like a vast green sea, and far down at the bottom of the mountain was Roosevelt Lake, which spread from eastern horizon to western horizon.

"The place always needs a little cleaning at first," Robert said.

He removed a key from his pocket and unlocked the hard wooden door.

Angie said, "This is perfect."

Robert looked over his shoulder and saw the expression on her face. She stood there on the porch gazing out at the wilderness that surrounded them. She looked utterly calm and at peace. She nodded her head lightly.

"What is it?" John said.

"This is it," Angie said. "We're going to find our cat. I can feel it; it's like a knot in my chest."

John and Robert exchanged glances. They were both aware of Angie's uncanny intuition, but rarely was she so specific, and they both kind of smiled curiously and then looked at her. She stood on the porch, the sunlight bright all around the screened-in area, out over the yard, the trees, all the way down to the lake. Crickets chirruped in the grass. A steady breeze stirred the treetops, and the screen bulged in and out as though the cabin itself was breathing.

What Angie didn't say was that she was certain, too, that one of them was going to die.

## TWENTY-SEVEN

The big cat stood perfectly still staring uphill through the trees. Its shoulders were tense, and it seemed ready to take a step forward. But it was staring at something up the hillside, something through the trees, something that seemed utterly unaware that a huge predator was stalking it. A breeze rustled through the treetops, but the cougar resisted the urge to smell the wind. Its head remained level and perfectly motionless.

The deer stood in a patch of sunlight that came through the forest canopy. It raised its head up and glanced nervously down the hill. Its ears stood like twin radars on its head, twitching and honing in on every sound along the forest floor. The deer's coal black nose was moist, and it detected a fluctuation in the scent of the forest.

Something had startled a squirrel two hundred meters down the forested hillside, and the squirrel scrambled up into a tree. Two birds were on a low branch of the tree, and the squirrel's jittery movement caused them to take flight through the forest up toward the deer.

Now the deer stood there in the dappled sunlight, cocking its head one way then the other, its ears poised and listening for any sound from down the hill.

The deer stood there like that for a good thirty seconds, making no sound at all, its head pivoting back and forth listening, listening . . .

The attack came from up the hill, which completely caught the deer off guard. It was so tensely poised listening for a sound from *down* the hillside that in the half-second between when it heard the mountain lion and was hit by the mountain lion, it actually bolted *up* the hill.

The cougar hit it at full speed and knocked the deer over in a blinding frenzy of fur, claws, and wildcat growling. The deer landed hard on its side, knocking the wind from its lungs. It made a short-burst groan and tried to stagger onto its feet.

The cougar hit the deer so hard that it was dazed itself, and it had overshot its mark. The cougar sprung around a hundred and eighty degrees without even looking and pounced down on top of the deer, which had almost reached its feet in the split second after the initial hit. The cougar's front two sets of claws dug into the deer's back, and its back left leg kicked wildly and swept the deer's back legs out from under it.

The deer groaned again, now pinned to the forest floor, and the cougar lunged forward and bit into the back of the deer's neck. The bite was just above the deer's shoulders, and it was powerful, but it didn't snap its neck instantly. The deer struggled and twisted and kicked its legs, and the cougar just dug in balancing itself over the smaller animal.

The deer thrashed and kicked like a fish on a pier, but the cougar held it down and refused to let go. The cougar's jaws pressed down harder, and it centered its balance so that the deer could not get a brace on anything.

The cougar wasn't centered well enough to break the deer's neck, but it was centered well enough to hold it firmly in place. The bite wasn't around the deer's throat either, so the action seemed momentarily stalemated. The cougar seemed to realize this, but it realized too that the deer wasn't going anywhere.

Gradually the deer tired enough that the cougar could break its neck. The cougar brought its front right paw forward and pinned it against the deer's head. It used its left paw to goad the deer into struggling, and with its jaws clamped tightly around the deer's neck, it wrenched the deer's head against its struggling body until the deer's neck snapped.

Once the deer was paralyzed, the big cat began to feed.

# Twenty-Eight

"You hungry?" Robert asked.

John looked up at Robert from across the inside of the cabin. Robert was at the counter in the kitchen. Sunlight shined in through the open windows, and there was a gentle breeze pulled in by one of two circulating fans in the living room.

"What do you got?" John asked. He was on the sofa, reading a magazine.

"Got a ton of these." Robert held up a Power Bar.

John motioned like he wanted one, and Robert tossed it across the cabin for John to catch.

"Where did Angie go?"

"She wanted to check the pump," Robert said.

John opened the wrapper on the Power Bar.

"Where is that?"

Robert said, "It's over at the side of the yard, at the edge of the woods, over on this"—he pointed to the right—"side of the cabin."

"You think it's safe for her out there alone?"

"She'll be fine," Robert said. "Chances are we'll be up here a week and won't find so much as a track."

"Yeah?"

"They're really elusive animals, John. Some professional trackers spend months searching for a single track. The chance that we'll find one specific cougar—*our* cougar—is really minimal."

"Do you think she's good?"

"Angie?"

"Yeah, man."

Robert Gonzalez poured a glass of water from a pitcher. "I've always thought she's the best field researcher I've ever known. She thinks like an animal. She has a good imagination, and she knows her business better than anybody else. If we're going to find our cougar, there's nobody that I'd bet on more to find it than Angie."

John stood up and walked over to the window on the right side of the cabin. He took a bite of the Power Bar and tried to spot Angie out in the yard, but he didn't see her.

"What is it with you and her?" he said.

"What do you mean?"

"I don't know," John said. "You probably understand her better than I do. You spend more time with her than I do; that's for sure. What is so attractive about these animals to her?"

"I don't know, man. Maybe it's the unknown. We fear the unknown. And I don't know of another predator in North America that we know less about than the cougar."

"And yet you've got a system by which you can get a handle on it, studying it?"

"Yeah, I mean, we get paid," he said. "There's academic respect, maybe even a little bit of fame in Angie's case. But I don't know; I think it's something altogether deeper for her. I mean her brother was attacked when she was a kid. She was there. It was like her brush with death. Maybe she revisits it the way guys coming home from Vietnam thirty-five years ago, sometimes would go back to Saigon a year or two later. It's like you just can't get away from it in your mind."

"That's a psychological truism isn't it?"

"To go back to the thing that almost killed you?"

"Yeah," John said.

"Maybe so; it's like you got a handle on it because you survived it once. It gives you a buzz to go back so close to death. I mean Angie lived. She made it through the attack. So that's what she expects will happen every time she encounters a cat. Maybe she feels like she knows the animals in a way that no one else ever really can. Hell, I don't know. I just know that she's one hell of a tracker. She knows this animal better than the animal knows itself."

••

Angie held a green garden hose coiled in her hand. The pump was an old hand-lever style, and she couldn't see any way that she could attach the hose to it. The pump had a wood-encased base, and the grass and weeds were grown up tall around the wooden base frame. Her fear of snakes rustling through the high grass in the yard was real, but Angie tried to brush that out of her mind in order to focus on getting the hose hooked up.

She placed the coiled hose on the wooden base, and she tried to lift the lever on the pump. It was harder than she had thought it would be, and so she stepped up onto the wooden base and tried to use both hands. She lifted the lever up, expecting water to come gushing out of the thing, when all of sudden the board underneath her cracked and she fell through.

"Son of a bitch!" she muttered.

Her left leg was down inside the wooden base, which stood a foot up from the ground; so she was in it up to her shin. It felt like she'd cut her leg, and she saw that the wood was rotted around the base. The nails that held the wood in place were rusty and exposed, and so Angie carefully removed her leg from the wooden base and stepped back two steps from the pump.

She looked at her left pants leg. Her khakis were ripped, and she lifted up her pants leg and saw that a shiver of wood had opened up the skin on her left shin.

"Damn that hurts," she said, grimacing.

She looked with disgust at the spot where the wood had rotted and broken through. The garden hose sat there on the edge of the wooden base frame, and it seemed to smile at her in the sunlight. She looked back at her leg, judging how badly the wound was going to bleed.

She glanced back over her shoulder. There was a wooden shed out behind the cabin. Maybe Robert kept a mower in there. It'd be nice to mow this grass, Angie thought.

She looked back at her leg, and then all of a sudden, there was a gurgling sound from the pump. Several belches of air came up from the spigot, and the pump hawked out some rusty-colored water. A second later, the water color turned over from the rusty color to clear well water. The pump stopped belching up air, and the water just flowed.

Angie reached her hand forward and felt the water's coolness. It was icy.

"Sweet," she said. She rolled her pants leg up past her knee, and she reached her shin forward and let the water clean the wound.

Everything was going to be alright. Angie looked at the green garden hose coiled on the side of the wooden base frame, and it didn't seem to be smiling at her in the sunlight anymore. It was looking at her smugly.

"What are you looking at?" Angie muttered, and she continued washing her wound until it stopped bleeding.

She lifted her leg and moved it out of the stream of icy water, and she let it dry for a moment.

The pump was over at the edge of the yard. There was pine straw on the wooden base frame from the ponderosa pines, and Angie more than once looked down into the forest, letting her eyes focus across the forest floor. She saw two birds fly from one tree to another, and she saw a squirrel scramble up a tree, but she didn't see anything that looked like a mountain lion.

She did all of this in a cursory sort of way because she didn't really want to dwell on the fact that she was becoming somewhat paranoid that a mountain lion may be stalking her at any given moment. It just wasn't natural, and even though this cougar had exhibited plenty of unnatural behavior in the past couple of months, Angie still held onto a fundamental belief that order existed in nature on a principle level, and that strange things didn't generally happen.

Angie was a scientist, and even though she was a deeply intuitive scientist, science operated on a cause-and-reaction principle, and monsters didn't well up out of nowhere and begin hunting people unless there was a very good reason.

If this mountain lion were stalking people, it did so because it had been conditioned to do so. Somewhere in its past, it had learned that humans were easy prey, an easy meal, and not a significant threat. It had probably grown up on protected sanctuaries where hunting was illegal, and as such, it had no reason to stay away from a human that it happened upon on a hiking trail.

"Aversive conditioning" was the phrase she'd used at the Fifth Annual Research Symposium for the Center of Applied Conservation Biology. These animals had to be taught to avoid humans, to stay away, that if it smelled or saw a human that the best thing for a cougar to do was to run away.

But that wasn't what was happening anymore. Hunting mountain lions was illegal in several states in the West, and where there weren't statewide bans on hunting the animal, there were generally hundreds of thousands of acres of protected forest land where it *was* illegal to hunt cougars. And with human populations on a staggeringly fast rise in the West, more and more people were putting up subdivisions in wilderness areas, and more and more people were walking on trails that would have been remote wilderness trails thirty years earlier.

All of this, though, was an explanation. Right or wrong, it operated on the principle that if there were an animal behavior problem (a cougar stalking people, for example), there were certain measures that could be taken to prevent such behaviors.

The paranoia that Angie felt while she stood there washing the wound on her leg, the tension in her shoulders, the shortness of breath that she felt, it was something altogether different. The paranoia was a result of fear, and the fear was a result of recent human attacks and killings, but the degree and intensity with which she felt the paranoia couldn't be easily explained. It was that gray area of human thought.

She *knew* that they were going to kill this cougar. She *knew* that someone was going to die. She *knew* it. But explaining *how* she knew it was beyond her scientific grasp. And yet it was there, floating along in her subconscious, and every time she saw a bird flutter through the trees or saw movement along the forest floor out of the corner of her eye, she turned and looked. She felt her chest seizing up just a little; she felt her breath growing thin and discordant. Would this be it? Was she breathing her last breath before the animal attacked her? Was she thinking her last thought before the cougar pounced on her and snapped her neck?

"Stupid, stupid, stupid," Angie muttered, looking at her wounded leg. And she wanted to yell out her frustration, her pain, her fear. "Stupid, stupid, stupid," she said.

She glanced over her shoulder at the spot in the grassy yard where she'd thrown the garden hose.

"I hope you're happy!" she said loudly, disregarding the realization that she sounded more than a little crazy shouting at an inanimate garden hose that was lying in the grass. She muttered, "Stupid garden hose."

# TWENTY-NINE

Angie spread the map out on a table on the porch. Robert and John looked on, and neither said anything about the clouds each of them saw forming to the south. The topographic map was four feet by four feet square, took up the whole tabletop, and it showed elevation gradations, hiking trails, creeks and springs all the way down to Roosevelt Lake.

Angie said, "I figure this afternoon we ought to map out a couple of grids that we can follow the next two to three days."

"We break the tracking work down into detail?" Robert said.

"Cover a grid per afternoon," Angie said. "Give us some reasonable ground to cover."

John and Robert nodded their heads. John held a contemplative index finger to his lower lip. Suddenly, a loud rumble of thunder rolled up from deep on the horizon, and it startled them all. It was distant but powerful, and all three of them looked up at the clouds rising from the southern horizon thirty miles away. Huge clouds climbed from mountains to the south looking white, dark blue, and almost black from higher to lower altitudes.

"Cumulonimbus," Angie said gravely. "You see the anvil-shaped head at the top of the cloud formation?"

"Thunderheads," Robert said.

"What does the anvil shape mean?" John asked stupidly.

"It means we're in for a storm," Angie said.

"It means they're monsoon clouds," Robert said.

A sudden breeze came up from the woods and pressed hard against the screened-in porch. The map started to flutter off of the table, and Angie leaned forward and pressed both hands flat against it, holding it in place. The wind died down, but there was no denying the moisture on the breeze. In Arizona, Angie had grown accustomed to being able to *smell* the rain on the air, the winds of change, twelve hours before a storm would strike. Life in the desert high country changed when a monsoonal storm hit.

"Well, technically, it would be a *pre*-monsoonal storm," Angie said. "We're not in monsoon season just yet."

"It may just pass us over," John said.

Neither Angie nor Robert responded to this statement. Angie focused on the map. She drew four grids north of the lake. She placed a roman numeral squarely in the center of each grid: I, II, III, and IV.

"We take grid three this afternoon," Angie said. "It's the closest to us. We break the grid into four horizontal sections, and we cover as much ground as we can. If a storm rises up, we can be back up here safely and quickly."

John started looking at the roof over the porch, judging how well the cabin would stand up in a storm. His eyes went back worriedly to the map. He reached forward and pointed at the map legend at the bottom right-hand corner of the map.

"What is the scale?" he said. "How many miles are we talking?"

"Each grid is about fifteen miles, north to south," Angie said. "Ten miles east to west. All we have to do is get a dart into him, and we can come back with the ATV and haul him up to the kennel. But for now, we're scouting, tracking, looking for signs of cougars. Robert and I know what to look for."

"And what's that?" John said. "What're the signs?"

"Cougar mounds," Angie said. "Tree markings and tracks would be the best, but there are more visible signs than a paw print in mud that'll help us determine if our cougar's up here in the mountains with us."

"And what if it's not?" John asked.

"Then, we all live another week," she said. "We take the helicopter back down to civilization. We let the Department of Game and Fish know what's going on. They'll let the governor know what's going on. We regroup, and if we have to come back up here, we do that. We establish a base camp here."

"You're convinced that it's up here," Robert said.

Angie nodded her head and looked into Robert's eyes.

"Our cat is up here," she said. She gazed out across the sea of trees.

John fingered his shotgun.

"We'll find him," Angie said. "Or he'll find us."

"What about the Chopper?" Gonzalez said.

Angie said, "That lunatic?"

"Yeah," Gonzalez said.

"He's out there, too," Angie said. "Somewhere."

They looked out across the forest treetops, south all the way to the lake. Another deep rumbling roll of thunder came up from the south; this one shook the windows hard enough to make them rattle in their frames.

•   •

The rains came when they were two miles out from the cabin on a trail in a forest so thick they couldn't see more than thirty meters in any direction.

"*Jesus,*" John muttered. "I'm cold."

The rain felt almost icy it was so cold, yet the air had been warm, so there was this sensation of going from warm dry air to cool, damp air in only a matter of minutes. And the rain fell hard. John looked up ahead of him on the trail.

Angie's hair was soaked. Her khakis were damp. She turned and looked at him, and almost had to shout to be heard, "We need to find some shelter! This may turn over to hail!"

"Right!" John shouted. They both looked at Robert.

"There used to be a camping shelter on up ahead," Robert said. "It's not much, but it may give us some protection."

They continued up the trail through the woods, and a few minutes later, they saw something ahead of them. Angie saw it first, and she pointed it out.

"Yeah," Robert said. "I see it!"

The rain hammered the trees, the earthy ground, soaking the trio in icy cold rain. Rivulets formed along the trail, quickly eating away at the earth. Angie saw something that looked like a couple sheets of dark plywood up ahead.

As they approached the camping shelter, she saw that Robert was right. It really wasn't much. A wooden platform was built up about two feet off of the ground. It opened like a rectangular clam shell and was about eight feet from right to left. A "half cave" is what outdoor enthusiasts called it. The side facing the trail was completely exposed, but they climbed up inside it, laughing with excitement.

"It's not much," Robert said over the rain.

"It'll do," Angie said.

The rain beat against the plywood roof and poured down the back of the lean-to. It was not much larger than a closet, but the group was happy to be out of the rain for a moment.

"Back-country hikers sometimes hold up here," Robert said.

Angie looked around. There were names carved into the wood.

Robert said, "It gets them up off of the ground."

"Yeah," John said. "You could put a sleeping bag in here, and it wouldn't be all that bad."

"Look at all these names," Angie said.

John read one that said: "Frannie blew me here 9-9-02." And then apparently Frannie had corroborated the statement just underneath that: "It was really fun—Frannie."

"Oh, man," John said. "People have screwed in here."

He seemed somewhat grossed out by the idea.

"Why is it," Robert asked, "that people write the most vulgar shit when they're carving stuff into wood?"

"Well, if you've only got five words to write in your lifetime, you're gonna write 'I wanted to get laid.'"

Angie said, "Or 'I got laid.'"

"Nice," John said. "Very succinct."

"Here's a nice one," Robert said. "'Sunny day—12-3-02.'" And there was a goofy looking sunshine carved into the wood with rays bursting out from it. The sun had a smile and eyes carved into it.

Suddenly, the forest exploded with the sound of hail hitting tree branches. The hail pounded the wooden roof of the shelter. Angie, Robert, and John tried to squeeze back further into the thing, and they looked out at the forest floor as it was quickly covered in little white pellets of hail.

"Well, wherever our mountain lion is," John said, "I hope he's got him some shelter."

The hail continued to pound the forest for the next ten minutes until the ground was white. Robert reached his hand out at one point to pick up a few pieces, and he was struck by the sharpness of the pouring hail.

"Ow!" he said, and he retracted his hand.

He looked at his hand as though shocked that Mother Nature had a little sting in her. He wasn't prepared for the fact that nature didn't give a damn about him and would sting his hand if he stuck it out at the wrong time.

"You alright?" Angie said.

He looked at his hand. "Yeah, I'll be alright."

"That's some serious stuff," John said inanely. "What is hail anyway?"

"It's the most destructive form of precipitation on Earth," Angie said. "Hailstones usually measure about a quarter inch to four inches in diameter."

The stones that covered the ground around the camping shelter were about the size of marbles, about a half inch in diameter.

"Some stones measuring up to six inches in diameter have been reported," Angie said. "That kind'a hail can kill animals."

John and Robert looked at her. The hail continued to pound the forest.

"I read a story a couple years ago about a hailstorm in Colorado that just wiped out an entire herd of cattle," Angie said. "Like ten thousand head of cattle, lying out in the field fifteen minutes after the hail started, most of them dead or near death. Terrible."

"It'll last like five minute," John said.

"Hailstorms rarely last longer than fifteen minutes," Angie said. "It'll turn over to rain soon enough."

They sat there silently, eyes bright, excited, and alert. Something about all of this was fun, even though they realized they had serious business ahead of them.

Angie sat there in the lean-to, her legs curled up in front of her, her arms and hands wrapped around the front of her knees. Her wet brown hair was pulled back in a ponytail, but strands of hair hung down on either side. Robert thought she was cute. He noticed that her blue eyes, which normally held such intensity, seemed bright and almost innocent. Angie was in her element, and she was having fun. The curve of her chin was rounded like an apple, and when she smiled, little crescent-shaped dimples rose on both sides of her face. She looked from Robert to John, and she patted at her wet hair.

"What's the worst storm you ever got caught in?" John asked.

"When I was sixteen," Robert said. "I was driving back from my grandparents' house in Santa Fe."

"New Mexico?" John asked.

"Yeah," he said. "We lived down in Albuquerque. It's about an hour drive, and I was coming home one night, and it was like the sky just opened up, man. It started pounding. Lightning, thunder. But the crazy thing was a bolt of lightning came down and hit the highway in front of my car. Sparks exploded all over the place, man. It was crazy."

"Scary," Angie said.

"Could you feel it?" John asked.

"The lightning?" Robert said. "No, it was far enough ahead of the car that I wasn't like struck or anything. But I was close enough to literally see the sparks fly up off of the pavement."

"Damn," Angie said.

"What about you?" Robert asked Angie.

"The last time I ever saw my brother was in a terrible monsoon," Angie said. "He was a funny guy, my brother. You know he had scars, from the attack and all, and when we were kids everybody made fun of him. He kind'a grew into it, though, by high school; you know, he found ways to make fun of his face. He'd dress up like a ghoul at Halloween and shit like that. I don't think he could have made it through those years without a sense of humor. He made people laugh, you know."

"He married young, right?" John said.

"Too young," Angie said. "I think a big part of it was that he was with the prettiest girl in school. He made her laugh, and it was a time when everyone was doing the non-superficial thing. I don't know, maybe she really loved him. I just remember that storm."

"What happened?" Robert asked.

"The plan was to drive out to the National Monument down in the Chiricahuas," Angie said. "He got her parents in a car, and I tailed behind them with her baby brother and sister. We got nailed by a storm south of Willcox, and it totally freaked out her family. They were shouting to let them off at the next town; only, the next town was in Mexico!"

"Damn," John said.

"I think all of the bravado and humor that he'd shown all those years just finally caved in," Angie said. "I mean he's married to this girl, you know, and they're your standard country club fair, and he's this *freak*, with his face, you know? I think it just scared them that their blonde-haired blue-eyed daughter had married this guy, no matter how good her intentions. I don't know; they got divorced six months later, and my brother moved to Hawaii.

"I think he was totally humiliated and couldn't stand to look at me, couldn't stand to look at *anyone* who had known him all those years. I don't know; it just sort'a stopped him in his tracks. I haven't talked to him in fourteen years. How screwed up is that?"

They all looked out and saw that the hail had stopped. The precipitation changed over to rain, and they sat there inside the shelter like three kids trapped in a storm on the walk home from school.

• •

The mountain lion caught their scent through the pounding rain while it was burying the deer. Its head snapped up, and it looked over the mound of leaves, branches, and pine straw. It was raining so hard it was difficult to see far through the trees, but the cat heard the sound of laughter and became tense and territorial.

The mountain lion licked its lips and looked down at the partially buried deer. A single hind leg stuck up from the pile like a hoofed tree branch. The big cat pawed at it so that it wouldn't be sticking straight up into the air and noticeable to any scavenger that might happen along in the coming hours. It was largely a clean site, and the big cat continued to pile up brush over the deer with its front paws, making it even cleaner.

It sounded like the laughter was coming from just over a ridge. The forest was alive with rain, and a creek formed to the left of the mound.

The big cat continued to pile up scrabble and branches over the deer. It circled the mound a couple times and looked cautiously up the hill. It sniffed the air. It listened to the pounding rain on the trees and the forest floor. There was a flash of lightning in the sky, and then a crash of thunder shook the tree branches.

A bird squawked angrily, desperately somewhere in the treetop canopy, and the cat listened hard, listening for the sound of humans again. The rain was intense.

The big cat detected movement up the hill. The trees were too thick to see quite what it was, and daylight was quickly fading from the storm-darkened skies, but the cat had heard this sound before, and the sound had soon been followed by a successful kill.

It was the sound of a human. It was the sound of a human *singing*.

• •

John sang Led Zeppelin's "Whole Lotta Love," playing air guitar with his shotgun. And all around them the forest was alive. They were soaked through to the bone, and they were ready to be back at the cabin where they could take a shower, dry off, and enjoy a nice dinner together. Perhaps, they could even build a fire in the fireplace while the storm raged outside.

There were three bottles of wine that Angie knew of (she'd packed them), and she could think of nothing better than being out in the woods with her boyfriend, one of her best friends, a good meal, a fire, and a warm dry cabin in the woods while a thunderstorm raged all around them.

But for right now, the trick was to make it back to the cabin. It was raining so hard it was somewhat difficult to keep up with the trail in front of them. Their hiking boots were soaked, and the trail was muddy, and so they kept slipping and sliding as they walked up the ridgeline.

Angie checked her water-proof Timex and saw that it was a quarter to six. *Jesus*, she thought. *We better hurry up, or we'll be stuck out here after dark.*

"Hey, Robert," she called through the pouring rain. "Are you sure this is the right trail?"

Robert had to yell over the pounding rain, "What's that?"

"The trail!" Angie shouted. "Is this the right trail?"

Robert leaned in close and said, "I think so."

Angie looked into his eyes and realized for the first time that they might be lost. The thought hadn't occurred to her because Robert was leading them, and it was his cabin, and these were supposedly woods with which he was familiar. And he'd been chipper ever since they left the lean-to about an hour and half earlier. But it should have only been a two-mile hike from the lean-to back to the cabin, and they should have covered that ground in forty minutes, an hour at the very slowest.

Angie saw the worry and doubt in Robert's eyes, even though he covered it up well with a chipper smile.

"I'm pretty sure," he said loud enough over the pounding rain.

Angie nodded, and they walked on for a while. John continued to sing. He apparently had the entire Led Zeppelin catalogue memorized. It made Angie remember her high school prom, when the DJ had played "Stairway to Heaven," which was quite possibly the hardest song in the world to dance to at a prom, and she and her friends had laughed at their own silliness and awkwardness of dancing to a song that started off very, very slow and ended very fast.

"Could you sing something else?" she said.

John must not have heard her because he kept on singing.

"John?" she said loudly over the rain.

John turned around and looked at her. He wiped back rainwater from his forehead, eyes, and mouth.

"And carry that rifle a little more carefully," she said.

"What?"

"Stop singing, man," she said.

John looked annoyed that she'd be requesting him *not* to sing. He was just enjoying himself, trying to make the best of a shitty situation. But he complied.

He muttered something, and Angie wasn't having any of it.

"What'd you say?" she said.

He turned around and looked her squarely in the face. "It's not a *rifle*," he said. "It's a shotgun."

Angie looked over his left shoulder. Robert had continued on up the trail, but he seemed to realize that they had stopped and so he stopped and turned around and looked at them in the pouring rain.

"What's the matter with you?" Angie said without hostility.

John looked into her eyes, and he seemed to realize she *wasn't* being hostile.

"I sing when I get nervous," he said. "You know that, Angie."

She realized he was scared and said, "Come here, baby."

She kissed him squarely on the lips, leaned back, and said, "Everything's gonna be alright. Okay?"

She looked into his eyes. He nodded as if to say "okay."

"I love you," he said.

Angie smiled awkwardly. "I love you, too," she said.

The rain poured on them, and they looked at one another.

John smiled a little crazy-eyed, and they carried on into the driving rain that continued to hammer the forest.

• •

The big cat followed the group of three through the pouring rain and the forest trees. It was uphill from them, watching them slip and slide through the mud. The cat moved in on them swiftly, drawing closer, but it stayed uphill tracking them with its eyes through the downpour, through the trees.

The cat was wary because it had never encountered three people alone like this in the woods, and it had certainly never *attacked* three people alone like this in the woods in a driving thunderstorm. The cat was curious, but it was fiercely territorial, too, and it had learned over the past year that humans were not dangerous, yet they scared away many other animals that it needed for food. As such, they *were* a threat to its survival, and they were easy to kill.

The cat watched the group of three disappear over a crest in the hill, and it cut short the distance between itself and the humans by taking a direct line over the hill.

When the mountain lion came over the hill, it was suddenly within twenty feet of the humans. But it was behind them and to their left, and the humans were completely unaware of its presence just twenty feet behind them through the trees.

Angie was at the back of the group. Robert was out front, and John was in the middle, and they walked single-file on what Angie could tell was no longer a trail at all. She stepped around a prickly pear cactus, and she looked ahead of her at Robert and John.

"I think this may be it up here," Robert called through the rain.

Angie checked her wristwatch and saw that it was twenty past six. The official sunset was about six-fifty, but because of the storm and the dark clouds overhead, it was already dark enough that she couldn't see more than thirty feet. Her shoes and socks were soaked through, and she felt that the socks had gotten all bunched up down inside her boots. The air temperature had dropped about thirty degrees since before the rain began earlier that afternoon, and it would certainly continue to drop as night set in. Temperature variations in Arizona—in desert environments in general—were dramatic. A daytime high of ninety degrees oftentimes yielded a nighttime low forty degrees cooler.

And they were in the high country, some six thousand feet above sea level. It was about fifty-eight degrees, and after nightfall set in, the temperature could easily drop to forty. By midnight, it may well be near freezing up here, and they were all soaked through to the bone. The prospect of spending a night outside in these conditions if the rain continued was daunting.

Angie's shoelace came untied, and she knelt down to tie it. She felt the rain beating against her back, soaking her through to the bone, and she took the soaking wet shoelaces up in her hands and tried to give them a tie. Out of habit as much as anything else, she glanced back over her left shoulder.

She saw something up the hill from her. The rain was pouring hard, and it was difficult to see very well, but something was up on the hill. It was so close it took a moment to register.

The mountain lion stood two feet left of a giant ponderosa pine tree, and it just stared at Angie. It was soaked, and Angie could not believe her eyes. She was hit with such a rush of adrenaline it was difficult for her to comprehend what she was seeing.

The cat was easily as long as a sofa from its head to the base of its tail. With the tail, the cat was over twelve feet long, longer than some cars.

Her hands shook as she loaded a tranquilizer dart in the rifle. She got the rifle up with its butt firmly against her shoulder. The cat just stood there; it had absolutely no fear of humans. Rain beaded down the steel of the rifle barrel, and Angie lowered her head to see down the gun's sights. Her breath was coming out thin and ragged, and she felt white-hot adrenaline. Everything on her felt weak, wet, and tired.

She had never in her life seen a mountain lion as large as this one. It was huge.

For a moment, time stood still. Robert and John had continued on through the woods. They didn't realize that Angie had stopped to tie her shoes. They didn't realize that Angie was standing there, staring at their cougar. They didn't realize that for the past thirty minutes they had been stalked by an animal twice the size of each of them, an animal nearly three times Angie's body weight.

Angie suddenly felt the cold. She felt her own feeble mortality gripping her. She realized that if she did not hit this animal, it would kill her. There was no guilt. There was no remorse. There was no law, other than the law that simply stated that the larger, faster, smarter creature in the next thirty seconds would live to face another day.

Angie's index finger wrapped around the trigger. She clenched her jaw. Her blue eyes were clear and fierce. She followed the animal through the sights of her rifle. The cat stared at her.

"*Come on,*" Angie muttered.

And she squeezed the trigger.

The hammer clicked, but there was no kickback. Angie stared down the rifle's barrel, but she realized that the rifle had misfired. Without moving an inch, her eyes looked at the rifle's hammer and saw that it had sprung. But the rifle didn't fire!

A wave of fear-driven nausea washed over her because she knew that she was going to die. It was like panic, but she was still alive. She was without a gun, but she was still alive.

Suddenly, she heard John and Robert shouting from behind her. The giant cougar just stood there on the hill, staring down at them. It seemed to gather that the two men were screaming and shouting at it.

John's shotgun fired with a loud *crack!* that echoed through the forest and the downpour.

They rushed up beside her. Robert's hands were shaking, but he was trying to get his .357 out of the leather holster on his right hip. He nervously yanked it out, and the gun fired and hit the muddy ground about three feet from his right foot.

Angie shouted something at him.

John dropped down on one knee, and he raised his shotgun up to his right shoulder. He took aim and fired. The sound of the shotgun blast echoed through the forest. The air filled with the acrid smell of ignited gunpowder. All three of them looked up and saw that the mountain lion was just standing there, still, standing there on the hill no further than a living room's distance away from them.

"Kill it, John!" Angie shouted.

John took aim a third time, fired, and the forest filled with the sound of his shotgun echoing. Robert held his .357 up shakily and squeezed the trigger. It, too, fired, and the sound echoed all around them in the forest. They could smell the gunpowder.

And then all three watched in horror as the mountain lion took two steps forward, coming toward them.

"Oh, my God!" Robert shouted.

"Run!" John screamed.

"*Don't* run!" Angie shouted.

The mountain lion took another four steps. It was only fifteen feet away from them, now. But all three were so scared they couldn't even begin to think about firing straight. John raised his shotgun up and fired again. They saw a splash of mud about two feet in front of the cougar where the bullet struck the earth.

Mud splattered up and hit the cougar. The cougar shook its head, and then raised its head up and snarled at them. Its front incisors were easily three inches long. Robert yelled at the cat.

Angie hoisted her rifle up like a baseball bat. All three stood their ground, screaming and shouting at the cougar.

The rain continued to pour. A bolt of lightning flashed across the sky and was instantly followed by a crash of thunder so loud it shook the trees around them in the forest. Rain splattered up from the ground.

Suddenly, John started running *toward* the cougar.

Angie screamed at him, but he was on the cougar in less than a second. He was yelling like a crazy man.

The cougar raised its right front paw and struck John's left hip. It looked like a child knocking a doll off the edge of a table.

Angie watched in horror as John flew five feet to his right and hit the muddy ground hard. The cougar just stared at them. John lay face down in the mud. He groaned.

Angie held her rifle up and slowly approached the animal. She tried to insert a fresh tranquilizer dart in the gun, but her hands shook too badly. She shouted at it.

"Go on!" she shouted. "Back off!"

The cougar took two steps to its right, but it kept its eyes on Angie the whole time. They looked like two fighters circling one another. Angie screamed and shouted and swung her rifle out at it. The giant cat was only a few feet away from her, but she got herself between the cat and John who lay face down in the mud.

The cat snarled and swiped at Angie. Angie jumped back, just missing the razor-sharp claws.

"Come on!" she roared.

Rain spattered the mud all around them. The big cat bared its fangs, its mouth wrinkling up in a snarl. It growled a loud wildcat growl that shook them all. And then suddenly, the cat coiled down and leapt at Angie.

The force of the impact was like being hit by a car.

The cat struck her squarely in the chest, and Angie flew backwards and hit the ground. All the wind rushed out of her, and her vision blurred over. Everything was a white haze for a moment, and she scrambled to get up on her feet.

The big cat had gone over her and landed back where John was laying facedown in the mud.

Angie struggled to her feet and swung around to face the cat. She was soaked with rain; half her body was now covered with mud. Her normally beautiful brown hair hung down stringy, soaked, and clumped with mud. Her arms hung like mallets on either side of her body; her fists were clinched. She looked pissed.

Her useless rifle lay ten feet to her left in the mud. Rain spattered on it.

Suddenly, a strong wind kicked up and swept through the forest, driving rain at them almost horizontally.

Angie reached down and grabbed a big thick tree branch that was on the ground at her feet. She hefted it up like a bat. The big cat stood there two feet left of John who was still facedown in the mud. The cat stared at Angie.

"Come on!" Angie screamed. "Come on and fight me, now!"

She swung the solid branch out into the air. It whickered around fiercely. The cat stood its ground. Angie looked into its golden eyes and felt twenty years of fear welling up inside her.

"*Come on!*" she screamed.

Angie's shirt was torn open on the front where the cat had clawed her. The left half of her body was covered in mud. Her hair hung down, stringy, clumped, and soaked.

"I'll kill you," she said. "I'll kill you!"

On the ground, John started to come to. He felt hot pain in his hip, and he felt the rain beating down on his back. The left side of his face was in the mud, and he slowly opened his eyes. He saw the giant cat standing there just two feet from him.

He heard Angie screaming somewhere not far away. He could smell the damp fur of the animal it was so close. There was a deep growling sound coming from inside the animal. The rain spattered on the mud all around him. He saw the mountain lion's claws, but he realized that the animal's attention was on Angie just ten feet away. He realized too that if the animal wanted, right that moment it could lunge down at him and rip his throat out without any difficulty whatsoever. But Angie was screaming at the animal. Angie was keeping the big cat's attention.

John wanted to get up and run, but he was afraid to. He felt he needed to lie perfectly still and hope that this animal wouldn't turn and rip his throat out. He felt mud on the side of his face.

Robert stood there frozen. Angie was five feet in front of him to his left. The giant mountain lion was ten feet in front of her. John's body was on the muddy ground right beside the mountain lion. Robert had a gun in his hand, but he was paralyzed with fear and couldn't move. His mouth hung open in shock. His head shook a little like he was having a seizure. His face was pale. He slowly looked down at the gun in his hand. He tried to lift it and saw that his hand was shaking terribly.

Angie screamed something at the animal.

Rain pounded Robert, but he lifted the .357 up. His hand was shaking so badly it looked like he had Parkinson's. But he got the gun aimed in the general direction of the animal.

Angie swung a tree branch at the animal. Robert felt his finger squeezing around the trigger. He saw the mountain lion crouching down ready to leap on Angie again. He closed his eyes and pulled the trigger. The gun fired. It kicked back.

There was a sound across the way. It sounded like an animal. Robert looked up and saw the mountain lion turn and run backwards about thirty feet. It was so dark out now that they couldn't see far through the pouring rain and darkened forest.

"You hit it!" Angie shouted. She looked back over her shoulder at Robert.

Robert looked at his gun, as though surprised that it had actually worked.

"You shot it, Robert," Angie said.

Robert came up beside her. He looked at her. She wiped rainwater away from her eyes, and they both looked at the mountain lion up on the hill, now. The cat had stopped and was staring down at them from the hill.

"Where?" Robert said. "What kind of shot was it? I didn't see."

"I think you grazed his back left leg," Angie said. She stood there, still poised in case the mountain lion came back down the hill.

John was climbing to his feet. Angie and Robert came over to him. Angie helped him up. John got his arm around her shoulder, and she helped support his weight. Robert stood there with both hands on his .357, and they all three watched the mountain lion on the hill. It stared at them a moment more, turned, and trotted quickly up the hill, vanishing into the pouring rain and darkness

• •

The group didn't waste any time. As soon as the cougar was out of sight, they gathered themselves together and started off in the opposite direction. Angie checked her wristwatch and saw that it was seven-twenty. It was so dark now they couldn't see much at all. The rain continued to pour, but they struggled onward away from the attack site.

Angie and Robert held John between them; John's arms were around their shoulders. They staggered along like that through the trees not really sure at all if they were headed in the right direction toward the cabin or not. They only knew they were headed in the opposite direction from the mountain lion, and that seemed the most important thing.

They kept seeing movement out of the corners of their eyes, just beyond the edge of darkness to their right and left. They half expected to see the mountain lion appear in front of them, ready to finish off what he had started.

"Have you ever seen a mountain lion do that?" John asked.

"Never," Angie said.

They carried on down a steep hill, slipping and sliding. There was a flash of lightning up ahead of them. They all saw the sparks and were soon enveloped in the enormous crash of thunder. The lightning struck a tree somewhere up the hill from them. A few seconds later, they caught the whiff of electricity and smoke as it wafted down the hill in the driving rain.

"That cat was almost twelve feet long," Robert said.

"It was more," Angie said.

John slipped and fell down and nearly brought the other two down with him, but they held him tight and kept him up on his feet.

"Sorry," he said.

And they continued on, now heading uphill sidestepping trees and cacti.

"The biggest mountain lion I've ever heard reported was two hundred ninety-five," Angie said. "The one we just saw was easily fifty pounds more than that."

She glanced down at her chest where her shirt had been ripped open. Her white bra was exposed, but no one really noticed. They *all* looked like hell and were just trying to stay on their feet and get as much distance between themselves and that cat as they could.

The air had grown cold and they were completely soaked, but they were pumped on adrenaline and fear. The temperature would catch up with them eventually, if they didn't find a trail, if they didn't find the cabin. Angie's hands were numb with cold, and she kept flexing her fingers and feeling the cold tingle through them. It was colds, but the rain and the wind made it feel even colder.

If there had been enough light, she would have seen that her hands were bright red from the cold. And still the rain continued to beat at them.

Suddenly, a tree branch snapped up ahead and came crashing down out of the darkness toward them. All three fell backwards landing smack in the mud and soaked earth, and the large branch lay there just a few feet away. It was a solid chunk of wood that would have killed them had it struck them squarly on the head.

"Shit," Robert said.

"Come on," Angie said. She knelt down to give Robert a hand. He took her hand, and she helped him to his feet, and then the two of them helped John up.

"How's your leg?" Angie said.

"It's my hip," John said.

He glanced down at it and saw that his jeans were torn open on his left hip. He could feel that he'd been bleeding, but he didn't think it was too bad.

"I'll be alright," he said. "At least I can move it. At least I can put some weight on it."

• •

They came to the clearing twenty minutes later, though it wasn't until they were halfway across the clearing that they realized where they were.

"This is it!" Angie said.

Robert and John immediately realized she was right.

"The kennel," Robert said. "What happened to the kennel?"

In the darkness and rain, they could see that the kennel was dismantled. They crossed to it and found one side had been hacked through with some sort of chopping tool.

Robert said, "The son of a bitch chopped up my kennel."

"Come on," Angie said. "There's nothing you can do."

Robert picked up one side of the kennel and tried to hold it up, but the pieces fell apart and clattered to the ground.

"The maniac tore up my kennel," he said.

John said, "Here's the trail! Here's the sign!"

He stood there in the pouring rain pointing at the little wooden sign with the arrow and the word "cabin" etched into it. All three saw the opening into the woods on that side of the clearing, and they saw the trail leading up the hill into the woods. They started shouting and cheering, and they hugged one another. Angie wanted to cry she was so happy.

"We're not home yet," Robert cautioned.

They all realized he was right. They still had a stretch of dark forest to make it through, and what if the mountain lion was waiting in ambush for them on the trail up ahead?

"Come on," Robert said, and he led them up the hill into the forest.

John was walking well enough that only Angie had to help him along, but the last stretch was the scariest. They knew they were home safe if they could only make it another ten minutes. But the forest was dense on both sides of the trail, and there were plenty of places for the mountain lion to lie in wait.

Angie kept looking up through the darkness and the rain, hoping to see the warm lights of the cabin windows. They could only see ten feet or so in front of them, but the trail was pretty clear to them now. They were almost home. Almost home!

Angie could hardly contain her excitement and only wanted to hurry faster and faster up the trail.

She looked at John and smiled, and up ahead of them, Robert shouted, "There it is!"

He pointed forward through the driving rain, and they all saw the warm lights coming from the cabin windows up the hill through the last bit of trees.

They crossed the last stretch of yard and climbed the steps. Robert held the screen door open for them, and John and Angie stepped through onto the front porch. They looked at themselves in the dim, glowing light coming from the windows. Robert put his key to the door and opened it.

They were home. They were alive.

# THIRTY

The man with the ax sat in a recliner on the far side of the living room. Robert had hardly stepped one foot in the door, when a ripping flash of lightning enveloped him, Angie, and John, and then unfurled a pummel of thunder that made all three shriek. The lights inside the cabin went out, but in the split second between when the lightning hit and the power went out, Robert took one step into the cabin and saw the man with the ax sitting there in the recliner.

Robert froze.

Angie and John bumped into him from behind and instinctively felt his fear. Robert's hands came up, palms facing outward in a defensive posture, and he took two steps back, effectively pushing Angie and John back out onto the porch.

"Yo!" Robert called to the man in the darkness. "Just take it easy, man. Everything's cool."

Angie and John looked over his shoulders, but the lights were still out inside the cabin and they could see nothing. Suddenly, there was another flash of lightning that lit up the whole house a moment, and all three saw Charlie sitting there in the recliner with the ax across his chest.

Angie turned and ran back off of the porch, out into the rain. John and Robert were not far behind, and they all stepped midway out into the yard. The rain continued to pour, and they stood there in the yard looking at one another.

"What is he *doing?*" Angie shrieked.

Robert pointed fiercely at the cabin, and said as though it was unfathomable but true, "The dude is sitting in there with an ax!"

"Oh, holy shit," John said. "Oh, holy shit. Oh, holy shit."

They were terrified.

"How do we handle this?" Robert said.

He was so afraid his limbs felt weightless.

The whole time they kept looking up at the cabin. They expected to see Charlie come to the door. They watched around the corners of the cabin in case he tried to slip out the back door and sneak around on them. The whole time the lights were out inside the cabin, and it just stood there in the darkness and rain like the crazy house in the Poe story.

"Wait a minute," Angie said.

John and Robert looked at her.

She started walking toward the cabin.

"What are you doing?" John said.

She raised a hand, indicating they should stay back.

The rain continued to hammer them. Angie took one step up the front porch steps. She looked up and saw the screen door swaying slightly in the wind and rain. Beyond that, she saw the front door to the cabin was still open. She took another step up the front porch steps and slowly reached her hand forward toward the screen door's handle.

She opened the screen door slowly, and it creaked with all the moisture and rust.

The front door to the cabin was open, and Angie could see the curtains ruffling in the windows inside from the breeze that swept through the front door. She tried to see across the inside of the cabin. All was darkness inside.

She tried to see across to the recliner on the far side of the living room, but she only saw the faintest outlines in the very dim light. She saw the area rug just inside the front door, and she saw the left arm of the sofa just beyond that, but then it was like the room disappeared into a vacuum of blackness, and she couldn't see anything more than seven feet inside the front door.

She *knew* the recliner was about fifteen feet across the living room from the front door, but there just simply wasn't enough light. She had no way to know whether Charlie was still sitting there in the recliner, or had decided to stand up and come to the front door to wait for someone to return.

Angie put one foot up onto the porch.

John and Robert stood at the bottom of the steps looking up at her.

She took another step up onto the porch. She slowly let the screen door creak shut behind her. She took another step across the front porch and found herself standing midway between the screen door and the open front door. She stood perfectly still.

Rainwater dripped down from her onto the porch as though she'd just stepped out of a shower. Her breathing was thin. She could almost see the contours of furniture inside the cabin. She felt her heart pounding in her chest.

Slowly, she looked back over her shoulder at John and Robert down behind her. They were still standing at the base of the steps, but were afraid to say anything lest they give away to Charlie the fact that Angie was standing on the porch.

She turned her head back and looked inside the pitch black cabin. She felt a stiff breeze rustle up from behind her. Her skin was soaked. The breeze pushed the front door of the cabin open ever so slightly, and this made it creak.

She gathered herself up and said firmly, "Rutledge?"

There was no reply; only the sound of rain hammering the roof of the porch and cabin.

"Charlie Rutledge?" Angie called firmly into the cabin.

She stood there for what must have been twenty seconds, listening to the sound of rain hammer the tin rooftop.

"*Angie?*" John whispered up at her. "*Do you see anything?*"

She stood there, her head craning right and left trying to see into the darkness. She could make nothing out beyond the oval-shaped area rug just beyond the door. She took another step closer to the open front door.

She was close enough now that she could smell the musty, aged dust odor inside the cabin. That smell mingled with the fragrance of varnished wood and the even fainter smell of old fires from the fireplace.

Angie was only one step from the doorway into the cabin.

Her left hand came up and touched the doorframe.

She leaned her head forward and slowly stuck it through the doorway in order to see inside the cabin. Everything was dark.

She said far less firmly than before, "Charlie Rutledge?"

Suddenly, the lights came up, and Angie just about fell over with a heart attack. The lights were crazy bright after peering into the darkness so intensely, and she was blinded and staggered backward.

"Angie!" John shouted, and he ran up the porch steps to her.

John and Robert thought she'd been hit. She was holding her hand in front of her eyes. John grabbed her.

"Are you alright?" he said.

"I'm fine," she said, squinting. "The light's blinding me."

They both looked inside the cabin. And they saw a note attached to the recliner where Charlie had been sitting.

Robert came up behind them and saw it, too.

The screen door slapped shut with a smack, and all three stood there on the porch looking inside at the recliner across the living room. The note was attached to the chair byway of a nine-inch hunting knife that was stuck through it.

• •

John went for his cell phone. It was packed in a pocket on the right side of his backpack, which stood over by the kitchen. Angie and Robert cautiously approached the note that was pinned to the chair. Both kept looking up over the chair toward the two bedrooms at the back of the cabin and up toward the upstairs loft and the two bedrooms at either end of the loft.

"There's no signal," John said.

He held his cell phone out in front of him.

Robert looked at him; Robert was standing in front of the recliner and the note.

"No," he said. "We're too far out. I've never been able to get a signal up here. I've never been able to even get a *phone line* up here. There just aren't any lines."

"How about your cell, Angie?" John said.

Angie knelt down and looked at the note on the chair. In crazy scrawled handwriting, it said:

Go home, Tree Huggers, before you get <u>killed</u>.

The word "killed" was underlined twice.

"Pleasant," Robert said.

147

He walked back toward the two back bedrooms at the back of the cabin, and he saw the open window in the bedroom on the left. He crossed to the window and closed it.

"Well," he said. "I guess we know how he got into the place."

John was still trying to get a signal on his cell phone, walking around the front of the cabin, holding the thing out in front of him like a remote control for a toy airplane.

"There's no signal," he said, growing desperate.

Robert said, "I'm telling you, John, you're not going to be able to get a signal up here, man. The nearest friggin' *road* is forty miles away."

"And you don't have a phone up here?" he said.

"Is that some kind of accusation?" Robert said. "Because it sounded like an accusation."

John looked at Angie for help. "Angie," he said. "We've got to try yours."

Angie frowned. "It's in my pack," she said.

John was already over her backpack. "Where?" he said.

"I think it's the front pocket," she said.

John unzipped one of the front pockets on her backpack and removed her cell phone. He activated it and then looked at the little signal meter. The signal was at the absolute lowest. He pressed 9-1-1, hit send, and held the phone up to his ear.

There was nothing.

"There's no signal," he said. He sounded hysterical. "You mean we're stuck up here? Until *when?!*"

"Dave Baker will be back in seven days," Angie said.

"Six days, now," Robert said.

Angie tilted her head a little and nodded. "Well, yeah."

John got control of himself. He said, "And in the meantime, we've got a mountain lion the size of a Buick out there. And some nut with an ax popping in and out of the place to say 'hi'!"

Robert said, "Well, the mountain lion might have a bullet in its back left leg."

Angie said, "And we don't know about this nut. Maybe he just wants to scare us."

She tore the note from the chair and held it up in front of her.

John said, "And maybe he wants to throw you on the ground and make you *squeal like a pig!*"

"We don't know what he wants, John," Angie said.

"Well, what the hell?! Do you think he wants milk and cookies? He was sitting in the chair with an ax across his chest! Not a friendly, Angie. Hello, Angie? Earth to Angie! Do you need it written in blood? The guy had an ax!"

There was a flash of lightning outside, and the glass in the window frames shook with the powerful thunder. The rain continued to pound the cabin.

Angie crossed over to the bathroom. There was a little whicker hamper right outside the bathroom door, and on top of the hamper there were about a half dozen clean, neatly folded bathroom towels. She picked one up and tossed it across to John.

"Well," she said. "We can't do anything about it right this moment. So you might as well dry off."

"Dry off?" he said.

"Hey, at least we're not stuck out there in the woods," she said. "It's pouring down rain. The temperature's gonna drop down near freezing by midnight. At least we found the place. At least we're safe from that cougar. Get a hold of yourself. This is the situation, and we have to deal with it."

"We've got three guns," Robert said.

Angie tossed a towel across to him, too, and Robert started drying himself off.

"We've got wood on the back porch," Robert said. "We can build a fire."

"If that lunatic comes back here," Angie said. "We'll confront him. We've got the three guns."

John said, "Yeah, but one gun doesn't seem to work, Angie, and none of us can shoot worth a damn."

• •

John was convinced that they needed to go. It wasn't that he was afraid so much as it was that reason had taken over his mind, and nothing seemed more *un*reasonable than staying in the cabin, isolated from the outside world for another six days. He hobbled back and forth in the living room.

Robert Gonzalez was bent over the fireplace, trying to start a fire. Angie was across the cabin at the kitchen table; on the table in front of her was her rifle, which she had completely taken apart in order to dry, clean, and oil. Robert had cracked a Duraflame starter log in half, placed it in the center of the fireplace, and stacked three split logs around and on top of it. The split logs were damp, but they were not soaked. He kept his woodpile on the front screened-in porch, and even there it was covered with a plastic green waterproof tarp.

He struck a match and lit the paper corners of the starter log. He stood up and watched as the log took fire. There was no electric or gas heat in the cabin; there was only the fireplace, and the cabin felt like it was about fifty degrees. Both he and Angie had changed over to dry clothes. John, however, was still in his wet clothes and seemed intent on refusing to accept the idea that they might have to stay there another six days.

"You say there's an ATV," John said.

Robert looked up. "Yeah," he said.

"Where is it?"

"John, man, I think you need to settle down," he said. "If I was you, I'd check on that hip of yours."

John glanced at his hip where his jeans were torn.

"I just want to know where the hell the ATV is," he said.

"What difference does it make, man?" Robert said. "It's not like you're gonna get on the thing and be able to drive down the mountain, in the storm, in the middle of the night."

John didn't seem to have heard any of this. He said, "It's in the shed out back isn't it?"

"Yeah, it's in the shed," Robert said. "And there's just enough gas in the tank to make it down the mountain, to make it down to Grapevine."

"Well, then that's what we need to do," John said. "We take the ATV down to Grapevine, and we call for help."

"John, Grapevine is nearly thirty miles as the crow flies," Robert said. "There is no road down to Grapevine. The only way to get to

Grapevine is to take backcountry trails not unlike the one we got *lost* on today."

Finally Angie said, "Come here, John. Let me look at your hip."

"Screw my hip," he said. "We need to get out of here. I'm taking the ATV, and I'm gonna drive it down to Grapevine."

"You'd get lost before you were a mile away from the cabin," Robert said.

"*And* you'd leave us stranded," Angie said. "I think you need a drink. I think you need something to take the edge off."

"*What edge?!*" he shrieked. "You guys are nuts!"

Robert said, "John, do me a favor, man"—he tossed a red first-aid kit at him, and John caught it—"Go in the bathroom and clean up your cuts. Just do that. Then, we'll maybe talk about taking the ATV down to Grapevine."

John held the first-aid kit in his hands. He looked from Angie to Robert and just shook his head.

"This is a conspiracy," he said. "You guys are a couple of fanatics! You're so *screwed up in the head* with mountain lions, you're willing to risk our lives to stay here!"

Robert and Angie looked at him calmly. He was hysterical. He looked like he was about to explode, and he stormed across the cabin toward the bathroom, grabbing his backpack along the way. He slammed the door shut.

Robert stood there flabbergasted. He looked from the slammed bathroom door to Angie at the kitchen table. She was calmly reassembling her rifle.

He crossed to the kitchen table and said in low tones to Angie, "What the hell is going on?"

Angie held the partially assembled rifle in her hand. She looked up at him. "He's losing it. I think he needs to settle down. The earliest we could take that ATV down, *if* that's what we were gonna do, would be tomorrow morning."

"Is that what you want to do?" Robert asked.

Angie whispered, "I don't see any reason why we have to. I mean it looks like his hip is gonna be alright. I thought he had seriously injured it."

"It doesn't look like it," Robert whispered.

They both glanced over at the bathroom door.

"I mean he's got some scrapes," Angie whispered. "But it doesn't look like anything's *broken*, you know?"

Robert nodded his head.

• •

Inside the bathroom, John looked at himself in the mirror and winced. He looked a little crazy. His eyes were wide and manic looking. His shirt was soaked. His hair was all over the place. He had mud and dirt on his hands, face, and arms. And his jeans were ripped open on his left hip.

He unbuttoned his jeans and carefully pulled them down over his hips. The cuts were pretty bad, but they were nothing life threatening. He turned on the sink, dampened a washcloth, and began to clean the wounds. Next, he used rubbing alcohol and toilet paper, and he dabbed the wounds with alcohol-soaked paper. The alcohol burned pretty badly, but he gritted his teeth and got it done. At this point, he could see exactly what the mountain lion had done.

There was a strip of claw marks on his left hip. They were about six inches long and a quarter of an inch deep at their deepest. He held a wad of toilet paper below the wound and carefully poured the rubbing alcohol over the claw marks.

Then, he threw all the mess into the garbage can, sat down on the closed toilet seat, and pulled his jeans off. There was a shower in the bathroom, but he knew that they had no hot water, and as such, the thought of taking a freezing cold shower was not appealing. Instead, he stripped down completely naked and stood up in front of the sink.

There was a bar of soap adjacent to the sink, so he just washed himself with the washcloth and soap.

*Screw it*, he thought. And he turned around and turned on the shower. He realized that he was just too filthy to wash himself at the sink. He put a clean towel on the commode seat where he could quickly reach it, and he stepped into the shower.

He almost howled it was so cold, and his body immediately began to tense up from the cold. He ducked his head under the showerhead, wet his hair and quickly ran some soap over his body. It was so cold it was almost unbearable, but he made sure to cover every square inch of his body with soap, and he watched the dirt run down off of him and into the drain.

"Jesus, that's cold," he said. And he killed the shower.

He reached out and grabbed the towel and just tried to wrap himself up in it to warm up. His nipples were like two tiny prunes, and his body was doing a whole-body shiver. He climbed out of the shower and dried off.

He pulled out a pair of clean long johns from his backpack, a pair of wool socks, a thick thermal long-sleeved shirt, and he got dressed. He stood up in front of the sink and combed his hair. He dabbed his hip down with the towel and made sure that it wasn't bleeding, and then he rubbed some Neosporin ointment from the first-aid kit onto the cuts.

It felt good to be clean and dressed in warm thermals and a pair of wool socks, even if the cabin felt like it was about fifty degrees. He brushed his teeth, combed his hair once again, and got all of his stuff together over in one corner of the bathroom.

*That* was when he looked out the bathroom window and saw the shed back behind the cabin.

The bathroom window was only about twenty inches wide, and it was about three feet tall. And John could see that it was still pouring down rain outside. But he could see across the backyard to the little aluminum shed beyond the back of the cabin.

An excited feeling rushed through him. It was the realization that the ATV was inside that shed. The shed was cream colored, and John could see that the roof of the shed was covered in pine straw. A single door stood five feet wide on its front; it all began to make sense to him. It all began to take shape in his mind. He could roll the ATV out of the thing, get on it, and drive it down the mountain.

He could make it to Grapevine, and he could call for help. Angie and Robert were too obsessed with this animal to see the picture clearly, the way that *he* was seeing it right that moment. Someone needed to take charge and call in extra help.

They thought *he* was crazy, that *he* was losing it, but it was Angie and Robert who were crazy. *They* were the ones that wanted to stay up here in the middle of nowhere Arizona without phones. They were the ones who wanted to hunt this mountain lion with darts. They were the ones throwing caution to the wind, when there was a lunatic with an ax who had *come into their cabin* and sat himself down just as pretty as you please.

And they couldn't be reasoned with.

For a moment, John gave himself over to dark thoughts that Angie had *wanted* to see him lose it like this. She'd been riding him ever since they'd started dating, but it was *she* that had the job, the money, the television spots, the newspaper articles, the chief of police as her buddy. It was a sick game she played, John realized. She pretended to be all calm and kind and thoughtful, but it was all just a game and ultimately she wanted to see him fall flat on his face because that was what all the men in her life had ever done: they'd let her down.

And she had come to expect it—even *wanted* it to happen—so that she could play the victim and earn everybody's sympathies, and then get more money, more friends, TV shows, fame, fame, fame. Another Porsche, maybe. Another hillside home.

"*The bitch*," he muttered.

And Robert? That little asshole had wanted to bang Angie as long as he'd known him. He was one of those university types that walk around with a canned smile on his face and plenty of flowery language while nursing an erection for every woman in the Biology department. *Why I ought to go out there and beat the hell out of him*, John thought.

*Probably wouldn't surprise me if he's already banged her*, he thought. All those field surveys, academic symposiums, nights in tents, nights in the cold. And suddenly John became furious at the thought of Angie and Robert fucking one another in a tent. He was *sure* it had happened!

"*Son of a bitch*," he muttered.

He thought, *I wonder who gets on top?*

Because that was the way it was in Biology departments, right? No one had any ethics. Everybody was screwing one another, and "loyalty" was such a quaint concept as to be archaic and jejune. Everyone could bury their cheating, lying, and scheming in fancy research grants. It was why *he* had been left out of the loop. *He* was too honest to fit into an academic department. People just couldn't handle him.

*I ought to kill them both*, he thought. *I mean what if he really is fucking her.*

The thought was so real, so bitter, so palpable that it made him nauseated with jealousy. What if she'd been stringing him along and quietly banging Robert behind his back (or not so quietly, perhaps)? After all, she was the one that insisted on keeping her own place. She was the one who asked him to sleep nearly thirty miles away in Oracle. What was she so afraid of?

Or was it fear at all?

That, of course, was what she'd led him to believe: that she'd been injured in relationships before, that men had always mistreated her, that men had hurt her. So, maybe she was just getting back at all those ex-boyfriends. Maybe she wasn't really afraid at all. Maybe she was banging Robert on the nights when John wasn't there at her hillside Tucson home.

He could picture her with her legs wrapped around Robert's back while he pumped away deep inside her.

"I ought to kill them both," he whispered aloud.

There was a flash of lightning outside that brightened the bathroom window a moment. Thunder boomed.

And then there was a knock at the bathroom door.

John could tell it was Angie without even opening the door.

"John?" she said, her voice sounding delicate and nice. "John, are you okay?"

John shook his head and crossed to the bathroom door. He turned the handle and opened the door. Angie stood there with a worried look in her eyes. John glanced over her shoulder at Robert who was sitting on the sofa in front of the fire.

Robert was cleaning his handgun.

Angie looked into John's eyes curiously.

"John, are you okay?" she said.

"Of course I'm okay," he said. "Why wouldn't I be okay?"

Angie glanced over his shoulder into the bathroom.

"You've just been in there an awful long time is all," she said. "I was just curious."

"Well, you know what they say," John said. "'Curiosity killed the cat,' Angie."

"What is that supposed to mean?" Angie said.

John shrugged.

"Bathroom's free," he said, and he pushed past her and crossed the cabin toward the kitchen.

## THIRTY-ONE

John had it in his head that at some point during the night he would try and make it out to the shed. He helped Angie cook dinner—a kind of beef stew in a large five-gallon kettle—and he pretended not to notice what he'd deep down known all along: that Angie and Robert were having an affair. Of course, he had to look deep to see that it was there. They wouldn't *consciously* let him know that something was going on, but he saw it in the friendly way that Angie handed Robert a bowl, or the pleasant way that she asked Robert if he'd like a glass of water, or the way she crossed her legs when she sat down on the sofa.

*She's practically inviting him to have sex,* John thought. His thoughts flooded with blood-red murderous revenge. Jealousy. Raw, ravenous jealousy.

"Thank you, Angie," Robert said. "That's pretty good stew."

"Well, it wasn't me," she said. "John is the one that came up with the idea."

*Did she just touch her nipple?* John thought. It looked like Angie looked right into Robert's eyes and touched the tip of her left breast. *Next thing you know, he'll be calling me "old sport."*

"I think I'm going to step outside and have a smoke," John said.

"I didn't know you smoked," Robert said.

"Only after dinner," John said. And he crossed to his backpack and removed a lighter and a pack of Marlboro Lights.

"Be careful out there," Angie said.

"I'm just going to be on the front porch," he said.

"Yeah, but we don't know whether our axman decided to stick around or has taken to the deep woods."

John looked at her curiously and said, "What is *that* supposed to mean?"

He didn't realize that he sounded paranoid. Angie exchanged a perplexed glance with Robert.

"Yeah, go on and look at him," John said.

He pointed an accusatory unlit cigarette at her. Both Robert and Angie had no idea what the hell he was talking about.

"I know about you," John said, pointing that cigarette. "Don't think I don't."

He turned, opened the front door, and stepped out onto the screened-in porch. It was still pouring rain, and he closed the door behind him.

As soon as the door was closed, Robert said, "What is he talking about?"

Angie stood up and took Robert's empty bowl from him.

"I think he's cracked," she said. She carried the dirty dishes over to the kitchen sink and began rinsing them out.

"Does he think that something's going on between us?" Robert asked.

Angie just shook her head. Finally she said, "We may need to go down tomorrow. I hadn't planned on John losing his cool like this."

"I just don't understand, Angie. What the hell is going on in his head? He was fine just a couple days ago."

"I think there are two things," Angie said. "I think he has borderline personality disorder, and he's paranoid."

"Is that a clinical diagnosis?"

"John has always been a sensitive guy, and probably the stress of being up here isolated, nearly dying today has gotten to him. I think he's just really afraid. I mean we're all afraid, you know? But I think that it just got to him. I think it rattled him. I think he's had a split. Now whether he's just kind'a *acting*, you know, to convince us that we need to get out of here or whether he's really screwed up, I don't know. It's probably not even clear to him."

"I've seen some crazy shit in my lifetime," Robert said. "I once saw a professional boxer have a nervous breakdown in the ring, start crying, and refuse to fight. The human mind can only take so much, before it just sort'a splits, you know? Maybe that's kind of what's happening."

"I don't know," Angie said.

"What was the other thing? You said there were two things."

She said, "I think he's jealous. I think he thinks that there's something going on between you and me, and that's only adding to his insecurity, which is already over the edge. I think he's really afraid. I love him. But I think he's really afraid."

Robert glanced at the closed front door.

• •

John took a draw from the cigarette and looked through the porch screen out across the yard. It was too dim to see much of anything other than that they were getting nailed with the worst storm to hit Arizona in at least two months. Rain covered most of the front porch, but John stood back as far from the screen as he could and was able to stay mostly dry.

*Maybe she isn't banging him*, he thought. Maybe they were just flirting with one another. It was only a matter of time though, right? *I mean*, John thought, *I'm a fucking loser. My writing career hasn't taken off in more than fourteen years, man. I've written a million words of trash, and nobody's going to take a chance on me. I just didn't get the breaks, man, and it's pretty fucking clear that I'm not going to get the breaks. It's pretty fucking clear that my life is an appalling failure.*

So, in that way, John reasoned that he'd be doing Angie a favor if he just lost it on her. She could get rid of the excess baggage. *Besides, they're crazy for wanting to stay up here. I'm doing her a favor if I go for help.*

It was all mixed up in his head—his motivations—but one thing was clear: he needed to get down the mountain. He needed to take the ATV, which was supposedly stored in the shed out back, and he needed to drive that ATV down the mountain to Grapevine. He could call for help there. He could let the authorities know that they'd been attacked by the mountain lion. He could let them know that Charlie "The Chopper" was threatening all of their lives.

John was building it in his mind that it was his *duty* to take the ATV down the mountain to let the authorities know what had happened. It was his *responsibility* for crying out loud.

He started laughing, holding the cigarette, standing there on the front porch, trying not to get rained on. *Oh, the irony!* he thought. They all thought *he* was the crazy one, but *he* was the only sane one of the bunch! *He* was the *voice of reason!*

"Who's really the crazy one here?" he said aloud. "I mean *really?*"

He looked around him on the front porch. He saw the green tarp covering the wood pile at the far end of the porch, and he realized that he could use that tarp as a rain poncho to go out back and check the shed. They thought he was out here just taking a smoke, but he could use the tarp to cover himself, and he could sneak around back of the cabin and check the shed.

If the keys were out there, he would be one step closer to getting down the mountain.

Cigarette in hand, John bent over the woodpile and tried to pull the tarp from off of the wood. It was caught in a couple of places, but he managed to lift the thing from the woodpile. A gust of wind sprayed him with rain through the screen, and the pile got coated.

He stuck his cigarette in his mouth, pulled the tarp over his head and shoulders, and started down the front porch steps out into the yard.

He walked on around the side of the cabin in the pouring rain with the green waterproof tarp covering him like some whacked out ghost.

• •

"Did you see that?" Robert said.

"See what?"

Angie looked at him from the kitchen sink. Robert rose from the sofa. He'd seen John moving around on the front porch with the tarp over his head. There was no light on the porch, and the light inside was bright enough that it was difficult to see well *outside* of the cabin, but he could have sworn he saw John with something like a tarp draped over his head, walking down off of the porch.

Robert went to the front door, opened it, and looked both ways on the porch. John was not there. Angie came over and looked, too.

"*John?*" Angie called, but her voice was drowned by the sound of rain hitting the tin roof of the porch.

John had gone on around the side of the cabin, and they couldn't see him.

"What is he doing?" Robert said.

But Angie was already rushing over to her backpack to grab her bright orange rain poncho.

"Come on," she said.

• •

Despite the tarp, John was still getting wet. It was difficult to see because it was so dark and because the rain was unrelenting, but he knew where the shed was, and he crossed the backyard toward it. The thought that the guy with the ax might be out there did cross his mind, but it filled him with a crazed excitement, and he roared out into the rain, "*Come on!*"

He staggered across the backyard toward the shed. The tarp kept tripping him up, and had anyone seen him, they would have thought he was completely crazy.

"*Bring it on, man!*" he shouted into the rain.

He reached the shed and turned the handle. It smelled like gasoline and motor oil inside the shed, and sawdust, and faintly in the recesses there was a fragrance of saddle leather. It was dry inside, but the roof was only about six feet tall, and he had to stoop to keep from banging his head. He let the tarp fall from his shoulders, and he saw the ATV over in the back left corner. He crossed to it.

It was dark, but he felt around the handlebars of the thing, and he felt a single key already in place in the ignition. He remembered ATVs from his childhood, and he knew that the thing probably had an electric starter button but that the key had to be turned over in order for the electric starter to work.

He played around with different switches, feeling in the dark, when suddenly the headlights came on. It was so bright it blinded him for a moment, and then he heard the faint sound of Angie's voice calling to him through the pouring rain outside.

"*The bitch*," he said. He hit the electric start button, and the engine fired up loudly inside the shed.

He turned the throttle, and the engine revved. With his right foot, he felt around for the foot-operated gears. He popped the clutch with his left hand and snapped the gears into place.

The ATV lurched backwards hard, slamming into the back wall of the shed. It made a horrible aluminum-wrenching-metal sound, and he thought for sure that the whole thing was going to collapse on top of him. But he managed to get the handlebars straightened out and got the ATV pointed in the direction of the front door.

He popped the clutch and was just about to put it into gear, when Angie appeared in the doorway. The headlights shined brightly on her, and then John saw Robert appear behind her left shoulder.

Angie held both hands up cautiously, telling him to hold back.

"*What are you doing?*" she shouted.

"I'm going for help!" John shouted over the roar of the ATV engine.

"John, you're going to leave us stranded," she cried.

"Get out of the way, Angie," he said. "You two are crazy!"

"John, I love you. Please don't leave us alone here."

"You don't love me." John thrust an angry index finger at her. "I know about you! Both of you! I'm not stupid, you know? I can see. Now, get out of the way!"

Angie knelt down on her knees in the middle of the doorway.

"Please, John." It looked like she started crying. The ATV lights shined brightly on her. The rain continued to pour. "I love you with all my heart. We don't want to hurt you. We're your friends, John. *I love you.*"

John sat there on the ATV, staring at her in the headlights. She was blocking his way through the door, just like she'd been blocking him from succeeding in his writing career their whole time together. Oh, it was subtle, alright. She'd never arouse suspicion, but *by God*, everything she did undercut his chances for success.

"Get out of the way, Angie, or I'll run you *down!*"

"Please, John." She was on the verge of tears.

He felt so humiliated, he almost wanted to get off the ATV. Maybe she really did love him. Maybe he was just afraid. Maybe all of this had been some huge misunderstanding. But he felt ashamed. He looked from Angie to Robert, and he felt sheer, unadulterated shame, and suddenly he started to cry.

"Get out of the way, Angie! You don't love me! Nobody loves me! All of you people have perfect lives, and I'm a loser! A goddamn loser! Do you know how that makes me *feel?* I am nothing! *Nothing!*"

"That's not *true*, John," Angie cried. "You matter! You matter to me—"

And then, by accident, his hand slipped on the throttle, and the ATV lurched forward. Angie was on her knees and unable to get wholly out of the way, and it shocked John so badly and he had so little time to react, that before he knew what had happened, the ATV struck Angie and raced out into the yard.

Robert managed to leap out of the way.

John was twenty meters out into the yard, and he turned the ATV around to see what had happened. Angie lay on her back by the shed's door. Robert looked stunned, his eyes moving from John on the ATV to Angie.

"*Angie*," Robert said.

John sat there. The rain poured on him. He couldn't believe what had just happened. He wanted to get off of the ATV and run to her. He wanted to make sure that she was okay. He wanted to say that it was an accident. But he did none of those things.

Instead, he looked up around the side of the cabin, and in the headlights of the ATV, he saw the path that they had climbed earlier that night, the path that led down to the clearing where the helicopter was supposed to pick them up. He turned, hit the accelerator, and raced away from the only woman who had ever actually loved him.

# THIRTY-TWO

Rain hammered him on the ATV. It was a cold, stinging rain, and he raced through the woods. The ATV's headlights shined through the pouring rain, illuminating the narrow path in front of him. He had no idea where he was going, but he figured he would follow the paths down the mountain.

That he was psychotic with fear and self-loathing didn't matter to him anymore. He didn't care. He had no money. He had just stranded (and possibly killed) the only woman who would ever love him. No editor would ever buy anything that he ever wrote. And on top of it, he was stuck out here—

"—in the *goddamn* rain!!!" He screamed "goddamn" so hard, the veins in his neck bulged, and his throat felt red and raw. He started coughing.

He could hear Angie's voice in his head. Her pleasant, friendly, underhanded, self-serving. . .

"I'm glad you're dead!" he roared. "I *hope* I killed you!"

And then he saw that image of her in his mind: that last image as he ran her down with the ATV. She was so sweet and kind, and she was on her knees crying for him not to leave her, not to leave them, that she loved him. And he was suddenly filled with white-hot rage.

"*The bitch!*" he yelled.

His hands rose up from the handlebars, and he swung out at the air. He was so filled with rage and self hatred that he wanted to die. His life was an appalling failure—

The ATV hit a bump, skidded around, and raced up an embankment on the right. John fell off of the thing to the left. He heard the whine of the engine, and he felt the wind rush out of him as he hit the ground. The ATV rolled and continued recklessly down the embankment, but John felt mud and the bright stinging pain of broken ribs.

Rain spattered the mud all around him, and he looked down at the headlights of the ATV pointed crazily down the hill.

He thought he saw something move out in front of the headlights. Whatever it was, it was low to the ground, and it moved across the path out in front of the ATV from right to left. John shimmied carefully down the embankment toward the path.

Once he got to the bottom of the hill, the ATV was only about fifteen feet in front of him, and he walked slowly up to it. The engine was still running, and he touched his hands lightly to the back right wheel to see if he could slow down its spinning. He couldn't. It was still in gear.

He stood up straight and tried to look around him in the forest. He was sure he had seen something, but the rain was so intense and his head was dazed from hitting the ground so hard that he couldn't be sure what he'd seen.

"*Here, kitty, kitty,*" he said.

But he didn't see any sign of the mountain lion, or anything else for that matter. He was soaked through to the bone. The ATV was overturned but probably not inoperable, and he was some fifteen minutes from the cabin.

But every time he bent a little to the right, there was the sharp stabbing pain of broken ribs along the right side of his rib cage. He just wanted to sit down and cry, but he couldn't because the pain was too intense.

"*Oh,*" he said. And he staggered out in front of the upside-down ATV, out in front of the headlights.

Real panic began to seize him. He realized that he needed to right the ATV, but he realized too that there was no way in hell that he would be able to ride the thing over this bumpy path for another fifteen or twenty miles. It felt like the broken ribs were pressing in on his lungs, and he was afraid that maybe a rib had punctured his right lung sac. That would account for the difficulty breathing.

It felt like fluid was filling up inside his lungs.

"Oh, man," he said. "You've really screwed up this time."

And he coughed up a helping of blood. He bent over a little and spat the blood on the ground.

That was when he saw the mountain lion step out in front of the ATV.

John stood about forty feet in front of the upside-down ATV, just at the edge of the headlights, and he saw the mountain lion right in front of the ATV. The mountain lion stood sideways across the path, and it looked down the path at him.

It was large.

The cat seemed a little surprised to see this man standing there. It had obviously been attracted to the sound of the ATV and the crash, but it was only now associating that sound with the human it saw forty feet away from it.

"Nice, kitty, kitty," John said.

His hands rose up in front of him in a defensive posture, and he backed slowly away. The big cat just stared at him. Because the headlights were directly behind the mountain lion, John could only see the black shape of it as it stood in front of the lights.

He glanced over his left shoulder to see what was behind him. He saw the path continued downhill, but it was so dark beyond the ATV's headlights that it was difficult to tell much of anything.

The big cat just stood there.

Maybe it would let him go. Maybe the encounter earlier had spooked the cat enough that it would be cautious around humans from now on. John took another two or three steps slowly backwards. The big cat just watched him.

"That's a nice kitty," John said. He could feel his broken ribs puncturing his lungs. He coughed reflexively, and his mouth filled with blood. He didn't want to spit it out, lest it provoke the cat into movement. For the time being, the cat was just standing there, and it may just as soon continue on up the embankment to the left and leave him alone.

John took another two steps slowly backward, and he spat the blood quickly over to his right.

The cat's head popped up with curiosity. It sniffed at the air. The rain continued to pour. The wheels on the ATV continued to spin, and then suddenly the cat just casually started walking up the embankment to the left. It climbed the hill quickly and vanished into the darkness and trees at the top of the hill.

John took a deep breath and swept his wet hair back over his head.

He stood there for almost a minute, looking up the embankment, waiting to see the cat step out from the shadows. He started slowly back up the trail toward the ATV, keeping a watchful eye on the hillside where the cat had vanished into the trees. John drew within a couple feet of the overturned ATV, still staring hard up the hill in case the mountain lion returned.

"All you got to do," he said to himself, "is get the damn thing turned over. You can go back up to the cabin. Just apologize to Angie. Tell them it was an accident."

He could hold up there and wait for the helicopter. Maybe Robert could take the ATV down the mountain in the morning. He could call for help in Grapevine. That seemed like a good option to John. He'd take whatever punishment he had coming. He deserved it. He was sorry. It was an accident.

He leaned over and tried to lift the ATV up on its side.

Sharp pains stabbed at his lungs, and he cried out. He coughed up more blood. He leaned into the ATV again and began to roll it over. The pain was so intense he couldn't believe it; it literally felt like someone was stabbing him. But he got the ATV up on its side. The wheels caught and the thing lurched forward, knocking John backwards onto the muddy ground with a *splat!*

And it killed the engine.

John sat there on the ground. The pain in the right side of his abdomen was more intense than any pain he had ever felt in his life.

John was hit with the urge to get to his feet. He could salvage this situation. He could make it up to Angie. Robert would understand; he was a guy. He knew how guys could get. Robert would understand.

If he could just get to his feet, he could get out of this. He would write a novel, and he would dedicate it to Angie. One day he would have a writing desk that overlooked a pretty backyard, and he and Angie would have a couple of kids together who would think their pop was the coolest guy on the block. One day, he would succeed. One day.

# Thirty-Three

Robert knelt down and saw that she was breathing. Angie lay flat just left of the doorway into the shed, and it was raining so hard that even though they'd both changed over to dry clothes, they were soaked again. Robert tried to pull her into the shed just to get her out of the rain. She groaned.

"Angie," he said, "just try and take it easy. Everything's gonna be alright."

Angie's eyes opened like she was waking from a terrible hangover, and she squinted and looked cross-eyed at Robert.

"What happened?" she groaned, and she reached up and felt her forehead.

Robert looked into her eyes. "I don't know," he said. "He just sort of ran you over."

Angie rubbed her face with her right hand and tried to lean up on her left elbow. Her left hand hurt; she looked at it in the dim light and saw that it had been run over. Robert looked up at the sound of the ATV racing away from the house.

"Is anything broken?" he said.

Angie moved her fingers around, flexing them. "I don't think so," she said. "I managed to get kind of out of the way."

"I don't even know what to say," he said. "I've never seen anything like that. He just ran you over!"

Angie coughed and managed to sit up. "I'll be alright," she said. "I've had guys do worse things than that. The *asshole!*"

She was angry, and Robert just shook his head. That she could take being run over by her boyfriend and still had plenty of fight was a testament to the kind of person Angie was.

"My head hurts," she said. "The jerk hit my head pretty hard."

"It looked like your head bounced off the front of the ATV, Angie," he said. "I'm surprised you're not bleeding."

"Help me up," she said.

He reached a hand forward and helped her to her feet. She staggered a little bit, trying to regain her balance there inside the shed.

"What did he do," she said, "afterwards?"

Robert glanced out into the backyard beyond the shed, and then looked back at Angie.

"Well, he sort of drove out into the yard," he said. "He turned around. And I'd swear he almost looked sorry. I really don't think he meant to do it, Angie. He couldn't have. Maybe his hand slipped on the throttle or something, and the thing just lurched forward."

Angie leaned over and put her hands on her knees. She spat on the ground inside the shed, and she looked like she might get sick. Her head was clearly hurting, but she didn't whine about it. She straightened herself up, brushed herself off, and said, "Well, we can't stay out here all night."

"Maybe he'll make it down to Grapevine," Robert said. "Maybe he'll call for help."

Angie looked at him and was about to say what she thought—that there was no way in hell John would make it down to Grapevine in this weather, at night, on trails he'd never taken before and did not know— but she resisted the urge to say something so discouraging.

"Maybe so," she said.

But they both seemed to realize that the odds of that happening were not very good. John had just lost it; he'd gone nuts, panicked, and then in a state of panic, *maybe* his hand slipped, and he ran over Angie.

"Come on," she said. "Let's get out of this rain."

They started out into the rain, across the backyard, back to the front porch and the safety of the cabin.

## THIRTY-FOUR

Rain hammered John Crandall, and every time he slipped or slid on the mud, he felt the broken bones in his ribcage pressing and puncturing in ways they were not supposed to. He wheezed and started to moan a high-pitched whine. The headlights of the ATV shined down the path, but the engine was dead and the whole thing was now turned on its side.

All he needed to do was get over on the right side of the thing and push it over from its side onto its four balloon tires. He felt around the handlebars and saw that the key was still in place. Rain spattered up from the metal on the ATV, and he knelt down a little and tried to brace himself into its side. His right hand gripped around the seat, and his left hand was on the ATV's left foot peg.

He tried to push using his legs, but the ground was muddy and his feet kept sliding.

"*Damn it*," he muttered.

He glanced over his left shoulder, up the embankment where the mountain lion had disappeared just a few moments before. He was afraid that the big cat would rush him while his back was turned to it, while his focus was on turning over the ATV. And he was in so much pain, was so injured, that he knew there'd be no way that he could defend himself against that thing.

But, for the moment, he didn't see it. He readdressed the ATV, placing his left hand on the left foot peg and his right hand just under the seat. He started to rock it a little, and each rock sent a knife-stabbing pain through the right side of his abdomen. He coughed up blood, down his mouth and over his chin, and he gritted his teeth and really leaned into the ATV, trying to overturn it.

The ATV rocked up just enough. John's feet slid. He roared out in pain, and felt the whole thing falling over onto its wheels, right side up. His hands slipped on the ATV, and he fell face-first down into the mud.

Something stabbed him inside so sharply that his eyes widened, and he gasped. It was so painful no sound came from him.

That the ATV was now right-side up was of no consequence to him, for the moment, because one of his broken ribs had run him through. It felt like someone had stabbed him with a nine-inch hunting knife.

*Oh, God*, he thought.

And the blood just poured from his mouth. He lay there in the mud, and the realization that he was probably not going to live another fifteen minutes washed over him. He tried to roll over on his back and felt the rain hit his face. That feeling was peaceful, and he made the decision that he would lay there like that and die.

He knew he was going to die, and the only concern he had was that the pain could somehow be minimized and that the peace and cool comfort of the rain falling on his face would continue. Every breath he took was labored as though only about fifteen percent of his lungs were working anymore. He just lay there sorry for all the mistakes he had made, sorry for all the weaknesses he had given into during his lifetime, sorry that he had run out on Angie and maybe even killed her.

"Dear, God," he whispered, "please forgive me."

And that was when he heard the mountain lion coming down the embankment. There was a low growl, and each step the creature took displaced mud and water coming down the embankment. John tried to raise his head up to see.

The big cat was walking casually down the embankment. It was about fifteen feet away from him. John's head fell back, and he only wished that the animal would be quick about it.

The big cat came to him. It stood near his feet and sniffed at him. It seemed to completely realize what a wounded animal he was, and it approached his side. John didn't move his head, but his eyes looked down over his chest at the head of the mountain lion. It was as large as a basketball.

"Oh, dear God," he whispered.

The mountain lion cocked its head inquisitively at the sound; its eyes were grayish-brown, almost a golden color like nothing John had ever seen. John looked into those curious eyes, and his lips trembled.

*I'm going to die*, he thought.

And, at just that moment, the mountain lion's head lunged down, jaws open, just below his sternum. There was a crunching sound, and John began to scream.

## THIRTY-FIVE

Near dawn, Angie stepped onto the front porch and saw the horseman coming through the trees. She heard the horses' hooves coming carefully up the hill. One man sat up high on a rust-colored horse, and there were two unmanned horses following closely behind him. It looked like they were tethered.

"Robert," she called through the open front door of the cabin.

Robert was on the sofa. Neither had slept, and Angie knew that he was awake. His head rose up, and he looked through the front door.

"What?"

"Come here," she said.

As the horseman approached the cabin, Angie saw that he wore a black cowboy hat. He wore a black oilskin duster, and the collar was turned up. She could not see his face well.

Robert stepped out onto the porch and stood beside Angie.

"Sheriff?" she called. She opened the screen door and stepped onto the wooden porch steps.

The cowboy emerged from the trees with the two horses tethered behind his riding horse. The assemblage walked slowly up the hill, the cowboy's face drawn down under his black hat.

The rain had finally let up an hour before sunrise, but the air was damp with moisture. Everything was wet, and Angie saw water fly up from the tall grass at the horses' legs.

"Doctor Rippard," the horseman said.

"Sheriff Tucker," she said. "What are you doing up here?"

The sheriff brought the horses up to the front porch and dismounted. His long black duster swept down to his boots, and he tipped his black hat back and looked at Angie and Robert.

"I figured you could use an extra hand," he said with a smile. His walnut-colored eyes glistened. "I've heard tell that there's a big ole mountain lion in these parts."

Angie's eyes shined. Her smile went wide, and she gave him a hug. Sheriff Graham Tucker laughed and hugged her back.

"Good God are we glad to see you," she said. She looked at the three horses. "You rode all the way up here?"

"I rode all night," Sheriff Tucker said.

"You rode through the storm?" Robert said. "You must be soaked."

"It's not that bad," he said, "after the first few miles."

The three ascended the steps, Sheriff Tucker's boots clomping on the wood.

·· 

Angie explained as best she could what had happened to John. She described his running her over as "an accident," but Tucker's eyebrows rose up as though to say he knew better. Robert cooked them breakfast, and they began to assemble a plan.

"First things first," Sheriff Tucker said. "Do we want to stay up here to save this mountain lion, or do we want to get you folks down to safety?"

"What about John?" Angie said.

Robert couldn't believe she cared for John after what he'd done, and he wanted to say as much. But he restrained himself and cooked the eggs. If Angie still cared for a boyfriend who ran out on her and almost killed her in the process that was her business, not his.

"What time did you last see him?" Tucker asked.

"It was around midnight," Angie said.

"Well, if he's on the mountain on an ATV, he might just make it down to Grapevine."

"What if he's lost? What if he's had an accident?"

"Good riddance," Robert said. "The ball-less coward ran out on you. He ran over you and didn't think twice about it."

"It might have been an accident," Angie said.

"And he might have meant to kill you."

"*Robert*," Angie said. "I think he was just afraid."

Tucker eyed the two of them. Finally he said, "Well, we have no way of knowing where he is. We could assume he's made it down the mountain."

"Why?" Angie said. "Why assume that?"

"Because he's not here," Tucker said.

"And he's not coming back," Robert added. "How could he show his face after what he did to you?"

## Thirty-Six

The mountain lion carried John's body to the old abandoned mine. It had fed on his chest, lungs, and spleen and was storing the rest in a cool, dry place.

The big cat stopped at the mine entrance. Its head pivoted around, and it looked downhill through the trees. It stared for twenty seconds, twitching its ears at every sound along the ground, and then it turned and started down into the mine.

It was cool and dry inside, and sounds echoed off of the rocky walls in a disorienting way. The mountain lion carried John's body about fifty meters into the darkness, dropped it, and then began to cover it up with dirt, rocks, and gravel.

The mine smelled odd. A coppery mineral stench filled the air. The mountain lion didn't mind the smell. What the cougar didn't like was the odd way that sound ricocheted off of the walls. He kept popping up from his burial job to listen to the strange sounds. The cougar couldn't tell from which direction any given sound was coming, and the minutest scratching was amplified and sounded closer than it actually was.

The cougar resumed burying the body, and after another fifteen minutes of tentative work, it sniffed at the mound, walked three times around it, inspecting it, and then walked back up toward the light. At the entrance, the cougar paused again and looked down into the mine. It listened to the sounds from around the forest. It wanted to make certain that nothing saw it and that nothing would claim its kill.

• •

Charlie Rutledge stood on a tree branch twenty feet above the forest floor, watching the mountain lion. He stood perfectly still, motionless, and he watched the big cat at the mine. It was the largest mountain lion he had ever seen, and he stood on the limb, blending in with the branches.

Charlie felt a breeze pick up, and he sniffed at the air, making certain that the breeze was coming down the mountain, down the hill from the mine and the cougar. The cougar was alert, as though it knew something was watching it, but Charlie knew that he had stalked the big cat in silence.

Two shiny hatchets dangled from either side of Charlie's belt, and he just stood on the branch, watching.

The mountain lion lay down in the sunlight and rolled over on its back. It looked like it was scratching its back, but Charlie knew that the process served two purposes. It was rolling in the mud and dirt at the mine's entrance to coat itself, to cover up its natural smell, and to leave its own scent to ward off other animals.

Charlie silently descended out of the tree.

## THIRTY-SEVEN

Angie stood by the horse and felt the morning sun burning moisture from the land. She wore dry denim jeans, and the grass in the yard was wet with humidity. The pine tree fragrance was strong. It came from the woods, carried on a breeze that cooled the sweat on her brow. Angie swept her hair back and looked at Sheriff Tucker.

"I haven't ridden one of these in years," she said.

Tucker was on the porch looking at a map. The map was spread out on a table. Beside Angie, the horse made a breathy sound and shook its head.

"Ain't nothing to it," Sheriff Tucker said.

Robert exited the cabin. He looked at Tucker, then Angie and said, "We ready?"

"I think so," Tucker said. He folded the map. "So, we'll cover the second quadrant today, see how we feel around one o'clock? Maybe push it down to the lake."

Angie nodded.

Robert said, "Sounds good."

Robert wore his .357 on his right hip. Tucker started down off of the porch, and he stepped up to his horse. His rifle was strapped to the side of the animal, and he put his foot in the stirrup and pulled himself up into the saddle.

The leather stretched under his weight, and the horse took two steps forward. The sheriff took the reins and turned the horse. Angie mounted her horse. Robert looked back at the cabin one last time.

Sheriff Tucker started down the hill toward the trail. From atop his horse, Robert looked at Angie.

"Everything's going to be alright," she said.

Robert nodded his head, and they both started after Sheriff Graham Tucker.

••

They found the ATV three hours later. It was at the bottom of a hill on a section of narrow trail, and a steep incline ascended to the right.

"John?" Angie called out. There was no response.

Sheriff Tucker stayed on his horse, but he approached the ATV. All three could see the drag marks up the side of the embankment. The ATV was dented up pretty badly, and it was covered in mud. Angie traced it out in her mind. She looked at the embankment and could see where the ATV had flipped.

"*John?*" she called again.

Prickly pear cacti dappled the embankment, and Angie got her horse to climb up the steep incline. She looked up the forest hillside, through the trees and clustered sunlight that reached through the forest canopy.

"See anything?" Robert called from down on the trail.

"It looks like the hillside continues on up over here, through the trees." She turned and pointed to the spot on the embankment. "The ATV hit the side of the hill here. It must have flipped and rolled down there."

Sheriff Tucker was off of his horse. He leaned down and inspected the ATV. He saw the cougar tracks ten feet away.

"We've got tracks," he said.

Robert and Angie dismounted. Angie walked carefully down the incline. Tucker squatted near the tracks and pointed to the spot where the mountain lion tracks had dried in the mud.

"He must have flipped the ATV," Tucker said, "before the attack."

Angie looked back up the incline and began to piece together what had likely occurred.

"He must have been coming down the trail and skidded up the side. The ATV rolled," she said. "Maybe he was unable to right it. The cougar might have caused him to lose control."

"Maybe it was standing in the middle of the trail," Robert suggested.

"Maybe," Angie said. She walked back up the trail. "These are drag marks," she said.

The marks went up the side of the hill where the cougar had dragged John's body. She climbed up the incline, and Robert followed after her. They both looked up into the forest.

"The drag marks end here," she said. "But you can see paw prints up here, and here."

She walked up into the woods a little ways.

"It must have repositioned him," Robert said. "It must have carried him wholly in its mouth."

"Judging from the drag marks, I'd agree." Angie nodded, then called, "*John?*"

Tucker was back on his horse; he climbed the embankment.

"Well," he said. "We've got something to go on. Let's mount up and follow these tracks."

# THIRTY-EIGHT

Charlie Rutledge stood over the entrance to the mine with a Bushman EZ-Grip double-edged chopping ax in his right hand. On the ground below him, the mountain lion looked like it had fallen asleep. Charlie was about twenty feet above him, and he could see the mountain lion's chest moving up and down, the slow breathing of the animal at rest. The cougar lay in the sunlight.

The ground underneath Charlie's feet was rocky, covered with loose sandstone, and he was careful to keep from slipping. The incline above the mine entrance was steep, and Charlie had circled around and then come down the hill one step at a time. The chirruping of crickets stirred in the grasses beyond the clearing.

Charlie knelt down. He was about three feet from the edge, and the drop down onto the mountain lion would be twenty feet. He wanted to make certain that leaping down onto the big cat was the best approach, and that he wouldn't break a leg in the fall.

*I'll catch the son of a bitch by total surprise*, Charlie thought, and he felt his fingers tighten around the ax handle.

He licked his lips and felt sweat beading on his forehead. He inched closer and closer to the edge. He could see the mountain lion down there below him. He hoisted up the Bushman EZ-Grip, and sunlight glinted off the shiny ax blade.

He calmed the butterflies he felt in his stomach and prepared to leap. The fall would be silent, and the ax blade would strike clean and true.

Charlie started to rise up from his knelt position. His left hand came up and gripped the ax handle just below his right hand. He hoisted the ax up in the air like a baseball bat. His lip grew rigid, and his eyes narrowed. He focused his aim on the big cat's shoulder blades.

There was a little indentation in the big cat's shoulder blades and because of the angle of the sunlight the little spot formed a dark circle. Charlie focused on it. He inhaled slowly, feeling his nerves aglow, and he exhaled.

*Now, Charlie, now!*

He leapt.

Suddenly, there was a sound from down the hillside. It was the sound of horses coming up through the forest. The big cat's head popped up at the noise.

Charlie was in the air, falling swiftly toward the mountain lion. The ax swung down with equal swiftness.

The cat sprung to its feet, and it felt Charlie just hundredths of a second away. Its head pivoted around and saw a man flying toward him.

Charlie roared. The ax blade whickered through the air.

The mountain lion bolted forward. But the ax blade struck the big cat, though not where Charlie had planned. The cat's movement enabled it to get away from a fatal blow, but the ax did catch the mountain lion's back right leg. Blood splattered across Charlie's face, and the ax blade struck the ground with a metallic *clank!*

Charlie hit the ground and felt the tendons in his right ankle snap.

The mountain lion roared loudly, and it stumbled forward into the forest just twenty feet from the mine entrance. The gash on its back right leg was deep, and the skin flapped.

Charlie quickly tried to right himself. He was on the ground. The ground was dusty. He could feel the sticky blood covering his face. He looked up and saw the cat just ten feet away. The cat swung around and looked at Charlie. It was not happy.

The ax lay on the ground five feet from Charlie. He hobbled forward. The mountain lion looked at him a moment more and then darted off down the hillside into the forest.

Charlie grabbed the ax in his hand and used it like a cane. He could feel the break in his ankle and knew that it was serious. He could not put weight on it.

He watched the mountain lion vanish into the woods. It was leaving a trail of blood, but Charlie knew that the wound wasn't fatal. The cat had gotten out of the way in time. Charlie's face was covered in blood, and his eyes shot down the hillside to the left. He saw three horses coming up through the woods. He could tell the lead horseman had spotted his movement. They shouted.

Charlie watched them a moment more, a terrible blood-soaked grimace on his face, his blue eyes darting left and right down the forest hillside. And then he turned, ax in hand, and lurched toward the darkness of the mine.

## THIRTY-NINE

"He went into the mine!" Robert shouted, and he kicked his horse into a gallop.

Angie shouted, "Wait, Robert!"

Trees raced by him in a blinding blur. The ground was red with pine straw and old leaves, but his horse galloped up the hill weaving in and out of trees.

Angie and Sheriff Tucker started after Robert. All three had seen the mountain lion bolt down the hillside, but they'd also seen Charlie Rutledge hobbling into the mine.

*He's going to get killed*, Angie thought. Up ahead, she saw Robert dismount his horse at the entrance to mine. She shouted over her horse's pounding hooves, but Robert removed his .357 from its holster. He fired three shots and raced into the mine.

• •

Charlie "The Chopper" Rutledge slinked along the wall inside the mine. He used the wall to brace himself. In his right hand, he used the ax like a cane, and he hobbled forward into the darkness.

Suddenly, he heard shouting back behind him, toward the entrance. He listened. His eyes moved around nervously in the darkness. His face glistened. He leaned, for a moment, against the wall to his left and wiped cougar blood from his face.

His right ankle throbbed. He knew that it would start swelling soon.

"They don't know what they're doing," he muttered. "They're trying to save the mountain lion. I'm going to kill them all."

His mouth was dry. He smelled sickly sweet with blood, and he only wanted to show them how stupid they were. Their ignorance almost cost him his life. He pushed off from the wall and lurched forward deeper into the darkness.

He groaned, "I'm going to throw that little bitch on the ground and give her what she's got coming." He swung out with his ax at the darkness in front of him. "I'll kill them all—every last one of them!"

Again, the ax whickered through the darkness, and Charlie lurched forward dragging his bad foot behind him.

• •

Angie brought her horse alongside Robert's and shouted at him, "*No!*" But he was already in the mine. Angie leapt down from her horse and ran toward the entrance.

Sheriff Tucker pulled up next and quickly dismounted. Tucker shouted at Angie, "Don't go down in there!"

But Angie, too, vanished into the darkness.

She screamed at Robert, "No, don't go in there!"

Tucker removed his rifle from the side of his horse. He checked the shells, flipped the safety, and started toward the entrance.

# FORTY

Charlie stood in the darkness of the mine. His head twitched at every little sound coming down the mine to him. He heard a young man's voice; he heard a young woman's voice. And further back he heard the deep voice of an older man. They were coming toward him.

He chuckled. It was perfect. He wouldn't even have to dig them a grave.

Suddenly, his foot struck something on the ground, and he almost fell over.

"*What in the world,*" he muttered. And he poked around at it with his Bushman EZ-Grip. It felt like a little mound. He hobbled around it on his one good leg, and he knelt down and began feeling over its surface. It felt rocky like a little pitcher's mound of gravel. And then his hand touched something that was not gravel.

"Oh, jeez," he said. He realized it was the body he'd seen the mountain lion carry into the mine. He smiled.

"Chopper!" the voice boomed from near the entrance. "Charlie 'The Chopper'! We know you're in here. Come on out with your hands up!"

Charlie listened to their footsteps echoing over the gravelly ground inside the mine. They were thirty meters away from him. Charlie turned and shuffled further down into the mine.

*Come and get me*, he thought. *I've got a little present for you!*

"Robert," the woman called. "Don't go down any further."

Robert said, "This lunatic broke into my cabin. He's trying to scare us, Angie."

Charlie heard the click of a handgun's hammer.

"Angie, Robert," the deeper voice said. "Be cool. You're playing right into his trap. Come on back out here, and we'll wait him out."

"Listen to the Sheriff, Robert," Angie said. "Charlie wants us to come down in there. You'd be a fool to go any further. He'll kill us."

Charlie shuffled a few steps more, found an indentation in the wall and stepped up inside it. He leaned back and turned his head to look up in the direction of the entrance. He couldn't see them well, but he could hear all the noise they made echoing off of the cavernous walls.

"Just come a little further," he whispered. And he hefted up the ax in his hand.

• •

Robert couldn't see well, but he held his handgun out in front of him and proceeded forward slowly. Angie was about ten meters behind him. Suddenly, his foot struck something on the ground, and he stopped. It felt like a little mound.

"What in the hell," he said.

Angie whispered, "What is it?"

"Feels like some kind of mound," Robert said.

"Come on," Angie said. "Let's get out of here. We can wait him out outside. We can smoke him out, build a fire, *something*."

Feeling along the base of the mound with his feet, Robert moved around it. Angie caught up with him and touched her right hand to his left elbow.

"Shhh," he said. "Listen."

They both stood perfectly still in the darkness.

• •

Sheriff Tucker wasn't having any of it. He stood a few feet inside the mine with his rifle hitched under his right arm. He reached his left hand around and lifted the gun up to his shoulder. He raised the gun to firing position and looked down the barrel into the darkness. He couldn't see a thing.

He lowered his rifle. He called, "Angie! Robert! Come on out of there! We'll wait him out, out here!"

He stood just beyond the light. He glanced back over his left shoulder out at the forest. He swung his head back around and squinted looking down into the blackness.

"*Shit*," he said. "Shit, shit, *shit*."

••

Angie's breath was thin, and her chest filled with adrenaline. Her heart felt like it was about to explode. Everything was pitch black around her.

"Goddammit, Robert," she said. "Let's get out of here!"

Her hand held his elbow; she could feel him shaking.

"*No!*" he said. "I will not back down from this. He is threatening our lives. I want you to see, Angie, there is one man who will stand up for you. There is one man who will not abide someone threatening your life."

"Don't be a fool, Robert!"

They both froze because they heard something coming toward them. Robert's gun came up, and he fired three times into the dark.

*Blam! Blam! Blam!*

Each gunshot ignited a brief flash of light, and in the flashes Angie saw a man coming toward them. His face was covered in blood, and he held an ax up readying to swing. His eyes were wide, and his teeth were clenched in a fierce grimace.

He swung the ax.

"*Look out!*" she screamed. She stumbled backward, tripping over the mound and fell to the ground.

There was a dull, wet *thud!* like a watermelon hitting the pavement. Angie heard a breathy gasp from Robert. She heard him fall to the ground.

"Come here, you little tree hugging bitch," Charlie said. "I'll show you what a real man can do for you!"

Angie's face felt like five million needles all touched it at once. She tried to get to her feet, lost her balance, and fell backwards. She heard the ax whicker through the air. It struck the ground two feet from her and sparks exploded.

In the flash of sparks, she saw Robert keeled over on the ground. He clutched at his stomach, and his neck was spotted with blood. Charlie with the ax stood over her, but everything was instantly dark again.

Angie screamed and scrambled away.

The ax struck the gravelly ground again, igniting sparks.

Angie screamed and leapt to her feet. She started running and hit the wall hard, bounced, and fell to the ground. Her face stung.

"Come here," Charlie said.

Angie shook her head, dazed. She looked around her, saw the brightness near the entrance, clambered to her feet again and ran. She saw Sheriff Tucker.

She shrieked, "*He killed him! He killed Robert!*"

Tucker looked into her scared blue eyes. He raised his rifle up to his shoulder and fired off three quick, controlled shots down into the mine.

He lowered his rifle and listened for any sound coming up toward him. Angie stood in the light, listening too.

Tucker raised the rifle to his shoulder and fired twice more into the mine. The sharp smell of gunpowder filled the air. He took a few steps back into the light. He glanced at Angie.

She stared into the mine. They couldn't see anything beyond the darkness. And they couldn't hear anything either.

"Jesus, Angie," Tucker said. "What were you thinking?!"

"*He's dead,*" she cried. "*Oh, my God!* Robert's *dead!* The Chopper killed him with an ax!"

He shook her.

"Get a hold of yourself," Tucker said.

She was hysterical. Angie recoiled. Tucker shifted his serious gaze from her, to the darkness of the mine.

He was nervous, but he grounded his energy, and he held his rifle firmly in his hands. If Charlie Rutledge came up out of that black mine, he was going to blast him back down to hell.

# FORTY-ONE

Three hours later, it was clear that Charlie Rutledge wasn't coming out of the mine. Angie had taken up a position on a rock. Her horse was down at the base of the rock, and she held her rifle cocked under her arm and stared into the darkness.

"He ain't coming out, Sheriff," she said.

Tucker tied up the other two horses adjacent to the clearing. He leaned back against a tree. One leg was propped up underneath him. His black cowboy hat was down over his eyes.

He didn't look up and might have been asleep save for the words he spoke. "He's got to come out sometime," he said.

"You might have shot him," she said. "Robert might have shot him before—"

"Shhhh," Sheriff Graham Tucker said calmly.

Angie sat there on the rock. She stared at Tucker. She stared at the mine. Her back hurt, and she readjusted the rifle. She was no longer using tranquilizer darts and saw the golden .22 shells glint inside the chamber.

She stood up and eased down off of the rock. Her legs had gone to sleep, and so she walked around to get the circulation flowing again.

She walked over to a section of woods where they'd seen the mountain lion take off down the hill. There was a green leafy bush, and Angie saw blood on it. She knelt down and inspected it more closely. She saw spots of cougar blood on the leaves and on the ground near the bush.

She glanced back at the sheriff.

"I'm going to stretch my legs," she said.

Sheriff Tucker looked up at her. His steely brown eyes glinted in the afternoon sunlight. His cowboy hat cocked back a little. He said, "Don't go walkin' off too far, now."

Angie nodded her head.

He said, "You hear?"

"I hear you," she said. "I'm just going to stretch my legs. See how far this trail leads into the woods."

It was the third time she'd mentioned the blood in the past three hours. He'd casually eyed the blood himself more than a dozen times, though he didn't say so to Angie. As far as he was concerned, the mountain lion would keep. Their real concern was Charlie down inside the mine; the lunatic had put an ax into Robert. He'd deal with the mountain lion later. For now, the sheriff wasn't leaving the entrance to that mine until Charlie came out.

Angie started down into the woods. A bird twittered on a branch to her right and then swooped down quickly and crossed the path right in front of her. Her nerves were on edge; she checked her rifle.

She glanced over her left shoulder and saw the sheriff was now fifty meters up the hill from her. He'd brought his cowboy hat back down over his eyes, but he was still leaning against the tree. Angie turned and looked further downhill through the forest.

Everything seemed bright along the forest floor. Everything had sharp edges. She could see individual strands of pine straw on the ground. A large lizard rustled over the ground. It startled Angie, and she stood still and watched the creature.

Its scales were mottled bright orange and black, and it climbed up a tree to her right. Her gaze went back to the forest in front of her. How far did the mountain lion go?

Maybe Charlie had delivered a fatal blow to it, and it had wandered a half mile down the mountain and died. Angie checked her rifle again. She realized the irony in her decision to switch from tranquilizer darts to bullets, now that they had a man to worry about rather than a mountain lion. She cleared her throat. A breeze started up in the treetops. Her face was oily, and the breeze came down through the trees and cooled her skin.

Her back felt sticky in her shirt. Her bra was uncomfortable. Her hair felt grimy and was pulled back in a ponytail. Her jeans were too tight.

Spots of blood dappled the ground every few feet. They grew increasingly thinner as she came down the hill. Suddenly, Angie realized she was beyond shouting distance from Sheriff Tucker. She turned around and looked back up the forest hillside but saw nothing but trees.

She knew he was up over that ridge just out of sight, but not being able to see him at all sent a chill through her. She hated being alone, but it was something she told herself she could do. Angie wanted to believe that she was a self-reliant woman, and in many ways she was. But she hated being alone. It was one of the few things that sent real panic through her.

It was why she settled on boyfriends who were beneath her. She thought of John. And she didn't feel anger. She felt love. She felt sad inside that he was gone, that she didn't do more to prevent it, that she was that much more alone in the world. No, she didn't feel anger. She felt remorse.

Angie held her rifle and took a long, slow turn, looking around her through the trees. She didn't see anything that looked like a cougar, but she knew that the animal was capable of camouflage that escaped the perception of alert prey.

She said slowly to herself, "What am I doing here?"

# FORTY-TWO

Charlie Rutledge *was* alive. A bullet had grazed his side, his ankle was injured, he was covered in blood, and he felt the cold chill of the mine sweeping over his face and hands. His hands felt cold and clammy. He touched the side of his shirt and felt the moistness of blood. Whether it was his or the cougar's he couldn't be certain.

Charlie started shivering.

How long had he been down here? It felt like several hours, but his head was swimming and so it might have only been forty-five minutes, or an hour and a half. Everything was black inside the mine, but over the course of time his eyes gradually adjusted to the dark. He could see well enough to keep from hitting the walls should he decide to stand up and walk.

He was sure they were waiting for him. That whore of a woman and the man with the gun. The woman he could handle, but he didn't know about the man. That son of a bitch would probably put a bullet in him without so much as a thought.

Charlie sat against a wall, his legs straight out in front of him on the ground. He began to feel around in the dark. He was looking for his ax. He patted the ground to the right of his legs and felt its handle. He leaned forward, and pain shot through his side. He grimaced and tried to raise himself up in some semblance of a stance.

Charlie slipped and fell back against the wall. Pain rippled through him.

*Not good*, he thought.

He reached down and felt around his ankle. He'd heard it snap, and he could feel it swollen to twice its normal size.

He wasn't sure how long he was going to last inside the mine, but he knew he stood a lot better chance of making it out of this situation if his ankle wasn't turning gangrenous in the next few days. The key was blood flow. As long as the blood flow in his ankle wasn't cut off, he'd be able to ride this injury out.

If the blood flow was severely impeded, though, that ankle would turn as black as the mine all around him. The tissue would be eaten up by bacteria, and his situation would be a hundred times worse.

He thought savagely, *I'm going to mess that girl up.*

He leaned forward and tried to get himself up on his feet. He used the ax and ax handle to pull himself up. He grimaced in pain, but he managed to keep himself balanced, and he rose to his one strong foot. Quickly, he whipped the ax around to support the weight that his bad ankle could not bear.

He could hobble forward fairly well, and so, carefully, he began to lurch forward, using the ax as a cane, dragging his bad leg behind him. He walked forward about ten steps.

Then, he paused and looked back.

*Not bad,* he thought. *Not bad, ole Charlie.*

He glanced up toward the entrance of the mine. It was no longer light out. Maybe they had left. Maybe the mountain lion had come. Maybe he could ease on out of this mine real quiet like and slip on down the mountain.

Suddenly, he heard whistling.

It was a man's long, slow whistling. Charlie leaned against the wall, and he squinted out into the darkness. Nightfall had set in, but he could see across the clearing fairly well.

He saw the sheriff. He was leaning against a tree. Everything had a blue sheen from the starlight and moonlight. The sheriff stood with one leg propped under him, leaning against a tree. Of course, Charlie didn't know he was a sheriff; to Charlie, he was just a son of a bitch with a rifle who was friends with Angie Rippard.

In the darkness, Charlie's eyes looked around nervously. He saw that the man had a cowboy hat pulled down over his eyes. He saw that he had a rifle hitched under his arm out across the thigh of the leg that was propped underneath him. In the darkness, Charlie could only see the sheriff's contours.

Except, he was whistling. The son of a bitch was out there, whistling away. Charlie looked around but didn't see the woman. That whore of a woman biologist. She was the cause of all this. She wanted to save the mountain lion. That kind of shit would run him out of business.

194

She was the epitome of every conservationist who had ever tried to bring him down. Goddamn woman biologist. He'd show her. He'd show her what she was good for.

"Oh, I'll show her," he muttered.

He'd show her exactly what she was good for. He'd show her exactly what she was put on this earth for.

He gripped the ax in his hands.

And then he recognized the song that the sheriff was whistling. That good-as-dead son of a bitch was whistling *Patience*. He was standing out there waiting for Charlie Rutledge to come out of the mine, and he was whistling *Patience*.

# FORTY-THREE

Angie Rippard stood in the shadows listening to Sheriff Tucker whistling Guns N' Roses' *Patience*, and she couldn't help but crack a smile at the big man. She was hungry and tired, and the night promised to be long.

When he was done, he sighed, yawned a long moment, and adjusted his rifle on his lap. He checked the safety and glanced for the thousandth time into the darkness of the mine. It was cool out, and he had on his duster, and so he adjusted the collar up around his neck.

Angie heard the horses moving around a little, adjacent to the camp that she and the sheriff had set up.

"You know if you stay like that, Sheriff," Angie said. "You're liable to become a permanent fixture of that tree."

Sheriff Tucker grunted, moistened his lips, and spat.

Suddenly, there was a long slow, deep rumble of thunder from far on the horizon. Angie's eyes rose up at the sound. She looked at the treetops, which started to rustle in the strengthening wind. She glanced at the sheriff. The sheriff tucked his head down behind his duster's collar like a bird settling into its nest before a coming storm.

Angie listened to the shifting sounds around the forest. She turned and glanced down the night-darkened hillside through the forest's trees. She thought she saw movement down the hill, but it might just have been the wind dancing with the branches, pulling shadows one way and then another. Then, the sky lit up with distant lightning, and a long slow rumble of thunder rolled out ahead of it. Angie shivered.

An owl hooted in a nearby tree, and Angie glanced back in the direction of the mine.

"We've got a storm coming," she said.

The sheriff looked at her, but said nothing.

The rain started in earnest twenty-five minutes later, and Angie realized they were in for one hell of a night. She tended to the horses, and Sheriff Tucker stood up and walked toward the mine entrance.

"Charlie Rutledge!" he called into the mine. "We're waiting for you, and we ain't gonna leave!"

Angie held her horse's reins in her hand. She stood beside it and patted its head to reassure it. She looked across the way at Sheriff Tucker. Rain poured down on the big man, on his duster, and his cowboy hat, and it poured over the brim as though around the lid of a barrel.

There was a flash of lightning, and Angie's horse started moving around nervously.

"Whoa, big fella," she said.

The horse took a couple more steps up the hillside into the clearing right in front of the mine. The rain beat down on them. Angie started to shout something at Sheriff Tucker, when a noise came from behind her. Angie swung around and saw the mountain lion standing atop the rock she had been sitting on earlier that day.

Lightning flashed across the sky.

She let the reins go, and the horse swung around and rose up on its hind legs. The mountain lion stood up there motionless, and all of a sudden, the sheriff was shouting at her to look out, to get out of the way.

The horse struck her broadside, and Angie fell to the ground. Her bare hands touched mud and rocky earth, and the horse came down and rushed over to the side of the clearing.

Angie heard the crack of the sheriff's rifle behind her, and she glanced over her shoulder and saw the big man standing in the middle of the clearing. He held his rifle up, and Angie climbed quickly onto her feet.

"Look out, Angie!" the sheriff said.

She ducked out of his way. Her rifle stood against a tree twenty feet away. She ran for it, but she saw the big cat take two agile steps down off of the rock and land powerfully on the ground. The big cat stood ten feet in front of Angie.

Because of the cat's position, Angie couldn't get to her gun. The gun was on the other side of the mountain lion.

She stared at the big animal. Rain pattered off of the ground around it, around her, around the clearing at the entrance to the mine. Two or three seconds passed, and Angie couldn't understand why the sheriff hadn't fired on it again.

She knew that if she looked over her right shoulder to see what Tucker was doing that the big animal would coil and pounce on her. She stood her ground and slowly raised her arms up over her head to make herself look as large as she possibly could to the creature. The big cat stared at her.

It took two steps forward, and Angie felt her whole world collapse. She wanted to scream at the animal.

*What the hell was Tucker doing?*

She saw her rifle leaning against a tree on the other side of the mountain lion, and then, the mountain lion veered to its right and stepped down into the darkness and the trees. Rain continued to hammer the ground, but Angie refused to look away from where the mountain lion vanished into the woods. It was probably standing just beyond the edge of the trees, circling the clearing.

She wiped rainwater away from her face and glanced once more quickly over her shoulder.

Sheriff Tucker lay face down in the mud. An ax rose from his back. The blade was buried between his shoulder blades. Angie swung around and ran to him.

"Sheriff!" she cried.

She knelt down over him. With her hands, she turned his face over, and she realized that he was dying. His eyes looked up at her, and his mouth tried to form words, but only a harsh little gasp of wind exited his throat. His lips moved up and down. Angie held him close, kneeling.

She looked around the clearing, expecting Charlie Rutledge to emerge from the shadows, expecting the mountain lion to pounce. But everything was still, except for the pouring rain. She glanced back toward the mine and saw nothing but darkness. And then she looked down into the sheriff's eyes. He was a handsome man, handsome in that rare way that honest men look. He had eyes that were true, and he was going to die in Angie's arms.

"No," Angie said. "No! Stay with me sheriff. Stay with me now!"

"*I'm sorry,*" he said, his voice raspy.

Angie said, "Oh God. Oh, dear God!"

The sheriff shook his head slowly back and forth and looked into her eyes.

Angie glanced around the clearing. She saw the sheriff's rifle lying seven feet away.

"Angie," the sheriff whispered.

Angie looked at him.

"I can't feel my legs," he said.

Angie looked at him frantically, but there was nothing she could do.

"I'm so scared," he said.

"*Sheriff?*"

Angie pulled him close and felt the life go out of him.

Lightning flashed across the sky, followed quickly by a terrible crash of thunder. Rain hammered them both.

# FORTY-FOUR

Charlie Rutledge hobbled down the hillside, slipping and sliding, but somehow managing to stay up on his one good foot. Two hatchets dangled from either side of his belt like shiny six shooters. He'd left his Bushman EZ-Grip in the sheriff's back. He lurched from one tree to another.

Rain poured down on him through the forest canopy. Charlie fell against a pine tree and stopped for a moment to catch his breath. He clung to the tree. He heard something coming down the hill toward him. It was weaving right and left through the trees, and Charlie realized it was one of their horses.

He hobbled out away from the tree, dragging his bad leg behind him. He threw his hands up to try and stop the horse. It was twenty feet away from him, coming down the hill.

"Whoa!" Charlie shouted. "Whoa there!"

At the last second, the horse saw him and came to a stop.

• •

Angie pulled Sheriff Graham Tucker's body over to a dry spot right inside the mine. She removed the ax from his back and sat him up against the wall. She folded his hands for him down across his lap. She stood up and looked at him. He was dead.

She looked out across the clearing in front of the mine, and she trotted out into the rain and picked up his rifle. She ran back to the dry spot a few feet inside the mine and checked the rifle. She saw that it was loaded.

Her horse had taken off down the side of the hill into the woods, but the sheriff's and Robert's horses stood leashed to a pine tree at the side of the clearing. Angie carried the rifle and walked over to the horse. She cupped her hand up over her eyes and stared down the hill through the driving rain.

200

She saw Charlie Rutledge.

He had stopped her horse and was mounting it. Angie unleashed Sheriff Tucker's horse from the tree. The horse took two powerful steps up toward the clearing.

A bolt of lightning ripped through the sky and struck a tree fifty meters right of Charlie. Sparks exploded into the air. A huge chunk of tree cracked and fell powerfully to the ground.

Angie swung up over the saddle of the big horse, cocked the rifle, and took off down the hill toward Charlie Rutledge.

• •

Charlie Rutledge balanced himself atop the horse and took off down the hill. He didn't think the woman had it in her to really cause him any harm, but he wasn't taking any chances.

The horse carried him swiftly down the hill, weaving right and left through the trees. The rain was cold and heavy, but he knew that if he gained any distance on her, he'd lose her completely.

• •

Angie was fifty meters to Charlie's back and right. She saw him through the trees, through the rain and darkness, and she heeled her horse faster, dodging trees right and left.

Her horse leapt over a log. Angie held on tight and drew closer to the cold-blooded killer. She held her rifle in her right hand and managed the reins with her left. She got the rifle up on her shoulder and fired off a shot.

The sound of the rifle ripped through the forest, but the shot missed. With her right hand, she cocked the rifle again and tried to take aim atop the galloping horse.

Suddenly, everything went out from under her. The horse made a terrible sound, and the ground flew up at Angie. She hit the ground, and the wind rushed out of her.

She rolled three times and struck a tree. Dizzy, she tried to climb quickly to her feet. She staggered and braced herself against the tree. She saw the horse climbing to its feet. She glanced back and saw the swath in the mud and the steep drop-off they'd slid down, and she thought for certain that her horse had probably broken its leg.

But the horse stood up. It shook its mane. It walked tentatively for a moment, but its legs seemed to be okay.

"That's a good boy," she said.

She reached down and picked up the rifle. She got back on the horse and started down the hill again, this time a little more slowly.

She couldn't see Charlie Rutledge anywhere, but she knew roughly where he had been, and so she got her horse pointed in that direction and started onward through the trees and driving rain.

• •

Three hours later, she was utterly lost. The horse walked onward slowly. The rain still poured, and she was soaked. She was cold, alone, and afraid. And she had no idea where she was in relation to the mine, the cabin, or the lake to the south. Everything was dark and wet, and she leaned forward and hugged closely to the horse's neck.

"Where are we, boy?" she said. "Where are we?"

# FORTY-FIVE

She saw him by the lake an hour before sunrise. The rain was thin, cold, and constant, but Angie's mind was so numb she didn't even feel it anymore. She was on a ridge about a quarter mile up from the shoreline. She looked down through the trees and saw Charlie Rutledge sitting on a log by the bank. He removed his boot from one foot. His back faced her.

His horse was ten feet to his left, and Angie quietly slid down off of her horse and began walking down the hill. Carrying Sheriff Tucker's rifle in her right hand, she called: "Charlie Rutledge!"

Rutledge swung around on the log. He saw Angie coming down the hill toward him, and he grinned. She was careful with her footing on the steep hill. Angie motioned with the rifle.

"You're just planning on riding out of here?" she said.

He acted like he wanted to get up, but Angie raised her left hand.

"Sit," she commanded.

She gazed out at the lake. It was wide and its surface was smooth, one hour before sunrise. It was ten miles across from where she stood to the bridge at Roosevelt Dam. She could see the bridge like a thin line far on the other side of the lake. That dam controlled water for three reservoirs forty miles northeast of Phoenix, Arizona.

Her ice blue eyes came back to Charlie.

• •

The mountain lion stood perfectly still, staring at the woman. Her back faced it. The cat stood in a thicket of trees forty feet down the shoreline from the woman and the man. It licked its lips, its golden eyes alert and clear.

The mountain lion took three silent steps forward.

• •

"You're a goddamned, no good whore," Charlie muttered.

Angie stared into his eyes.

"Women like you are going to be the downfall of our country. There was a time when you knew your place. There was a time when you realized you were nothing. You and your fancy degrees and elected positions. Women are nothing! Do you hear me?"

She felt sorry for him. She felt pity for him, but she kept the rifle aimed at him and remained quiet and listened. Even as exhausted as she was, she still clung to the hope that there was something good in the man. But this man just went on spewing out anger and hatred.

"You're nothing," he said, "and if it was up to me, I'd rape you right here on the spot. Because it's the only thing you're good for. And apparently you ain't even good for that. You can't keep a man. You don't deserve the job you have. You ought to be lying on your back. That's the one thing you're good for in this lifetime."

Angie listened to his insults.

"You're a goddamned ignorant—"

"Enough, Charlie," Angie said.

Charlie stared at her with hatred in his eyes. Angie didn't doubt that this man would rape her. Her heart pounded in her chest because she realized if she let up, he would probably turn the tide and do exactly that. He would rape her, spit on her, kick her in the ribs, and then laugh at her as she lay there dying. Some men were just that cruel. Some men, it seemed, had a black void inside their chests where they should have had a soul.

She just wanted to shake him, shake him out of his evil, and make him see the world the right way, make him realize that she was just a person, just like anyone else, and she was only trying to make it through this life.

"On your feet," she said.

Charlie sat there realizing he could win this little game.

"I don't think you've got it in you to shoot me," he said.

"Don't you have any good in you," she said. "I don't want to kill you, but you've killed two people, Charlie. You killed two of my friends, and you're going to pay for that. Now, we're going to walk all the way around this lake. I'm going to climb up on that horse. I'm going to keep this rifle aimed at you. And you're going to walk. You're going to pay for what you've done."

Charlie smirked. "Like hell," he said.

"On your feet." She motioned with her rifle. "Come on."

"My ankle," he said. "I can't walk. I think I broke it."

"You're telling me you can't walk?"

"I'm telling you my ankle's hurt."

Angie took a step closer to him, and then realized it might be a trick.

"Come on," she said. "On your feet."

Charlie braced himself on the log and tried to stand up on his one good leg. Angie stood less than five feet from him. She could see the pain in his eyes, and then he looked into her blue eyes as though asking for her compassion. And again, Angie felt sorry for him. She took another step closer and then saw Charlie's mouth tense up.

He spat in her face.

Angie stepped backward a couple steps, raised her left hand up, and wiped his saliva from her face. Charlie threw his head back and howled with laughter.

"No good, goddamned woman," he shouted. "That'll teach you. Why don't you come over here; I'll bend you over this log and give you a ride like you never had!"

Angie was about to lose her cool, but she just stared at this horror of a human being with wonder and pity in her eyes.

"That's what you need. That's what your problem is; you ain't been fucked properly. I'll give it to you; I'll make you *scream*."

Charlie stood there laughing at Angie Rippard like it was the last laugh he would have in his life.

"Stupid goddamned woman," he kept saying. "Stupid goddamned *woman!*"

He howled, tears filling his eyes. It was the laugh of a man with no regard for life. His face was red, and he started coughing he was laughing so hard.

"Jesus Christ, you ain't got the balls to kill me," he howled. "*Literally!*"

Angie stared at him, wonder giving way to anger. She felt mocked. She felt shamed. She couldn't believe that anyone could be so willfully evil. But he stood right there in front of her being exactly that. She raised the rifle and said, "Shut up!"

"Ain't got the balls to kill me!"

"Shut the hell up. I mean it!"

"She means it!"

Charlie spat at her again, his phlegm hitting her chest, neck, and chin.

Angie said, "Oh, you sorry son of a—"

Suddenly, she heard something about twenty feet behind her. Charlie went on howling, but Angie pivoted around and looked up the shoreline through the trees. She held the rifle in her hands. It was difficult to see. Charlie's voice dropped to silence, and Angie swung back around.

That was when the butt of the hatchet struck her powerfully across the left side of her head between her ear and her temple. The pain was sharp and blinding, and Angie's mouth went slack, the rifle fell from her hands, and she crumpled to the ground.

Charlie stood over her, the hatchet in his hands.

## FORTY-SIX

Robert Gonzalez staggered out from the entrance of the mine and fell down on both knees in the clearing. He had a frantic look on his face, and his shirt was soaked with blood. He was alive, but he had seen something there at the end that made him think otherwise.

How long had he been down? Several hours? Since midnight?

It was light outside now, a new day, and he remembered chasing Charlie Rutledge into the mine, and it had been light then, too. He reasoned that he'd been out cold for hours.

Robert looked around for his handgun, and his eyes came to rest on Sheriff Graham Tucker.

"Sheriff?"

It looked like the sheriff was sitting against the wall just inside the mine. Robert must have passed him as he came out, but he was in such a state of mind that he didn't see him.

"Sheriff Tucker, you okay?" Robert said.

The sheriff sat there with his hands folded over his lap. Robert lumbered up onto his feet and started walking toward him. The sheriff looked to be sleeping. Strange, Robert thought.

He suddenly swung around thinking Angie might still be out here.

"Angie?" he called. "Doctor Rippard?"

But the only reply was a morning dove's coo in a tree beyond the clearing. Robert glanced at his stomach. His shirt was ragged and bloody. He approached the sheriff.

Robert knelt down in front of the sheriff and started to reach his hand forward to touch the sheriff's foot. He glanced at the bearded man's face, at his closed eyes. The sheriff's mouth kind of slumped to one side like he was dead asleep, and Robert shook his foot to rouse him.

"Sheriff," he said.

The sheriff's leg was stiff. Robert realized that he was dead.

"Shit." He stood up and looked the other way.

Walking another ten feet away, he turned and looked at the sheriff. His hand came up to his mouth.

"Shit, shit, shit," he said. And suddenly, he started looking around frantically. He felt very alone. Was he the last one? Did Charlie Rutledge get Angie, too?

His legs went weak. Robert's breathing became thin and his hands shook. The fear that he was stuck out here alone, that Charlie Rutledge had killed the sheriff and Angie—it made his mind reel.

"Shit, shit, shit."

He walked over to the edge of the woods and looked down the hillside. His horse looked up at him; it had broken its tether and had wandered down the hill.

"Angie?" he called down into the woods.

He felt trapped; he didn't want to call out too loudly because it might alert Charlie that he wasn't dead. That is, if Charlie were still alive.

He walked down the hill, petted the horse, and led it back to the clearing. Part of him didn't want to leave the clearing, didn't want to wander away. What if Angie had just walked away for a few minutes and came back while he was gone?

But her horse was gone, he realized. Maybe she was gone for good; why else would she take her horse? Maybe she thought he was dead.

He looked all around him up the hill above the mine. He looked at the sheriff again, sitting there stiff as a board.

His horse shook its mane. Robert had to make a decision.

Then he saw Angie's rifle lying by the rock.

## FORTY-SEVEN

Charlie reached down and grabbed the sheriff's rifle from the ground. Angie lay flat on her stomach, her face buried in the dirt and leaves. Charlie rose up on his one good leg and stared up into the woods in the direction from which they'd heard the sound. He latched his hatchet onto his belt and pointed the rifle into the trees along the shoreline.

"Come on, you son of a bitch," he muttered.

A wind started up across the lake and reached the trees along the shoreline. The treetops rustled and the branches swayed, and Charlie squeezed his finger around the trigger and fired three shots into the woods.

Staring through the trees, he waited to see any movement. There was none. He glanced down at Angie who lay unconscious on the ground. Licking his lips, he rubbed his mouth nervously with his left hand, and hobbled around the clearing making certain that if the mountain lion had been there, it was scared off now.

"Go on, get out of here!" he shouted to the trees.

On the ground behind him, Angie moaned. Charlie checked the chamber, saw there were six more shells, and fired two more shots into the woods. He held his hands up over his head and shouted: "Go on, get out of here! *Yahhh!!*"

He held the rifle and fell silent, listening for any returning sound from the forest. There was only the sound of water lapping lightly on the shore, and so Charlie turned and looked at Angie Rippard lying face down in the dirt.

He sort of shrugged his shoulders and laughed.

"Jesus Christ. You're going to get it now."

Charlie knelt down behind her and felt the back of her thighs through her denim jeans. He held the rifle in his right arm, and his left hand rose up to her butt.

"Jesus H. Christ."

Angie moaned and started to stir. Charlie stood up over her, swung the rifle around, and then brought the butt of the gun down hard into the base of her neck. Angie sprawled out again and ceased moving.

Charlie checked the clearing once more, then looked back at Angie.

"Oh, my God," he whispered nervously.

Charlie hobbled around in front of her, grabbed her right hand, and dragged her across the clearing toward the log. He braced himself on the log and rolled Angie over on her back. Her eyes were closed, and there was a line of damp blood on the left side of her face where he'd struck her with the butt end of the hatchet. He could tell it was already beginning to swell up, and he reached down, popped the button on the front of her jeans, and managed to unzip her pants.

"Oh, I'm going to give it to you," he said.

He yanked her pants down to her knees. Angie tried to open her eyes but only groaned.

"Don't you make a sound," he whispered, leaning in close to her right ear.

He reached down and snatched his hatchet from his belt. He cut her underwear off with the hatchet blade, wadded them in his fist and flung them on the leaf-covered ground in front of her. He suddenly realized he was so excited he was breathing shallow ragged breaths. His dirt-stained hands shook. He stood up and got Angie bent over the log. Her nakedness was exposed.

Charlie's eyes were wide, and he licked his lips.

He hobbled around the clearing nervously, excitedly. Angie lay over the log, her jeans down around her knees.

He glanced around the forest and continued to shout up into the woods, his voice echoing over the trees, up the hill, and out over the lake.

"Yah! Yah! Go on, get out'a here!"

He fell silent and listened to the silence of the forest, and then he started shouting again.

When he was convinced that the mountain lion was nowhere nearby, Charlie swung around and looked at Angie. He hobbled over toward the log and unzipped his pants. He got around front of the log between Angie's face and the lake, and he knelt down and lifted up her head. Saliva dripped from her mouth, and a low groaning sound came up from her chest.

"You see this blade here," Charlie whispered. "It'll cut right through your throat. Now, I'm going to give it to you, and you're going to take it. But if you struggle, if you fight it, if you try and get away, I'll cut your throat and leave you here to die."

He held Angie's face up. Her eyelids fluttered open. She was not really conscious but managed to slur, "Fuck you."

Charlie grinned.

"That's my girl," he said. And he let her head fall limp again. He hobbled back around the log, back behind Angie, and he dropped his pants to his knees and stared at her nakedness. He was so nervous he was having trouble getting an erection, but he kept working it until he was ready. He leaned in close behind her.

He had trouble finding the spot and so just thrust up and down behind her, feeling her naked and warm beneath him. His dirty left hand came up to the base of her head, and he leaned in close and sniffed at her hair.

"There it is," he said.

He pushed it in, writhing slowly back and forth, and though only half conscious, Angie's body tensed up.

She murmured, "Please no."

"Hush now," Charlie whispered. "Hush now, my sweet."

He leaned in behind her, the hatchet in his right hand. He touched the blade to her throat. Charlie thought he heard something and swung his head around. He looked back up the hill and saw nothing but the trees staring down at him, and so looked back around at Angie's back, grabbed her hips, and pulled himself in as far as he could.

Angie cried out a little, becoming more and more conscious, realizing what he was doing to her.

"*Goddamn*," Charlie said.

He started to break a sweat, and the skin of his thighs slapped against Angie's backside. She groaned in pain.

Charlie said, "*Hush now!* Hush now, my sweet!"

Angie was becoming fully conscious, and the pain was so intense that her face locked in a grimace. Charlie's hands shook. He was going fast now. He held the hatchet out to the right side of Angie's face and kept saying stupidly, "Hush now. Hush now. Hush now."

The attack came without a sound from the right side of the clearing.

Charlie had a quarter second before he looked up and saw the mountain lion coming at him. He screamed, and the mountain lion struck him full force over his right shoulder. He fell away from Angie and was on his back. The cougar leapt on top of him.

"Get away!" Charlie shrieked.

He batted dumbly at the animal and tried to roll over to his left. He groped around for his hatchet, which had flung out of his hand. Angie fell away from the log and looked back just as the mountain lion's head came down toward Charlie's chest.

Charlie's screams filled the air, and Angie managed to get her pants up around her waist. She glanced quickly around looking for the rifle. It was on the ground to the right of the mountain lion.

Suddenly, the mountain lion's head swung back toward Angie and parts of Charlie flew through the air, hitting the water behind her. Angie stood and held her hands up over head.

"Whoa, now!" Angie shouted. She staggered backward toward the lake.

The mountain lion took two steps away from Charlie, pivoting to face her. Out of the bottom of her eyes, she could see Charlie's chest torn open. Blood gurgled up from his mouth, and his hands flailed around futilely. The mountain lion licked its lips, and its solid golden eyes stared at Angie.

"Whoa, now!" Angie said. Her hands were held high above her head, and she took three more cautious steps backward.

The mountain lion stood its ground, just watching her. Angie continued to shout with all the strength she had left, while holding her hands up over her head. She took a few steps away until she reached the edge and felt cold lake water filling her shoes.

The mountain lion stared a moment more. Suddenly, Charlie coughed up a huge mouthful of blood and bolted upright. The mountain lion swung back around, its right front paw landing squarely on his chest. It pushed him back onto the ground, stared into his eyes an instant, and its head lunged down, its mouth wide. It ripped the front of Charlie's face off in one powerful bite.

Its head swung back and forth mauling him, tearing his face and head apart. Charlie's arms fell dead at his sides.

Angie grimaced and staggered backward out into the water. She knew that mountain lions were expert swimmers, but she would much rather take her chances in the water than on the ground against this animal. The mountain lion flung parts of Charlie all around the clearing, and then lunged forward again and tore into him savagely.

Angie was knee deep out in the lake before the mountain lion lost interest in Charlie and took two steps away from him and toward Angie. She thrust her hands up in the air and shouted, "Back away! Go!"

The mountain lion raised its nose up and sniffed the air.

Angie said, "No! Go away!"

And then at the top of her line of vision, she saw Robert up on the hill fifty meters away. The cougar's back was to him, and in a split second, Robert saw Charlie's body, saw Angie backing into the water, and saw the cougar bearing down on her. The cougar was only twenty feet from her and was ready to pounce.

"Don't kill it!" Angie shouted, her voice echoing across the clearing.

On the hill, Robert raised Angie's rifle to his shoulder.

"Don't shoot it," she pleaded. "The cat saved my life!"

The cougar took three more steps, crouched, and prepared to leap at her. Angie's hands came up defensively. The cougar sprang.

The rifle blast erupted from the hillside.

Angie felt the weight of the animal strike her chest, and she fell backward into the water with a splash. She was underwater a moment, shrieking, flailing her arms about, expecting the mountain lion to tear into her. She opened her terrified eyes underwater and saw the cougar.

But it wasn't clawing at her. It wasn't moving. Angie found the ground under her feet and rose up from the water. The mountain lion lay before her. It was shot, but it wasn't dead. Its golden eyes looked up at Angie.

Robert ran down the hill.

Angie staggered up from the water, pulling at the mountain lion's shoulders, pulling it up from the lake. The animal was huge and must have weighed three hundred pounds. She was only able to lift it partially up onto the bank.

Robert shouted at her to get away, to back away from the animal, but Angie dropped down on her knees and held the mountain lion's head.

"Oh, my God," she cried. "What blood is this? Whose blood is this? Oh, dear God!"

She looked around frantically, holding the animal in her arms.

The cougar's head and shoulders weighed forty pounds. Its mouth moved up and down slowly. Blood poured from it. The rifle shot had struck the cat somewhere near its shoulder blades, and the magnificent animal lay there dying in her arms.

Robert reached the foot of the clearing and stopped. He looked around him at Charlie, at Angie, and at the cougar.

Angie rocked back and forth with the animal held close to her chest. She moaned, crying, "No, no, no." Tears streamed down her face, and she looked up at Robert.

The mountain lion was dead.

In her arms, it lay lifeless on the shoreline.

Robert, stunned, looked around him and said, "The ground is wet with blood."

Robert had a look of desperation on his face beyond words. He started to help her up.

"Get away from me!" she screamed.

Robert backed away. "Angie," he said.

He realized that she would have rather died than to have had this animal die in her arms.

Angie looked at the animal's body, and she felt shame, humiliation, and revulsion. It was dead and there was something horrifying in the realization that she couldn't bring it back, that it would lay there and she was powerless to bring it back to life, to ensure that it would live another day. It was just all gone in a single breath, and Angie was filled with frustration and rage.

"It was going to kill you, Angie."

"I would rather die. I want to die. I'm sick of this life and all the selfless, cruel, thoughtless *animals* allowed to *live!* Where is a God in that?"

"It wasn't your fault. None of this is your fault!"

"I'll tell you whose fault it is," she said.

She stood up and crossed over to the rifle that lay beside Charlie's dead body.

"What are you doing?" Robert leapt to his feet.

Angie pulled the gun barrel around and nuzzled it into the soft flesh under her chin.

Robert leapt at her, swinging his right hand around.

His hand hit the barrel.

The rifle shot echoed out across the lake.

Robert screamed, and Angie fell back away from him. The rifle clattered to the leaf-covered ground.

"Angie!"

She lay on the ground. Robert cried out "Angie!" once more and fell to his knees on the ground next to her. He grabbed her in his arms and pulled her up close to him. He felt the dampness of blood on her face against his own, felt her shaking with tears in his arms, and held her close until he was certain that he felt her own arms rising up around him, holding onto him as though it was the last thing on earth that mattered.

They held each other while Angie wept.

# Epilogue

ARIZONA COUGAR KILLS FIVE was the headline the Charlotte *Observer* used two days later. The Arkansas *Democrat* played the story up from the biologists' angle: CONSERVATIONISTS KILL COUGAR. And the *Detroit Free Press* headline read, END TO ARIZONA TERROR: COUGAR DEAD. There were color photos of Dr. Rippard on an ambulance gurney, being lifted into the back; she looked like she'd been through a war zone.

It took a couple of days for the story to catch on, but the national media realized the politics and power of Rippard's story. Probably the most emotional photograph was the very first one; a freelance photojournalist with *Arizona Highways* magazine stood on the side of a dirt road photographing Apache Lake fifteen miles northeast of Tortilla Flat, Arizona. Everything was dry and dusty, the late afternoon light at just the right angle on the lake to make for a great picture. The man turned and saw Angie and Robert on horseback coming down the dirt road out of the mountains. They looked like they'd been through a bombing, clothes torn and bloody, hair matted. The photographer snapped three pictures, and one ended up on the cover of *Newsweek*.

Angie looked like a soldier bracing a near-dead comrade. There was something noble and true in that image, something that spoke volumes about Angie Rippard's character.

The doctors at Banner Baywood Hospital gave a press conference that night at nine-fifteen MST. Rippard and Gonzalez were in stable condition. And though they were asked, the doctors couldn't comment on the fate of the mountain lion. That came out the next day when Rippard allowed a single reporter from the Phoenix *Tribune* into her seventh-floor hospital room. She gave him twenty-five minutes, and she knew that his story would hold until she was healthy enough to leave the hospital on her own.

She described it as the single most unusual case of a cougar attack on humans that she'd ever seen. Even in the hospital bed, she advocated compassion and conservation for the North American mountain lion. She called it "a bad case" and "tragic," and she felt "lucky" to have made it out of the mountains alive. And those were the words that cycled through newspaper and television reports the next ten days.

Governor Horace G. Redmond III called the event "a tragedy beyond reckoning" and said that he and his wife's prayers were with Angie and Robert whose "actions rose above the standard definitions of the word 'hero'." Horace G. ordered National Guardsmen to go up into the mountains north of Roosevelt Lake, and National Forest Rangers worked with military and civilian authorities to locate the mine, the cabin, and the bodies down by the lake. Angie began a two-week-long cycle of rabies vaccinations just to be safe.

By the fourth day in the hospital, she was walking up and down the hallways in her hospital gown, pushing her IV unit along with her. Robert's room was at the end of the hall.

"How you doing?" she said from his doorway.

Robert lay in his bed, and he turned and smiled at her.

"I'm tired of this hospital bed," he said good naturedly. "Look at you."

That night, she sat next to his bed, and they played a game of Scrabble. Robert was pretty well medicated, his speech slow, his eyes slowly blinking, but he stayed in the game until they reached the triple-word-score squares.

The fourteenth word Angie played was "brave," and Robert looked up and saw tears forming in her eyes as she placed the tiles on the board.

"Hey," he said. "What's the matter?"

Angie wiped the tears back stubbornly.

"I don't know." She sniffed. Leaning forward, she placed her hands over her face and just sobbed.

It was one of those cries that was so intense that it almost hurt, but when it was over, she felt like she was breathing through new lungs. There was a single light behind the head of Robert's bed, and he lay there quiet, reverent, letting her work it out of her system.

He held his Scrabble tray of letters and just watched her, listening, waiting to see if there was something he could say, *should* say.

He only said, "Everything's gonna be alright."

She looked at him, her eyes puffy and red. Then, she leaned forward and kissed him. Robert did not fight the kiss, but he did not return it either. He only looked into her eyes and felt the weight of so much pain in her gaze.

"I'm sorry," she said.

"No. Don't be. Maybe in time, Angie. But not now. We're going to make it through this. *You're* going to make it through this."

She held her hand up over her eyes as though trying to cover up the shame of crying, in letting her emotions control her. This kid, this graduate student, well, he'd seen her at her highest highs and at her lowest lows, and there was something so nakedly vulnerable in that realization that she felt broken inside to the point of crying. She didn't have anything to hide, but she wanted a part of herself always to remain hidden.

She wanted to save something for herself, but he'd pretty much seen it all. She felt her loyalty and her emotions mixed in her mind, and she only wanted someone to hold onto.

•  •

The Avis car rental center was a mile from the Kahului Airport, but they offered a shuttle that picked up customers just outside of the airport terminal. Angie helped a young girl and her mother load their suitcases onto the shuttle because she herself had only a backpack and one suitcase. She smiled affably and took a seat at the back of the shuttle bus.

Everything was green on the island of Maui. The air was thick and moist with humidity, and bright sunshine peaked out from behind large puffy cumulous clouds that drifted off of Puu Kukui, the mountain on the west end of Maui. Angie leaned back in the seat and let the fresh breeze roll in from the open window. She could smell the ocean and the fragrance of rain coming down over the sugar plantations southwest of Kahului.

There were only two left; it seemed the land was too valuable to waste on sugar crops. Hotels were in their future.

Angie rented a black convertible and drove with the top down along State Highway 380 and onward west along Highway 30. It was a two-lane stretch of blacktop with double-yellow center lines, and once west of the harbor town of Maalaea, the highway carved along steep ocean-side cliffs.

The wind whipped through her hair, and Angie looked out at the Pacific through Wayfarer sunglasses. Seven miles across the Auau Channel, the island of Lanai rose like a giant tortoise shell from the sea.

That fall afternoon from her fourteenth-floor balcony, Angie gazed out over pools and beaches, watching sailboats navigate the Auau's blue water. She put her legs up on the patio table and sipped an ice-cold margarita.

She ate the best seafood of her life that night at Leilani's. The outdoor table overlooked a green lawn, white sand beach, and a sunset straight out of a Hollywood movie. After dinner, she drove down to the waterfront town of Lahaina. There were shops and bars and restaurants and taverns, and an old man stood on a street corner, selling kittens from a wooden box.

"How much?" Angie asked.

"Two dollars," the old man said.

Angie reached in the box and retrieved a little calico hardly larger than her hand. The poor thing cried, and Angie held it close to her chest, saying, "There, there, little fella. Everything's gonna be alright. You just need a little milk."

The old man smiled and placed her two dollars in his pocket.

"Which way is Lahainaluna?"

"Lahainaluna Street?" the old guy said.

"Yes," she said. "My brother lives up there."

"It's just two blocks that way." He pointed.

Angie walked away, holding the kitten close to her chest, and she thought of something funny she could say when her brother opened his door. The lights from shops poured out onto the sidewalk, and somewhere in the distance, a ship's bell clanged merrily in the night.

## THE END

# CLAWS 2

2010 C.E.

staceycochran.com

Stacey Cochran is a writer, producer, and teacher. His books include *The Colorado Sequence*, *Amber Page and the Legend of the Coral Stone*, and *The Kiribati Test*. He was a finalist for the 1998 Dell Magazines Award for undergraduate fiction writing and a 2004 finalist for the St. Martin's Press/PWA Best First Private Eye Novel Contest. He teaches writing at North Carolina State University, and he hosts an author-interview TV show in Raleigh. He is married to Dr. Susan K. Miller-Cochran, and they have a son named Sam.

Made in the USA